THE OUTSIDER

THE OC

THE

C. THE O.C. THE

THE OUTSIDER

SCHOLASTIC INC.

New York   Toronto   London   Auckland   Sydney
Mexico City   New Delhi   Hong Kong   Buenos Aires

ISBN 0-439-66059-9

12 11 10 9 8 7 6 5 4 3 2 1   4 5 6 7 8/0

Cover and interior designed by Louise Bova
Printed in the U.S.A.
First printing, August 2004

THE OC

THE OUTSIDER

Adapted by Cory Martin

Based on the television series created by Josh Schwartz including the episode "Pilot," written by Josh Schwartz; the episode "The Model Home," story by Allan Heinberg & Josh Schwartz and written by Josh Schwartz; the episode "The Gamble," written by Jane Espenson; the episode "The Debut," written by Allan Heinberg & Josh Schwartz; the episode "The Outsider," written by Melissa Rosenberg; the episode "The Girlfriend," story by Debra J. Fisher & Erica Messer and written by Josh Schwartz; and the episode "The Escape" written by Josh Schwartz

THE OC

THE OUTSIDER

1

Fifty-three miles from the beaches of the Pacific, the sun had set on the dark streets of Chino. In the heart of the city, Larch Street was the darkest of them all. Of the ten streetlights on the block, five flickered on and off, and three were out completely. This part of Chino was always hazy, never really bright and never really dark. On the sunniest of days, the streets were clouded with exhaust sputtering from beat-up cars and the lawns were filled with discarded furniture. Even the California sun couldn't make it bright. But nothing could make it dark either. The nights were flanked by police helicopters hovering with searchlights overhead, and the wail of sirens and the flashers on police cars cast too much light on the dusty homes. Life in Chino was plain and far from extraordinary. In a county of orange, Chino was gray.

Ryan Atwood had lived in the gloom of Larch Street most of his life, and never traveled much further than the brand-new Italian restaurant they had built in the next town over. Not that he had ever eaten the gourmet food, his family was too poor to eat out much, but he had found a liquor store next to it that would let him buy cigarettes without an I.D. Ryan was only sixteen, but with his strong build and confident rebel façade, Ryan passed for twenty.

He had just returned from the liquor store with a fresh pack of cigarettes for himself and Theresa, his best friend and sometime girlfriend.

"You're back."

Ryan gave her his look, the look that she couldn't resist. The look that said it all without any words. He handed her a cigarette. She lit hers off of his as she pulled her long brown hair off her face.

Theresa and Ryan had known each other since they were kids, and it was part of their routine as friends, at least since they had gotten older, to smoke a few cigarettes on her back porch while just talking. Ryan took a drag off his cigarette.

Today had been a rough day. Not that any day had ever been great, but today it had just gotten to Ryan. His family life was less than perfect. He had woken up to his brother, Trey, stumbling in drunk and A.J., his mother's boyfriend, slapping him across the face to wake him up. His mom had skipped work yet again, and he had had to call in sick for her. He started to tell Theresa all the details, but . . .

Two houses down, Ryan could hear the fighting. Theresa knew what he was about to say. They inhaled deep from their cigarettes — puffed smoke rings at each other and smiled when the rings crossed and disintegrated.

A.J. and his mom were at it again. They did this when they drank. It was their idea of fun, and it was just the way it was between them. A.J. would drink a twelve-pack of Pabst Blue Ribbon and his mom would drink as much tequila as she could stomach. Then they would yell and scream, essentially about nothing. And when it got quiet, Ryan knew they had made up and taken it into the bedroom. Sometimes Ryan was embarrassed. Especially when he saw Mr. Ramirez across the street, with his two young daughters, trying to shield them from the mess that was his family.

Theresa put her head in Ryan's lap as they continued smoking under the gray light of the moon. Ryan was comforted by her brown eyes and the smoothness of her skin as he stroked her cheek.

Ever since his father went away to prison, Ryan's mom had had a string of abusive boyfriends. A.J. was the latest and, in Ryan's mind, he was the worst. He supported her drinking and even perpetuated the problem. A.J. never worked and was constantly mooching off Dawn. He was a living contradiction. He never wanted Dawn to work, yet he expected her to pay for everything. He preferred her drunk in bed with him than off at work. He practically kicked Trey out of the house. And now, Trey was rarely around. He stayed out drinking all night, or slept over at girls' places just to avoid the misery that was the Atwood home. Ryan despised A.J. for taking away his brother. The one person he could share his misery with was gone and in

Ryan's mind it was all A.J.'s fault. Ryan and A.J. fought constantly. Ryan wondered if some day he would turn out the way his parents had. He wondered if he would inherit more from his mother than her dirty blond hair and her clear blue eyes. And he hoped that he would choose the right path in life — the one that would take him out of this town. But that was just Ryan dreaming. He hoped for a better life, but he knew that life in Chino would never lead to much. He knew that the longer he stayed in this town, the further away his dreams became.

"Tonight, let's pretend . . ." Theresa began as she sat up. ". . . that none of that. Out there. Matters." Ryan and Theresa weren't dating at the moment but he knew he would be welcome to sleep in her living room.

Ryan smiled. Theresa knew him from the inside out, and knew he was saying he'd be all right. Tonight they would pretend. Theresa smiled back and walked off, leaving Ryan alone on the porch.

Theresa and Ryan had been best friends since they were kids. During the summer they used to play hide-and-seek in their dark neighborhood. Sometimes they would pretend that they were hiding from the cops. That they were on the run from the law, and together they would escape without being caught. They pretended that the "ghetto birds," as they called the police helicopters that combed their neighborhood, were after them and they would run from backyard to backyard, over rusted fences, and under jacked-up cars. And they would hide. And when Ryan's mom would scream for him to come home, Theresa would sneak him into her room and they would have their own little sleep-over. Ryan would fall asleep with Theresa in his arms, listening to the screams from his house. He would wonder when things were going to get better. When he could go home and feel safe. They made a pact to stay friends forever.

"Open the door. You stupid slut." Ryan's mom and A.J. were still going at it. For the first time in his life he wished they would fall silent and take it to the bedroom. For the first time, that thought was not repulsive, but a comfort. All he wanted was quiet.

But they didn't stop and there was no silence. Ryan went inside Theresa's house.

"Here you go." Theresa met him in the living room with a pile of blankets.

"Very familiar."

"What?" Theresa questioned.

"That." Ryan nodded toward his house. "Always the same thing. I used to sleep in your room."

Theresa remembered all right. She wished it were the same. But it wasn't. Things weren't the same. They hadn't been for a while and they both knew it.

When they entered high school, things grew different between them. They were no longer just friends. The awkwardness of puberty set in and they found that their friendship had become much more than a friendship. They were both attracted to each other in ways they had never felt before.

There was something awkward about them sleeping in bed together. But they didn't deny their feelings. They pursued them. The night they both made love to each other for the first time in their lives, was a night neither one would ever forget.

Theresa remembered.

"Can we just forget about all that?" she said. It was too painful now that they weren't together.

Ryan gave her a look that said *sure*, as he pushed his dirty blond hair out of his eyes and took off his leather coat and hooded sweatshirt. "Good night."

Ryan climbed onto the couch and under the blankets wearing nothing but his wife beater and jeans.

Theresa walked to her bedroom alone, wondering, would their on again, off again relationship ever be on again. She looked back and saw Ryan's eyes close. For now, and maybe forever, it wasn't.

"Ryan, get up."

Ryan moved a bit.

"Let's go."

Ryan woke, expecting to find Theresa standing over him, but saw no one. Was he dreaming?

"Get up, you piece of crap."

It was Trey. His brother. Standing outside the window that opened above the couch. He looked at the clock. Two A.M. Ryan didn't know why his brother was there.

"Come with me."

"It's two in the morning. Where?"

"Can't go home. Can't stay here. Come on."

Ryan could hear his mom and A.J. Only this time they were in the bedroom. But it was loud and almost mean. Ryan was repulsed. He wouldn't be able to fall back asleep anyway.

"Fine. I'll be out in a minute."

Ryan put on his clothes and folded up all his blankets. He thought about leaving Theresa a note, but figured he'd just come over for breakfast in a few hours and he'd explain then. Theresa would understand.

Ryan met Trey outside the house.

"Where are we going?"

"Hey, can't a big brother take his little brother out for some fun without a lot of questions . . ." Ryan gave him a brooding look like he always did. ". . . or that look. We're going to a party."

Trey led Ryan through several backyards until they came to a house Ryan had never noticed before. This wasn't where Trey normally hung out. Ryan knew that and was suspicious, but he followed anyway.

"Atwood. You showed up." Some guy ran up to Trey and herded him to the back of the small house.

Ryan stood alone.

This wasn't the first time he had been abandoned by Trey to fend for himself. He went over to the fridge and pulled out a beer. Just as he was about to take a sip, some big guy with a shaved head and a lot of tattoos grabbed the beer from his hand.

7

"That's a buck. No one drinks for free. Especially not anyone who comes here with Trey Atwood."

Ryan didn't know what the big guy meant by that, but reached into his nearly empty pocket and pulled out a crumpled dollar bill. He paid and got away from there as fast as he could. He wandered through the house. Not that he could wander very far. Houses in Chino weren't big. There was usually a master bedroom plus one or two kids' rooms and a bathroom. Ryan was waiting outside the bathroom when he heard noise coming from one of the bedrooms. Ryan thought he heard a girl screaming for help, and his immediate reaction was to charge in and rescue her. To take her by the hand and lead her to safety, to hold her in his arms and comfort her, to take the guy and punish him. But he scaled back his efforts and when he was able to quietly open the door just a crack, he found that the screams were screams of ecstasy. The girl stared him down. *What the hell are you looking at?* Ryan froze. This was not what he'd expected and he didn't know what to do. The door slammed in his face. He hated awkward situations.

The bathroom door opened. Ryan went inside to be alone. He sat for a moment and chugged his dollar beer. Life was hell, Ryan thought. How did he end up in situations like this? All his life, nothing had gone the way he had hoped. As a child he used to dream that one day he'd get out of there. Live on the beach. Have a family. Be happy. But his dreams were always knocked out of his head by some sort of shouting match or slap on the face.

"Five thousand. By morning." Ryan's thoughts were interrupted by shouts from the adjacent room.

The house was old and poorly constructed. He could hear through the wall.

"I mean it, Atwood. This time. No money, you're dead."

Ryan stood still.

"You'll have your money," Trey shouted. Ryan could hear him kick something over and slam the door behind him.

Ryan thought about hiding in the bathroom for the rest of the night. Or sneaking out the window. But what kind of brother would he be? As much as he hated the family he had, he could never abandon Trey. That wasn't the way Ryan was. Under his tough exterior, Ryan still cared. And Trey was his last glimmer of hope. His last shot at any sort of real family.

There was a knock at the door.

"Come on. We have to pee."

Two girls were pounding on the door. Ryan finished his beer and walked out. He headed into the kitchen, dollar ready, and grabbed another beer. Trey found him just as he was opening the can.

"We're out."

Ryan chugged his beer and set the empty can on the counter.

Ryan followed Trey as they ran through the streets of Chino past their house and Theresa's and down and over a few blocks until they reached the tiny strip mall where Trey liked to buy his beer. There was a convenience store, a video store, and a "cambio" money exchange, where his mom sometimes got cash advances on her paychecks. When she had a job, anyway.

Trey went into the convenience store leaving Ryan in the parking lot. Ryan pulled his pack of cigarettes out of the inside chest pocket of his jacket. He opened it and noticed the lucky one Theresa had turned upside down. The tobacco stared at him. Ryan laughed to himself. She always did that when he wasn't looking. Ryan didn't believe in luck or superstitions, but Theresa believed and insisted. She feared what would happen if they didn't follow the "rules." She thought their lives were full of luck. *"If we think our lives are bad right now, imagine what they would be like if we didn't have luck."* Ryan could hear Theresa's favorite line. He still didn't believe, but he smiled at the thought of her. Ryan felt guilty about leaving in the middle of the night and made a promise to himself to bring her her favorite McMuffin in the morning.

Trey came out with two forties wrapped in brown paper bags. Ryan finally pulled a cigarette from his pack and lit it.

Trey and Ryan walked over to the darkened side of the building and sat on the sidewalk sipping their beers. Ryan wondered how Trey was going to get the five thousand dollars. Was that guy really going to kill him if he didn't? Trey didn't have a steady job and he knew his mom didn't have that kind of money anywhere. Ryan wondered if he should get a job. If he should quit school and help his brother out. But then he realized that Trey didn't know that he knew about the money. And he wasn't sure how to bring it up or if he even should. There were some things brothers just couldn't talk about. With these two, *most* things were those things.

They didn't talk. They had moments. Moments when their mom was passed out drunk on the couch, or A.J. was screaming at them. Moments where they knew what the other was thinking and didn't have to say much at all. They would look at each other and know they had to get out of there. Tonight was one of those moments.

Ryan looked at his brother — the pressure of the situation evident on Trey's face. He knew that the guy from the party really did have connections and if Trey didn't pay up his debts, he'd be gone. Ryan wondered how he'd make it without Trey. They had already lost their father to prison and that was bad enough, but death? That was permanent. Ryan would be alone forever. The thought pained him. Trey fidgeted with his beer, slowly peeling the label. Ryan watched his brother's hands tremble. He wanted to reach out and calm them. Trey had given up on himself a long time ago, but Ryan knew his brother still had hope for him. Trey had always wanted to be the model big brother, but he just kept taking the wrong turns and ending up at dead ends. This was the biggest dead end Trey had faced. Ever.

"You know how to fight?" Trey asked.

"Ah, yeah," Ryan answered, confused.

"Oh."

Trey fidgeted again, but the label was already gone. Ryan looked at his brother.

"How 'bout girls? You okay. You know how to . . ."

"Yes," Ryan answered, starting to understand.

"You use . . ."

Now Ryan understood — Trey's last attempt at being the model big brother. But he didn't want this to be the *last* attempt. He whispered "yes," not wanting to lose his brother.

"I'm sorry."

"For what?" Ryan asked, already knowing the answer.

"You know. Everything."

"Yeah." Ryan took a sip of his beer and watched down the street where he could see drunk Mr. Alvarez stumbling home. "You ever think we'll get out of here?"

"Used to. Now? No."

"Yeah, dreams."

The brothers sat quietly for a moment. Thinking. Was it true? Were they stuck here forever? They both knew the answer was yes.

"Hey, you listen to me. I haven't learned much in my life. Or ever told you how to live. But the one thing I know — dreams don't come true."

12

Trey slapped Ryan on the back. A love tap. A brother-to-brother moment.

Trey's words sat with Ryan. For the first time in his life, Trey had said something that made complete sense to him. Trey was right. Having dreams in this town got you nowhere.

Trey and Ryan finished their beers and tossed the empty bottles into the abandoned lot behind the strip mall. The sound of shattered glass echoed into the dull night. They both laughed and for a moment they forgot where they were, the lives they had, their family. For a moment, they were just two brothers. Two brothers having fun. But then, their smiles faded. Moments like this never lasted long. Especially when they knew they had to go back home. Ryan reached for his pack of cigarettes.

"We're not going home yet," Trey said suddenly, picking up a small metal rod from a pile of debris.

"What else we going to do?" Ryan asked as Trey flipped the metal rod in his hands. It was four in the morning and everything was closed.

"You ever steal a car?"

"No."

"Well, come on."

Trey led Ryan down the side street next to the mall where they spotted a car, seemingly abandoned.

"There." Trey pointed at the gold Camaro lightly covered in the dust of the Chino air. "That's ours."

Ryan looked at the car. He couldn't believe what his brother was suggesting. On this crappy street, where the buildings were covered in graffiti sat someone's pride and joy. Ryan knew enough about cars to know that someone had put a lot of time and money into rebuilding that Camaro. And they were about to steal it.

Ryan thought Trey was joking, but then he remembered the money. And the threat. And . . .

"Shhh. We're getting out of here. No looking back." Ryan sensed his brother's determination. Trey had had enough. He no longer cared about the guy or the money or Chino. Trey was leaving and he was taking Ryan with him.

Ryan knew they were going to do this. He thought about running in the opposite direction. Heading back to Theresa's, jumping into her bed and sleeping next to her like they used to as kids. But Trey had warned him, no looking back. The past was the past. They were getting out of there. Leaving Chino once and for all. Ryan started toward the car with trepidation. He was scared.

Ryan pulled Theresa's lucky cigarette out of the pack. If there was ever a time that Ryan needed luck, right now was it. He lit it and took two drags. He blew one smoke ring and tossed the cigarette to the ground. This was it.

The streetlights' haze cast an eerie glow upon the car. He looked at his brother and begged the question, *you sure?*

"I'm your brother, if I don't teach you this, who will?"

Trey swung the metal rod at the driver's side window. Shattered glass hit the dirty asphalt and the two brothers jumped in the car as it began rolling down the street. Ryan feared this wasn't going to end well. He wanted to get out of this town, but not in a stolen car. The radio blared. The music pumped. His breath suspended. Ryan and Trey locked eyes. Trey laughed. Ryan froze. They were free. Ryan felt trapped. They had done it. Ryan couldn't believe it. They were family. Brothers. And together they were gone, onto the open road, down the block. Into the world. Alone. Together.

The sirens wailed. Red and blue cop lights strobed through the back window. Trey stepped on the gas. Ryan held on to the door.

"We'll make it."

They narrowly avoided two trucks passing in front of them. Another car swerved to avoid crashing into their tail and several others slammed on their brakes. Trey screamed ecstatic, they had made it. But not for long. The lights found them. Several cops had joined the chase. A sea of red and blue swarmed behind them. Trey swerved and tried to escape, but one of the cop cars smashed into their side. The glass of the gold Camaro shattered upon impact.

Trey hit his head on the steering wheel. Blood flowed. Ryan sat quietly and wondered if this was the end. If life as he knew it was over. The cops emerged from the car and pounded on the window.

Trey got out first with his arms above his head. He was a pro at this. Ryan's hands trembled. He had never been arrested before. Would he be taken to jail? Juvie? He was afraid. Ryan watched as Trey was cuffed and placed in the back of the police car. Trey resisted and the cop slapped him. Ryan listened as Trey was read his Miranda rights. The words jumbled. Ryan could barely hold himself back from helping his brother. Another car arrived on the scene and Ryan was cuffed. The cold metal sat tightly on his wrists. His skin pinched and twisted. The pain radiated. The cop shoved him into the car. The lucky cigarette hadn't been so lucky. This was the end.

The police car drove away and Ryan caught his last glimpse of Trey. They locked eyes and said goodbye. Perhaps, forever. The gray of Chino drifted by his window as he was driven away. Ryan thought about Theresa, alone, waking to find the couch empty. He should have left a note.

2

Salt-misted waves crashed along the sands of Newport Beach. The local surfer boys had been out in the water since six A.M. when the sun had begun to rise over the heart of Orange County, breathing life into the city. High above Balboa Island and the Back Bay sat an expanse of McMansions. Expensive cars polished to mirrorlike finishes sat in driveways and infinity pools glistened in the yards. Children rode to the beach on skateboards while their parents headed to work in Range Rovers. As the sun rose higher, Newport became a tiny metropolis bustling with money and beauty.

In the heart of it all, Marissa Cooper's house sat high up on a cliff overlooking the shore. She had lived there most of her life. Always next door to the Cohen family. And always with a view of the ocean from her window. Life in Newport was always the same — like the weather, seventy-two and sunny. Nothing ever changed. Lately, Marissa had gotten bored with the view. She was starting to wonder what life outside the orange curtain was like.

Marissa's best friend, Summer, had no such concerns. "This is perfect," she said as they laid their towels on the sand.

It was another day at the beach. Marissa and Summer took off their tops and skirts to reveal their tiny bikinis. They were two beautiful California girls. Marissa's tall, thin body glistened in the sun and Summer's glowed. Both girls were stunning. The guys out in the surf whistled and waved. Summer excitedly waved back, but Marissa was a little less excited. Her boyfriend, Luke, was surfing, but he barely even acknowledged her presence. He was too busy waiting for the perfect wave. Luke was part of the O.C. crew that surfed every morning, played beach volleyball all day, and went to water polo practice at night. Marissa and Luke had been together since the fifth grade. She had never had another boyfriend and he had never had another girlfriend. The whole town knew them as Marissa-and-Luke, always spoken in a single breath. They had become one in the eyes of Newport and that was starting to bother her.

"Coop, how cute is Saunders?" Summer said as she eyed Luke and his friends. Saunders was one of Luke's good friends and Marissa knew him too well. He was always with Luke.

"Cute, but good luck trying to carry on a conversation with him."

"Whatevs — he's still cute."

Marissa laughed. Saunders was cute, but he was probably one of the dumbest guys she had ever met. But that was Summer, always buying the book because the cover was pretty, but never getting past chapter one.

As Marissa watched Luke shake the blond hair out of his eyes, she wondered about the upcoming school year. Over half of the summer had already passed and she wasn't looking forward to another year at Harbor High. Nothing new ever happened in Newport. No one moved in and no one moved out. She had gone to school with the same group of kids since she was in kindergarten, had the same best friend since second grade, and the same boyfriend since fifth. Marissa was looking for something new. Something to add a little fun to the monotony that was her life. And she thought she'd found it. Marissa had woken up this morning hungover. Drinking had become her escape from Newport this summer.

As Marissa lay on her back in the sun, she tried to forget about the headache pounding behind her eyes. That was the one downside she'd found to drinking. She remembered the first sip she ever took. It was the day after school had let out in June. There was a big party at her friend Holly's house and all of the usual gang was there. Saunders's older brother had bought them a keg and Luke gave Marissa her very first beer. At first she had been repulsed, but as she began to drink more she realized that the beer made her lose her sense of control. The release was euphoric. She had spent most of her life in control. And when she was buzzed, she didn't worry about the way she looked or the way her mom criticized her hair or that she wasn't ready to have sex with Luke. She'd learned to just enjoy the moment and have fun with her friends. Sometimes Marissa wished she could stay drunk forever and never wake up hungover.

As Marissa pushed her feet through the sand, she wondered what the plans for the night were. Probably the same thing as always, she thought.

"Hey, Coop." Summer sat up on her towel. "What are you wearing to the show?"

"I don't know." The National Charity League fashion show, one of the biggest summer events in Newport, was in two nights and Marissa was the chairperson. She and her friends had been planning the event since school had let out and most were ready for their hard work to finally pay off. But Marissa was starting to doubt its importance and wondered if a sick child or an abused wife really cared whether or not she wore Prada or Chanel.

"What about to Holly's?"

"Umm." But Marissa hadn't really thought about that either. Holly was having another party, this time after the show. Secretly, Marissa was kind of tired of all these summer beach parties. They were the same thing every time. They would sit around and get drunk and watch as Luke and his crew would pull some stupid prank or go night surfing. Marissa just wasn't in the mood. Sometimes she felt like staying home and doing nothing, but she was too afraid to say no to her friends. She never said no, so now she was kind of in a trap — always stuck going along with her friends even if she didn't want to.

Summer, who was getting antsy, decided the "umm" meant they must go shopping.

"Let's go to Fashion Island. I'm, like, starting to fry anyways. Plus, I so need a new top."

Marissa nodded and the girls began packing up their beach gear. Luke saw them and surfed into shore. His tan, toned body glistened as he walked over to them.

"Hey, babe. Did you see that last one I caught? I totally got air."

"Yeah," Marissa replied unsympathetically. She really hadn't been watching. She had been wondering when — and if — things could ever change. When — and if — someone or something would show up and turn her world upside down. But the sight of Luke in his board shorts made her realize that it wouldn't be anytime soon.

"Where you going? Not going to stay and watch me rip?"

"We're going shopping," Summer chimed in as she twirled her long brown hair up and out of her face.

"Sorry," Marissa said.

"No worries," Luke replied as he leaned in and gave Marissa a quick kiss. "I'll call you later."

Fashion Island was the epitome of sunny California shopping. Valet parking, palm-tree-lined parking lots, sculptures, gardens, and fountains — all out in the open air. Stores like Neiman Marcus, Macy's, and Bloomingdale's were situated among the boutique and designer dress shops.

They valeted their car and headed straight to Neiman Marcus, Marissa's favorite store. The way the store was laid out, the limited numbers of each item, and the designer names made things seem unattainable yet perfect. As she walked around and looked at all the displays, she felt like all her problems could be solved by the right purchase. That the right pair of shoes could lengthen her legs and the right dress could make her slim. That the right top could make her stand out. Marissa thought about all these things and wondered what she could buy to make her forget that school was approaching and the monotony would continue. She wanted something to break her out of the rut that was Newport Beach, but she wasn't really in a shopping mood. Yesterday, two men in suits had showed up at her house looking for her dad. When Marissa told her father, he passed it off like it was nothing. But Marissa knew there was more. As she stood looking at the giant price tags, she wondered what kind of trouble he was in.

"Oh my gosh, how cute is this dress?" Summer was in a frenzy over a selection of Emilio Pucci dresses. Their bright colors and swirled patterns weren't really Marissa's style, but on Summer they looked good. The smile on Summer's face made

Marissa forget about her dad for a moment. She started looking through the dresses.

"So cute," Marissa replied. Sometimes Marissa wished she was as carefree as her friend. That she could get away with bright colors and trendy outfits, but she knew they wouldn't look right on her. She was a classic girl, Chanel and Hermès bags. People expected her to be classy, presentable, and just about perfect. But inside, Marissa was screaming to break free. She didn't want to be perfect. She wanted to be herself.

"This is so you." Summer was holding up a black classic-cut Donna Karan dress. Marissa knew it would look good on her but she was becoming disheartened. She wanted people to notice the real her. The crazy and fun side. Not the in-control and classy side. But that would never happen when even her own friends couldn't imagine her any other way.

Marissa grabbed one of the tamer Pucci dresses and held it up. "What do you think?"

"It's cute, but . . ."

"But what?" Marissa snapped. She knew what Summer wanted to say, *that the dress was not her style*, but she didn't want to hear it. She wanted to get the dress and show the world who she really was. She liked punk music and she wanted to dance. Usually Neiman's made her happy, but today the shopping trip was turning out to be a disaster.

"Nothing. Never mind. It's cute. You should totally get it." Summer knew that something was wrong, but she didn't feel like getting into it.

"Yeah. I should." Marissa was glad Summer didn't say more. That's what she liked about her. She always knew when and when not to say certain things. That's why they were best friends. They knew each other inside out.

Marissa took the dress into the dressing room. It fit perfectly. She liked the way the cut in the front showed off her slight cleavage and she loved the way the pattern disguised the tiny pouch she swore was her stomach. Not that she was a big girl by any means — in fact, she was tiny — but years of criticism from her mom and six months of swimsuit weather in sunny California made Marissa a little self-conscious. And although the dress wasn't exactly her style, today it was the answer to all her problems. Her escape.

Summer picked out a cute little miniskirt and top and the girls were ready to check out. But when the clerk tried to ring up Marissa's purchase, her credit card was declined. She couldn't understand why. Her father was a finance manager, and he always paid the bills on time. Then she remembered the two guys in suits and she wondered if they had anything to do with it. Frustration and panic set in.

"Miss, sometimes this happens with cards. The magnetic strip goes bad. Don't worry. Do you have another?"

But Marissa didn't have another one on her. She

had only brought one credit card to the beach this morning. Her dad had the rest.

"No, I don't. Um . . ."

"Here, I'll get it." Summer stepped up to the counter. "Don't worry. My dad will never notice. You can have your dad write him a check tomorrow or something."

Marissa felt uneasy. Her instinct told her not to let Summer pay.

"No, that's okay. I'll just come back later. Can you put this on hold, please?"

The clerk took the dress and placed it on the counter behind her. Marissa backed away, embarrassed.

"You sure?" Summer asked again as she handed the clerk her black American Express.

"Yeah. I'll meet you outside." Marissa walked off as Summer paid for her purchase.

On her way out Marissa passed through the makeup section. One of her favorite areas of the store. Endless rows of beautiful color. Compacts full of confidence and lipsticks made of light. Heaven, she thought. As she browsed through the makeup she came upon the Chanel nail polish. Bold and beautiful. A hundred choices. A thousand ways to escape. And there in the middle of it all was a bottle of dark pink polish screaming her name. Freedom. That is, until she remembered that her credit card had been declined and she wouldn't be able to buy anything. But she couldn't resist. She took the tiny bottle and slid it into her purse. If she couldn't have the dress, at least she'd have the polish.

Back home, Marissa stopped by her dad's office. She knocked on the door and Jimmy motioned for her to come in.

"Hey, sweetie. How was the beach?"

"Good. Summer and I went shopping afterwards."

Marissa waited for him to ask, "What did you get?" but he didn't. This was a ritual they had established when she was a little girl. She would go shopping and when she'd come home he'd ask her what she'd gotten and she'd try on all her new clothes. He'd tell her how beautiful she looked. And Marissa would prance around the house like a princess in a new gown. She loved the attention her father gave her. She was daddy's little girl and she looked up to him.

But now, as she sat in his office, and he didn't even ask her what she'd gotten, Marissa started to wonder if she was still his little girl. If things between them were falling apart. What had she done wrong?

"Aren't you going to ask me what I got?"

Jimmy was taken aback. He had forgotten the ritual.

"Sweetie, I'm sorry. What did you get?"

She wanted so badly to hold up that Pucci dress and try it on and model it for him. He would understand her reasoning, her desire to be anything but

26

the Marissa everyone expected. But she didn't have the dress.

"I didn't get anything."

"But you always do."

"When the credit card works," Marissa said coldly. "I saw a dress. It's on hold. Can I just have cash?" She held out her hand — she knew how this worked, but Jimmy just snapped and yelled.

"No! I'm not an ATM, Marissa."

This was the first time he had ever yelled at Marissa about money. He had always given her anything she wanted.

She flinched at the sound of his voice. She knew now that whatever rituals and closeness they had shared in the past were slowly deteriorating. Marissa walked out of the office. Not mad, but sad. She missed the way things used to be between them and she wondered if her dad missed them too. But what she really wanted to know was why her father wouldn't tell her what was going on.

A phone rang somewhere in the house and Marissa's little sister, Kaitlin, yelled for her.

Marissa went to her room to take the call. It was Luke asking if she wanted to hang out that night.

She didn't really feel like talking, so she quickly agreed to his plans and got off the phone. Another boring night in boring Newport, Marissa thought, how exciting. She lay down on her bed, kicking off her rainbow flip-flops. Thoughts of her father raced through her head. Why was he acting this way? They used to talk about everything, and now she felt like he was holding something back, that the two-way communication they used to have was turning into a one-way to nothing. Tears formed in her eyes, but she held them back when she heard her mom, Julie, coming up the stairs.

"Marissa, honey. Can we try on dresses now?"

Marissa sighed and wiped her eyes as her mom entered the room.

Julie went straight to the closet and started pulling out dresses for the fashion show. Marissa watched as her mom held each dress up to her own body. Julie did this all the time. When she first noticed this habit, Marissa didn't understand it, but gradually she realized that when her mom was growing up she didn't have dresses like these. In a way, Julie was living the adolescence she never had through her daughters. Sometimes it bothered Marissa, but sometimes she found it endearing that her mom only wanted the best for her.

"Here, try this Donna Karan."

Marissa looked at the dress. It was similar to the one Summer had picked out for her earlier at Neiman's. When would she ever be free to be herself? Marissa wondered. But she wasn't about to fight her mother, so she put on the dress and stood in front of the mirror. The black fabric held her small body perfectly.

"Oh, Marissa, it's so forgiving. It hides everything."

Marissa stared at her image. So plain and perfect, she thought. Just what everyone would expect. She looked fine. But she felt ugly and unspecial. She felt big and plain. She thought about the dress she had left behind and wondered if she would ever be able to buy it. She wanted to put it on and prance around in front of her father and feel special.

"Okay, next." Julie held out another dress. Very classic, pale pink.

"I think I like this one," Marissa said as she held out the bottom of the black Donna Karan.

"I know, but, Marissa, you must have options. Especially when you can afford them. Now, take that off and try this on for me."

Reluctantly, Marissa took off the dress and slipped on the pink one. Marissa looked in the mirror. It was all right. Nothing special.

"Ugh. No. Look how your hips jut out on the side. It's too tight. Take that off."

Marissa looked in the mirror again, but she didn't see it. What hips? She stared a bit longer before taking off the dress. Were her hips really that big? Maybe her mom was right. Maybe she should start running twice a day now. But were smaller hips really the answer?

Marissa slipped on the next dress. She liked this one, but Julie criticized again. Now her breasts were too small and the back hung too low. Jimmy knocked on the door.

"Marissa, you look beautiful."

Thanks. She smiled sarcastically. *You should've seen the dress at Neiman's.* She was still upset with him. Julie stepped in and cut Jimmy off.

"Jimmy, she has to look perfect. And that dress is not it. Don't encourage her to stop. We've got ten more dresses to try."

But Marissa didn't want to try on any more dresses. She was tired of all this fashion show business and thought the black Donna Karan would be just fine. Julie wouldn't hear it, but Marissa refused to cooperate anymore.

Julie stormed out of the room. "All this work I've done to give you the life I never had . . ." Her voice trailed off.

Jimmy noticed Marissa's unease. "Don't worry. She just wants the best for you."

"I know. But sometimes . . ." Marissa stopped herself. She knew that if she continued she might start crying and she didn't want her dad to see her crumble. Not when she knew he had problems of his own right now. Even if he wouldn't tell her about them.

"Here, I brought you something. I'm sorry about earlier. You know I love you. I didn't mean to snap."

Jimmy held out a stack of hundred-dollar bills. "Go buy that dress."

Marissa hugged her dad and held him tight. Even though she knew there was still something wrong, she felt like daddy's little girl again.

"Thanks, Dad. I love you too."

Jimmy got up and left Marissa alone.

She looked at her watch. It was already six o'clock. Luke would be over in two hours. She didn't want to go, so she called him and canceled their plans, something she had never done before. She told him she had to stay home and watch Kaitlin. It was a lie, but he believed her. He said he could pick her up later, but for some reason Marissa said no thanks. For the first time in her life she didn't want to be where all the action was. She had a dress to buy, and she just didn't want to see all her friends. She didn't feel like eating seafood or drinking at Holly's afterwards — she had a new escape. Instead, she told Luke she'd call him later if her parents came home early.

With that phone call out of the way, she raced to Neiman's, charging up the escalator stairs two at a time. The stack of hundreds burned in Marissa's hand — things might just be all right. The same clerk was there from earlier in the day. She recognized Marissa and brought out her dress.

"Are you sure? Don't you think it's a little too much for you?"

Marissa looked at the cash. She knew the dress wasn't her style and she'd probably never wear it, but she didn't care. She *had* to have it. It was her ticket out of Newport if only for a night.

"Nope. It's perfect."

She held it in her arms. She felt elated. The dress was hers.

* * *

When she returned home, her dad was waiting.

"What did you get?"

Marissa was ecstatic; she hadn't been this happy in a while. And for the first time in weeks her dad was acting normal.

Jimmy waited patiently as Marissa darted up the stairs to change. She couldn't wait to show him the dress.

As Marissa walked down the steps, Jimmy stood and watched. His mouth dropped slightly. He had never seen his daughter in such a bold dress.

"Marissa, you look beautiful."

And even though Marissa knew what Jimmy was thinking — *the dress is not her style* — she was happy to have their ritual back.

"Thanks." Marissa pranced down the steps and gave her dad a giant hug.

All alone in her room, Marissa wondered what to do. She hadn't been alone in a long time. Usually she was with Luke, and if she wasn't with Luke she was with Summer or the girls, and if she wasn't with anyone she was on her cell making plans for later. It had been a long time since she had sat in silence, and she kind of enjoyed it. But what next? She thought about reading a book, but realized the only thing to read in her room were a few magazines and she'd read them all several times. Then she remembered the nail polish she had taken earlier and pulled it out of her purse. She started painting her nails. The bright pink matched her new dress perfectly.

She turned on her stereo and cranked up the Clash. Her favorite song came on and she started dancing around her room, belting out the lyrics. It had been a long time since she'd felt free.

As she danced, Marissa caught a glimpse of herself in the mirror. Her dress was beautiful and her nails were bold. And even though she knew deep down that she could never get away with wearing the dress anywhere but her room, she felt perfectly imperfect. And alive. And beautiful.

She felt like the real Marissa and just for a moment she felt that things could be different. That life in Newport could change. That her destiny lurked somewhere around the corner.

And as the song ended and her feet stopped moving, she fell onto her bed, elated. She wanted to stay bright and bold and beautiful. And never take off the dress or chip the polish. For once, she felt like herself and it felt good.

Her cell phone rang. It was Luke, but she didn't pick up. She couldn't. Not tonight. Tonight she was alone. Alive. Longing for something new.

3

Juvie was silent at this hour. Ryan could almost see the cold seeping out of the walls of the damp, dirty cell. His gaze drifted into the blackness above his cot as he thought about his brother. The leaking faucet next to his head dripped the tempo of a dead end. Ryan couldn't sleep. His mind raced. He knew that as bad as he had it here, Trey must have it ten times worse, and as bad as Trey had it he could only imagine how bad his father had it. As his eyes slowly closed, he wondered if he'd ever see either of them again.

After just a few hours of sleep, Ryan was awakened by the clanging of keys on his cell door. One of the guards slid the door open with a bang.

"Atwood. Let's go."

Ryan groggily sat up in his cot. He was being summoned. He slipped on his white Juvie-appointed shoes and followed the guard out into the visiting area, where he watched as families and friends caught up on lost time. Ryan wondered where he

34

was going. He knew no one had come to see him and he was sure that the only person who knew he was here was his brother, and he was in jail. Once again, Ryan was alone without anyone. The guard ushered him into a private room away from the smiling families and the happy friends. Ryan entered with his head hanging low.

"Hey, Ryan. Sandy Cohen."

Ryan looked up from the ground and saw a well-dressed man sitting at the table in the middle of the room.

Ryan sat on the bench across from him. The man barely looked up as he rifled through a file. Ryan assumed the file was his. He was right.

"The court's appointed me your public defender."

Great, Ryan thought. Someone from the other side.

"You could do worse."

Not really, Ryan thought as he remembered his mom and A.J. and his brother and the reason why he was here in the first place, and now, Sandy Cohen, in his nice suit. It couldn't get much worse than this. Ryan barely heard what Sandy said next.

All he wanted to know was, "Where's my brother?"

Sandy rifled through another folder on his desk.

"Trey? Trey's over eighteen. Trey stole a car. Trey had a gun in his pants. An ounce of pot in his jacket . . ."

And Ryan couldn't listen anymore. He knew his

brother was gone forever. That he might never see him again. Ryan blamed it all on A.J. If A.J. and his mom hadn't been going at it, Trey never would have stayed out and woken Ryan and dragged him to the party and run into the guys he owed money to and stolen a car and Ryan wouldn't have left Theresa alone. Ryan would have woken up to a slap in the face. His mom would be drunk and he'd call in sick for her. Trey would eventually stumble home from some girl's place. He . . . well, he would bring Theresa her McMuffin and everything would be normal. Ryan clenched his toes in his shoes, trying to hold back the anger and the fear. He forced back the tears as he dragged his toenails along the inside of his shoe, trying to show no emotion. He was good at this. He had done it all his life. He'd learned if you show no emotion, no one can hurt you.

But Sandy sensed the tension in Ryan's body and tried to change the subject.

"Trey's not my concern." Sandy leafed through some more papers as he attempted to connect with the kid sitting across from him. Sandy felt for him. He'd been there before. At one point he had been Ryan. The kid from the wrong side of the tracks. Dad gone and Mom never around. But he'd pulled himself out of it and he saw the same spark in Ryan that he had once had. Sandy looked over Ryan's transcripts. His grades were low and his attendance poor, but his test scores were in the ninetieth percentile. Even his own son hadn't scored that high. The kid had potential.

"You given any thought to your future? Any plans?"

But Ryan was still in his own world. Wondering if things were ever going to return to normal. For the first time in a long time, he wanted to go home.

"Hey. Dude. I'm on your side. Anytime you wanna help me out I'd —"

Ryan snapped out of his world and looked up at Sandy.

"Modern medicine is advancing to the point where the average human lifespan will be a hundred. But I read this article that said that Social Security is supposed to run out by the year 2025. Which means people are going to have to stay in their jobs until they're eighty." Ryan paused a beat. "So I don't want to commit to anything too soon."

Smart kid, maybe too smart, Sandy thought as a smile appeared on his face. He asked the guard to give him and Ryan some time alone. The guard walked out and Ryan and Sandy sat in silence for a moment as Sandy gathered his thoughts. He wanted to help this kid.

"Look — I'll plea this down to a misdemeanor. Petty fine. Probation."

Ryan nodded and waited for the "but." There was always a "but" in these situations.

"But know this: Stealing a car because your big brother told you to — that's stupid. And it's weak. . . . You want to change that?"

Great, Ryan thought. Another lecture from a man who barely knows me. Sandy continued on, but all Ryan could think about was Theresa. She was probably awake by now, looking for him. He felt bad. He wanted to be with her. Hold her in his arms and know that things might just be okay. Why did he have to leave with Trey? Why did he believe him when he said they were going to get out of this town?

"I'm serious. Smart kid like you — you gotta have a plan, some kind of a dream or —"

Now Ryan had had enough. He couldn't take much more of the lecture. Sandy Cohen did *not* understand him. No matter what he said. The only one who would ever understand his situation was Trey. And he was gone.

"Where I'm from — having a dream doesn't make you smart. Knowing it won't come true?" Ryan remembered Trey and their discussion the night before. "That does."

Ryan pressed his toes against the sole of his shoe and fought the emotion. Sandy was speechless.

The guard returned and walked Ryan back to his cell to change. He was free to go home until his hearing.

Sandy waited with Ryan outside Juvie. It was fairly quiet. Then the choking sound of a beat-up Chevy Nova interrupted the silence and Ryan knew that it was his mom. She sped into the parking lot and hit the brakes just as she went up and over the sidewalk curb right in front of them. Ryan was sure that his mom was at least a little drunk — if not a lot — and feared what would happen if she got too close to Sandy. He might smell the alcohol and turn her in, then she would be taken away. Ryan would be left with no one. His entire family stuck in jail. The thought scared him.

"What the hell did I do to deserve this family? You wanna tell me that?"

If he sniffed hard, Ryan could almost smell the tequila on the wind of his mother's breath. He turned his head. Sandy saw the shame in Ryan's eyes and tried to ease the situation.

"Hi, Mrs. Atwood. I'm Sandy Cohen, Ryan's attorney." He extended his hand and stepped forward. But Dawn stayed close to her car, ignoring the gesture. Ryan was relieved. Sandy would not smell the wreck that was his mother.

"You shoulda let him rot in there. Like his dad's doing. And like his brother's gonna. Let's go, Ryan."

Ryan took a deep breath, nodded thanks to Sandy, and started toward the car. Sandy fidgeted a moment, uncomfortable with the situation, and started to speak before he had a chance to think.

"I'm gonna give you my card."

He looked back at Dawn, who slammed her head on the door frame as she got into the car.

"And my home number . . . if you need somebody. If things ever get to be too much . . . call."

Ryan took the card from Sandy and slid it into his pocket. He didn't say it, but deep down he felt a sense of relief. No one had ever offered him help before. Sandy's gesture wasn't lost on him. He got in the car without turning back and drove away with his mom. Sandy watched him go and wondered if the kid would be all right.

The Nova skidded to a stop in the Atwoods' over-grown driveway. Dawn got out, slamming her door. Ryan followed close behind. They entered their tiny trailer-sized home. Everything was old and worn down. An indication of the life they had, Ryan thought.

"I can't do this anymore, Ryan! I can't! You wanna throw your life away too — I'm not gonna watch it."

The car ride home had been silent, but Ryan knew this was coming. He knew his mom was pissed. No matter how mad his mom had ever got-ten at him or his brother, she always had something to say. Dawn opened a cabinet and pulled out a bottle of tequila. She poured herself a shot and continued yelling. Ryan tried to apologize but it didn't help.

"I can't do it. I want you outta my house. I want you out."

Dawn downed the shot and lit a cigarette. A.J. emerged from the bedroom.

"You heard your mother, man. Get your stuff and get out."

That was it. First, A.J. started all this and now he

was kicking him out of a house that wasn't his. Ryan had had enough. He lunged for A.J.

"This isn't your house, man."

And the fighting began. Ryan threw the first punch, but A.J. was quick and bounced back. He grabbed Ryan by his white T-shirt and threw him to the ground. Ryan lay there in shock. Waiting for something. Anything. But nothing happened. His mom swallowed another shot and took a drag on her cigarette. She didn't even look at him.

Ryan got up and went to his room. He pulled out the black backpack he'd had since third grade, the only luggage he'd ever owned, and began stuffing it with his belongings. When he'd finished he took one last look around, though he didn't know where he was going; he wasn't sure he'd ever be back. He muttered *goodbye*, more to himself than anything here, and walked down the hall, past Trey's empty room and out the front door.

He got on his bike and rode down the street. Past Theresa's and the Ramirezes'. Past the overgrown yards filled with car parts and the Larch Street sign. He thought about turning back and going to Theresa's, but he couldn't do it. He had to get away. Fast.

He rode all the way to the liquor store in the next town over. Dropping his bike on the pavement, he walked inside and bought a new pack of cigarettes with some of the last money he had. Outside, he sat on the small concrete wall surrounding the parking lot and thought about what to do next. He picked up the pay phone and called everyone he knew. Even Theresa. But she wasn't home and she didn't have an answering machine. He kept calling. No one was home. No one wanted him. He kicked the phone out of frustration and searched his pockets for any change. He had to keep calling. Just one more quarter. But his pockets were empty. The only thing he found was Sandy Cohen's card. The one with his home number on the back. Ryan was desperate. He called collect.

Back in Newport, Marissa had just returned from another day at the beach when she noticed her neighbor Sandy speeding off in his BMW. She wondered where he was going in such a hurry. The Cohen family had never been of much interest to her. But there was something about Sandy's urgency that made Marissa pause. Part of her wanted to be in that car speeding away to something new and part of her was just plain curious. Maybe Mr. Cohen was part of some mafia, she thought, and he was running around like Tony Soprano. But then she laughed. Sandy was too kind and honest to do something deceitful, and Newport was too traditional — and clean — to let criminals into town. She giggled at her crazy thought and went inside.

Upstairs, in her bedroom, Marissa got ready for another evening in Newport. She and Luke had made plans to go to dinner and meet everyone at Holly's later. As she went through her closet, she came upon her Pucci dress. Maybe tonight she could pull it off. But when she tried it on and looked in the mirror, she couldn't do it. It wasn't her style and everyone would notice. As much as she wanted out of Newport, she still wasn't ready to be different.

As he sat on the wall waiting for Sandy to arrive, Ryan pulled out the pack of cigarettes he had just bought. He grabbed one and was about to place it in his mouth when he heard Theresa's voice echoing in his head, *If we think our lives are bad right now, imagine what they would be like if we didn't have luck.* He flipped the cigarette over and placed it back in the pack. Desperate, sure. But maybe luck would find him soon.

Sandy pulled up in his brand-new BMW and before Ryan knew it, they were headed far away from the world Ryan had known.

As they drove, the gray of Chino slowly turned into the gold of Newport Beach. Chevys and Fords transformed into Mercedes and Range Rovers. Dirt-filled lawns morphed into perfectly manicured golf courses. Never-ending concrete freeways gave way to warm golden sand. Children played on the beach and couples watched the sun set. The sky was empty and clear. And the air was warm.

By the time they arrived inside the gates of the Cohens' private community, the sun was just about to set. Sandy slowed as a golf cart crossed in front of them. Ryan looked at Sandy. He'd never been in a neighborhood where golf carts and BMWs shared the same street. In fact, he'd never seen either of them before in his life. Chino wasn't exactly known for its golf courses *or* fancy cars. Ryan was almost speechless, but too curious to keep his mouth shut.

"This . . . this is a nice car. I didn't think your kind of lawyer made money."

Sandy laughed a bit. This kid really *was* smart.

"We don't. It's my wife's."

Now Ryan was even more curious. "What does she do?"

"You see this?"

Sandy gestured out the window at the mansions surrounding them. Ryan took it all in. He was in awe.

"All of it?"

Sandy thought for a minute.

"Pretty much . . ."

Ryan had definitely never seen anything like Newport Beach or the houses that were passing outside his window. He had once thought that Theresa lived in a nice house, with the screened-in front door her mother had put up to let a breeze drift in during the summer and the metal siding Ryan had helped her brother Arturo hang one summer. It was better than most in the neighborhood. But this was different. *This* screamed money and comfort. Ryan wondered what he was doing here and thought about running away.

Sandy pulled into the driveway of one of the

bigger houses on the block. Ryan started to get out, but Sandy stopped him.

"You mind waiting here a minute? I gotta lotta esplainin' to do."

Ryan said nothing. What was he talking about?

"That's what Ricky always said to Lucy when — never mind. I'll be back."

Ryan nodded. Sandy turned off the car and was about to step out when he reached to take the key out of the ignition. He suddenly became very self-conscious. Here he was leaving a kid who had just attempted to steal a car twenty-four hours ago alone in his BMW. On the other hand, he wanted to show Ryan that he trusted him.

"It's no fun if the key's in the car," Ryan said.

Sandy smiled, appreciating Ryan's awareness, and got out of the car, leaving the keys behind.

Ryan sat in silence, disbelieving the situation he was now in. Leather seats, air-conditioning, a radio and CD player. No damp, dark cell. No drunk, screaming mother. No drunk, angry A.J. Just music on the Bose speakers.

Inside the house, Sandy had begun explaining the situation to his wife, Kirsten.

"You brought him *home*?"

As expected, Kirsten was not exactly overly thrilled about the prospect of a thief staying in her home. Her nice home. Where everything was metic-ulously planned *and* quite expensive — the Viking fridge and stove, the Spanish tile on the floor, and the granite countertops. But as mad as she was, Kirsten wasn't completely surprised that Sandy would be so willing to take in the stranger. That's why she loved him. He had a heart of gold.

"It's only for the weekend. Until Child Services opens on Monday."

Kirsten thought about it for a moment.

"He sleeps in the pool house."

"We have five extra bedrooms we don't even use." But Kirsten glared at him. And Sandy knew this was not a fight he could win. The pool house it was. Kirsten headed out of the kitchen.

"Where are you going?"

Kirsten turned around. "To put my jewelry in the vault."

Sandy was about to open his mouth, but Kirsten interrupted, "Where do you think I'm going? The boy's going to need fresh sheets. And towels. A toothbrush . . ."

Kirsten walked out of the room just as their son, Seth, walked in. Seth tried to stop her. "What boy?"

But Kirsten just replied, "Ask your father."

Sandy knew he was going to have to explain this one to Seth too. Seth walked over to the cabinet and began to pour himself a bowl of Cap'n Crunch. Sandy stared at him with a blank face, not sure what to say. Seth thought he was staring at his cereal.

"A bit minty, I know. But it doesn't get soggy. Look."

46

Seth took a bite and left his mouth wide open. The cereal crunched in his teeth. Sandy nodded. He got it.

"Seth, there's this kid, Ryan. A client of mine. I, well, your mom and I have decided to let him stay here for the weekend. He doesn't come from a good family, and he's got nowhere to go right now. So, we're going to watch him."

Seth thought about this for a moment.

"Interesting . . . like a little brother," he finally said.

His mind raced. He always wanted a brother. Someone he could mold and teach and . . .

"Uh. Not quite. He's your age."

Seth's face dropped as he shoved another spoonful of Cap'n Crunch into his mouth. He was not happy.

"Right. The sixteen-year-old male. My best friend. Thanks, Dad. We'll get along swell. Just like cat and mouse, fish and bear, lions and . . ."

"Seth, that's not —"

"No, it's great. I'll just be in my room."

Sandy tried to convince him to stay, but Seth had already gone upstairs to read his latest comic books.

Outside in the driveway, Ryan was getting bored. He needed to smoke. He opened the pack and saw the lucky cigarette. Theresa's voice filled his head. Luck, he thought, what a strange thing. He wondered if she was home right now. If when he got inside he could call her. If Sandy would even let him.

Next door, Marissa emerged from her house. She was about to call Luke, when she noticed Ryan at the end of the Cohens' driveway.

Their eyes locked.

She smiled at him. Ryan was stunned by her beauty. Tall, tan, and thin. Light brown hair and green eyes. Gorgeous.

Marissa noticed him staring at her. She was curious and uncomfortable. She had never seen him before.

"Who are you?" she asked.

Ryan tried to play it cool.

"Whoever you want me to be."

"Okay," she answered.

God, that was lame, Ryan thought and put the cigarette to his lips.

Marissa thought about the lame response but let it go as she watched him. She was in awe. He was different. She needed to say something cool.

"Hey, can I bum a cigarette?"

Ryan walked over and handed her the pack. She pulled one out and placed it between her lips. They hesitated for a beat, then leaned in to each other and allowed the ends of their cigarettes to touch. A spark caught between the two.

Marissa's heart skipped a beat. This was better than any Pucci dress.

"So. What are you doing here? Seriously."

Ryan wasn't quite sure how to answer. The

truth? Or a lie? But he didn't have much time to think.

"I stole a car. Crashed it into a telephone pole. Actually, my brother did. And since he had a gun and drugs on him, he's in jail. I got out but then my mom threw me out, 'cause she was pissed off and drunk, and so Mr. Cohen took me in."

Marissa started laughing. This guy wasn't serious, was he? Ryan was taken aback.

"No — for real. You're their cousin from Boston, right?"

Now Ryan understood. She wasn't laughing at his situation — she simply didn't believe it. He got it.

"Boston. Right."

Ryan was about to ask her name, but suddenly Sandy was on his way down the driveway. Marissa immediately tossed her cigarette into the bushes. Ryan continued to smoke his.

"Hey, Mr. Cohen. I was just meeting your nephew."

Sandy was a little surprised, but then he caught on. This boy was good.

"Ah, yes. My favorite nephew, Ryan. All the way from Seattle."

But they weren't free and clear.

"Seattle?" Marissa asked quickly.

But Ryan was quicker. "My dad lives there. Mom lives in Boston."

Sandy felt the tension in the air and quickly changed the subject.

"So we're all really excited about the fashion show fund-raiser tomorrow."

Not the fashion show, Marissa thought as she looked into Ryan's eyes. Her escape was standing in front of her and all she could talk about was the one thing she dreaded the most. God how she wanted to run home and put on her new dress and show Ryan that she was different. But Sandy went on and she was too polite to stop him.

As Sandy and Marissa continued talking about the details of the fund-raiser, Ryan tuned out. He couldn't help but get lost in Marissa's beauty and the sound of her sweet voice. No girl he had ever been around talked with such sophistication and grace. Not even Theresa. Ryan looked down at the open pack of cigarettes he had shoved into his pocket. The lucky one was gone. He looked into the bushes and saw Marissa's cigarette still smoldering. She had smoked it. He panicked. Did that mean she would get all the luck? Or would they have to share it? He looked up at her and felt a connection again. The spark. Was this what luck was?

Marissa turned to Ryan.

"Hey, you should come by. Check it out. If you don't have other plans."

He was exactly what she needed to make the fashion show sound fun again.

Ryan shrugged maybe. He was playing it cool. Marissa smiled at him and just as he was starting to believe in love at first sight, or some other cliché like that, Luke pulled up in his fully loaded truck and

Marissa said goodbye. Ryan couldn't keep his eyes off the two of them as they pulled away.

"Who was that?" Luke asked Marissa as they drove out of sight. She hesitated.

"No one. Just the Cohens' cousin." But she knew better. He was more than that . . . he was different.

Luke nodded and flexed his chest muscles under his Volcom T-shirt. He was a tan, blond, blue-eyed jock — too naïve to be threatened by another guy. Luke started to talk about the amazing waves he and his friends had caught that afternoon. Marissa barely listened as they headed off to dinner at the Crab Shack. She couldn't get the image of Ryan out of her head. He was better than any Pucci dress she could ever own.

Sandy and Ryan headed up the driveway and into the house. Ryan took a drag off his cigarette. Sandy noticed.

"There's no smoking in the house."

Ryan paused. No one had ever told him not to smoke. He wasn't used to adults with rules, but he wasn't about to get in any more trouble. So he tossed it onto the driveway.

The inside of the house was even more spectacular than the outside. Ryan was speechless as he followed Sandy through the kitchen and out to the pool house. There he met Kirsten who showed him around his room for the weekend. She was polite, but distant.

Ryan wondered if the Cohens had other guests staying with them. They had to have guest rooms in this enormous house of theirs. Maybe he wasn't the first kid Sandy had brought home. Maybe the others got the guest rooms and he had the pool house. But at least it was a bed, Ryan thought.

Sandy and Kirsten said good night and left Ryan alone. He took off his jacket and his boots and neatly placed them on the chair in the corner. Then he removed his jeans and folded them on top. He climbed between the clean, soft sheets of the bed. The room was silent. This was nothing like home.

As Ryan lay awake in this strange place he thought about his dad and A.J. and Trey and his mom and wondered where his life would take him. Would he ever see them again or were they gone forever?

He finally fell asleep holding the leather band around his neck, the last thing his father ever gave him before he went to prison, the last time he could remember being part of a family.

4

From his bedroom window, Seth stared out at the pool house. He couldn't sleep. He wasn't sure about this strange kid sleeping in his backyard. Did he really have to meet him?

As he paced around his room, Seth wondered what kind of trouble this guy was in. He wondered if Ryan was tough and mean — he'd read somewhere that some criminals who'd been through the justice system became hard and calloused and virtually unable to function in normal society. Seth thought he should be used to this by now; after all, his dad was a public defender and dealt with criminals all the time. But he'd never brought his work home. And Seth had never known anyone who'd gone to jail, let alone someone his own age who'd gone to jail. Seth wondered what was so special about this guy — why had his dad brought him home? And why did he have to sleep in the pool house? They had five other bedrooms they never used.

Seth tried to get Ryan off his mind as he went

53

back to reading his new book, Salinger's *Franny and Zooey*. He had picked it up this afternoon after he'd given a sailing lesson in the harbor. There was something about Franny that intrigued Seth. He liked her distrust for guys who brought the right girl to the right bar on the right game weekend. The book mocked society's standards, and he loved it because he didn't fit society's standards. He empathized with the way she could categorize the girls on the train by the schools they attended, because he did the same. He could skate down the pier or along the boardwalk and pick out the water polo jocks, the deb girls, the Pacific students, the stoner/surfer guys, and the kids who lived in the numbered streets. Newport was full of labels. The game was easy for him. And it wasn't that he liked labels, it was that he found it interesting that all the other kids did. They lived for labels.

Seth had no label. To most people, he didn't really exist. People knew *of* him, but no one knew the real Seth Cohen. He was the captain of the sailing team. Comic Book Club. Film Preservation Society. But he was the only member of all three. He thought about how he had practically begged his parents to let him go to boarding school this year — they had refused. They said a family needed to stay together and it wasn't right for a kid to grow up on his own far away from home. It'd be too rough. But what they didn't understand was that life here was rough too. Right about now, if they had let him go away to school, he'd have left for the start of the school year and not returned home until Thanksgiving. Unfortunately, he was here. Now he had to deal with Ryan and the impending school year at Harbor. Not exactly his idea of the idyllic Newport life. But he was stuck. Seth went to his record player and put on his vinyl copy of the Cramps. He was about to crank up the volume when he heard a faint noise.

Through the vent in his wall, Seth could hear his parents talking downstairs. Their faint voices whispered like a summer breeze.

He pressed his ear close to the vent and listened.

"Promise me just this weekend. We're not a halfway house, Sandy. Did you see his eyes? They were red and . . . he looked so . . ."

"Sad," Sandy said as he completed his wife's sentence.

"Not what I was going to say, but okay."

"He's all alone. He's got no one."

Seth pressed his ear closer to the vent. He knew what it was like to feel sad and alone. Maybe he and Ryan would have something in common, he thought. Maybe they could become friends. Hang out. Do guy things together. Go sailing. Look for girls. Skateboard. Read comic books. Play video games. This friend thing was so new to him. Seth had never really had any friends. And this would probably never work out the way he wanted, but the idea that he, Seth Cohen, could be friends with a hardened criminal . . . it was a cool thought.

"And he's got no one, because he . . . ?" Kirsten started.

"He stole a car. With his older brother," Sandy answered succinctly.

Even better, Seth thought. A car thief. Tough *and* cool. This could almost be worth not being able to go to boarding school. If he showed up at school in the fall with Ryan as his friend, he was bound to get some respect.

"He's not a criminal mastermind. You should've seen his mother. Drunk and cursing. And the poor kid just standing there. Lost. Unsure of himself and his situation. Kirsten, I couldn't just leave him — she kicked him out."

Seth hadn't expected his dad to say anything like that. He was waiting for the drugs, the booze, the sex, and the parties. Real criminal stuff. Maybe he and Ryan wouldn't have so much in common after all. How would he talk to a kid who was kicked out by his parents? He could never imagine his own parents kicking him out of the house. Abandoning him. Life without parents was inconceivable to him and *he* had a giant imagination. Where would he go? What would he do? How far could he go on a skateboard? He had no car, and his sailboat was reserved for Summer. If he ever got kicked out he'd be lost.

He'd probably end up having to hide out in one of his grandpa's new developments. In some mansion that wasn't quite finished. Without TV or a stereo. Almost in complete isolation.

"It'd be me and you, Captain Oats," Seth said to a small plastic horse he took off a shelf and sat on his desk. He looked at his cell phone. No missed calls and an empty phonebook. "I suppose that's not so unusual, though, huh?"

Seth plugged in his iPod and began to download some new songs.

The voices downstairs quieted. The only sounds now were the crickets chirping and the waves hitting the shore far below. The summer breeze pressed against the palm fronds. Their green leaves rattled against the window.

Seth peered out the window at the yard below. What would he say to Ryan? He needed a plan. Something that would make him seem cool and collected. Not nervous and geeklike. Something that would make him the antihero superhero. Everything he'd always dreamed. But how, he thought. This plan had to be better and more consistent than his plan to sail to Tahiti with the love of his life, Summer Roberts. And he'd been working on that plan since third grade. He was doomed.

The Summer plan had been in the works ever since the day she entered his class in third grade. She sat two rows in front of him and every morning he would watch as she hid her My Little Pony in the bottom of her desk. She would smooth its hair and kiss its head and tuck it away when the teacher wasn't looking. The pony was her comfort and Seth understood. Her parents were going through a divorce that year, and one morning he saw her dad give her that pony. This was when Seth discovered the real Summer. The sensitive Summer who was smart and witty and vulnerable. The Summer he was in love with. The Summer he knew existed behind all the designer clothes and the popular reputation she now had. The Summer he would someday talk to and sail with to Tahiti.

But Ryan was not Summer. He had no extensive plan for Ryan. This was going to be hard. He had a plan for Summer. And he wasn't even on her radar. Then again, he wasn't on Ryan's either. Maybe he could avoid Ryan all weekend. Sneak through the house. Grab some cereal. Hide upstairs. Oh, who was he kidding? He'd have to talk to him. And what would he say? They had nothing in common besides the fact that they were both alone. And as comforting as that sounded, loneliness hadn't gotten him very much so far.

Seth needed a real plan. A foolproof, one-hundred-percent-successful plan.

"So, Captain Oats. What's it going to be? The plan? A new car? A rare edition of Wonder Woman? A six-pack of beer?"

But the horse didn't respond.

"Figures. The one time I need you to have my back, you go silent."

Seth got up from his bed and started searching through his desk drawers. But there was nothing there. No plan for how to talk to a criminal. No book on how to make friends. Just a bunch of maps and waterway charts. Sextants and brochures on

58

Tahiti. If Summer were a criminal, she'd be his best friend.

He needed more time. Like nine years worth. And he had approximately eight hours until Ryan woke up. He really was doomed.

"Take a rest, pal. This could get ugly." Seth sighed as he placed Captain Oats back on his shelf.

It was time for business. And that meant playing Death Cab for Cutie on repeat. A few great books. *Kavalier and Clay*. And his favorite — *On the Road*.

He flipped through the books, looking for answers. Not quite sure what he would find, but he thought there had to be something. Wasn't literature just the history of human emotion? Kerouac had to have an answer. He'd spent months on the road meeting lots of people. He would know how to deal with a criminal. How to make friends. How to be cool. Handle awkward situations. The right things to say at the right time.

Seth flipped through the pages, but he was drawing a blank. He couldn't find the perfect line or passage that would show him the way. He continued reading. Searching.

Maybe Ryan was like Dean, a sort of jailkid just waiting to become an intellectual. A misfit with the hopes of becoming something greater. And if that were true, this might not be so hard. Seth considered himself an intellectual. They could discuss literature, music, the arts. Engage in heated arguments. Banter. But what if Ryan didn't want to talk?

Was this good enough? It was nowhere near a

perfectly charted course to Tahiti. The knowledge of trade winds. A brand-new sextant. It wasn't solid. He needed a solid plan. Operation Criminal Friend was going to be hard to execute without a good plan.

He turned to *Kavalier and Clay* and began flipping through the book. Illustrations popped out at him, but nothing seemed right. Would he have to start from the beginning?

Maybe he would have some cool thing he did like Josef Kavalier to break the ice. A moment where he and Ryan could bond over something they had in common. Just something that would take the edge off. He didn't smoke, so he couldn't exactly make a new cigarette out of the butts of old ones, but maybe he could do something else. Something that would make him seem cool. They could play Jenga and he'd let Ryan win. But was that lame? He'd only ever really played with Captain Oats before and, well, he never talked back.

Or maybe he could show Ryan his comic book collection. He had some that were collector's editions. Quite impressive. But what if Ryan hated comics, and thought they were lame?

He had lots of music. Emo bands. Independent rock. Punk. Did other kids listen to the same things he did?

Seth felt hopeless. The weight of the world on his shoulders. He couldn't find one good answer. One solid plan.

The bed bounced under him as he fell on it.

More than ever he felt like a loser. An outsider. Incapable of ever having any real friends. He was sad. And mad. He wanted to run away, but he couldn't. He'd thought of that earlier. He had nowhere to go. No one to run to. He was alone. Without a good plan.

At least it couldn't get any worse.

He'd just have to wing it.

One day he would look back on this moment and laugh. When he and Ryan were old pals, like brothers, he would make him read these books. Find an answer for him. And together they would laugh at all the trouble Seth went through for just a simple hello.

Seth looked out his window at the dark pool house and the darkness that covered Newport. Everyone was asleep. Who was he kidding? This would never work. He was Cohen: The geek no one talked to at school. Clark Kent without a cape. Peter Parker before the bite. On the other hand . . .

"You ready, buddy?" Seth said as he pulled Captain Oats back off the shelf and put him next to his bed. "Get a good night's sleep. Tomorrow starts Operation Criminal Friend."

The horse said nothing, but he had to stand tall.

"We can do this. And if it fails, there's always Summer and Tahiti. . . ." Seth said as he closed his eyes for the night.

5

Eight hours had passed and Seth still had no plan. The California sun rose high above the Pacific Ocean and rested upon the Cohen house. He peered out his window. There was no sign of movement around the pool house.

"All right, Captain Oats, it's doomsday. Are you ready?" Silence. "That's what I thought. Fine, you stay here. I'm going to face my destiny."

Seth threw on a T-shirt and headed downstairs. In the kitchen he found a note. His mom had gone into the office and his dad was out grocery shopping. Great, Seth thought as he read the last line: *Show Ryan around the house and make sure he gets some breakfast.* How did I become the tour guide of the Cohen home?

Seth dropped the note on the counter with a groan, then grabbed a bagel and sat down at the kitchen table. He found the Arts and Leisure section among the pile of newspapers and began to read. His morning ritual. But this Saturday was different. He couldn't concentrate. Not with Ryan outside sleeping in the pool house. The jitters and the nervousness from last night returned. Operation Criminal Friend was starting to seem like the worst idea ever.

How was he going to talk to Ryan? He didn't have Captain Oats and he wasn't Kavalier. Why had his parents left him here all alone? When they got back he'd have a talk with them. This was unacceptable behavior. They were supposed to be working for him. Not the other way around.

Seth tossed the Arts and Leisure section onto the table and gathered his breakfast. He couldn't sit any longer in silence just waiting for the criminal creature to wake up and come inside and eat him alive. He had to do something. He needed a distraction. So he went into the other room and started to play his favorite video game. Seth was content — at least for now.

Outside, Ryan woke up — startled. Disoriented. For a moment, he crouched under his blankets, waiting for A.J.'s slap or a scream from his mother telling him to call in sick for her, but it was peaceful. Just the cry of a seagull and the sound of the ocean. Ryan looked around and remembered where he was. Was this a dream? He pinched himself to make sure it wasn't. The pain stung. This was no dream.

Ryan slowly pulled on his jeans as he took in his surroundings. The pool house was almost the size of his entire house in Chino. He couldn't believe he had slept here. Then he remembered Marissa, the girl next door, and his ride with Sandy Cohen, and felt dizzy for a moment. He scraped his toes against the floor. A reflex.

He stepped outside only to find that the house was even more spectacular than he thought. The infinity pool, the lush grass, the ocean view. This was truly paradise. And way too much for Ryan to handle on an empty stomach. He headed toward the back door to find some breakfast.

When he opened the door, Ryan found himself face-to-face with Seth. Not exactly, but it felt that way. They were the only ones in the room. He was a little surprised, but then he remembered that Sandy had mentioned he had a son. This was probably him. But Ryan didn't know what to say except, "Hey."

"Hey."

This is it. This is really it, Seth thought. Okay, play it cool. Just maybe ignore him for a beat. Seth turned back to the plasma screen TV and continued to play his game.

Ryan stood awkwardly waiting. Was he allowed in?

Seth thought of his mom's note. Be nice, he thought. Okay.

"This is the new PlayStation," Seth said with the best intentions. Ryan took a step forward.

"I know."

Maybe Ryan knew more than he thought. Now he felt bad. Did he offend him? He had to do something to make up for it.

"Wanna play?" he asked weakly.

Ryan hesitated a bit, then, "Sure."

Ryan sat down on the floor next to Seth and picked up the extra controller. They started to play and just as Ryan was about to maim Seth's ninja, Seth hit pause. He'd remembered his mom's note again. Ryan was probably starving.

Ryan looked confused. What had he done?

"Do you want some breakfast?"

Then Ryan understood. He nodded yes. Seth jumped up and ran into the kitchen. He opened a cabinet and started listing off every cereal known to mankind. Ryan was in awe. At his house, they were lucky if they even had one box. Ryan told Seth he'd have whatever he was having. He didn't want to make things complicated or difficult.

Seth returned with the cereal and the boys resumed play. They both really started to get into the game and were beginning to warm up to each other as they continued fighting onscreen. This isn't so bad, Seth thought. Maybe Ryan wasn't a hardened criminal after all. Maybe he was more like Dean, just a jailkid waiting for his chance.

As the boys continued laughing and playing, Sandy arrived home from the grocery store and stopped dead in his tracks at the door. An unfamiliar sound. The boys' laughter. He couldn't believe it, but he was thrilled. He stood back a moment and watched the guys continue to play.

"Hurry! They're going to kill us!" Seth exclaimed.

"How about a little backup?" Ryan asked.

And Seth went to town. Both boys hit the buttons furiously, but to no avail. They threw their controllers in the air. They'd lost. It was time for a new game.

Seth got nervous for a second. He had to choose the game wisely. He didn't want to seem lame. He made a mental note of all the games he owned. And then he had the perfect idea. This game was cool.

"You wanna play *Grand Theft Auto*?" Ryan stared at him. "It's really cool. You can steal cars —" Then Seth caught himself. Had he really just said that to Ryan, the criminal? The boy who was here because he stole a car? Now he was doomed. He'd ruined it. Things had been going so well. He tried to save himself. "Not that that's cool. Or uncool. But —"

Sandy saw his son bumbling and doing the Cohen thing — speaking on tangents that only dig the hole deeper — and he stepped in to the rescue.

"I see you two met." The boys glared at each other and nodded. "What are you doing sitting inside? It's beautiful out. Seth — why don't you show Ryan around?"

Great, Seth thought. Now he could take Ryan out and introduce him to all the friends he didn't have. Or better yet, he could show him all the different groups of kids – the stoner/surfers and the water polo jocks — and show him how he fit right in.

"Yeah, Dad, 'cause it's so great here. . . . There's

so much to do. . . ." Seth was feeling down on Newport and didn't feel like venturing out, but then he realized Ryan was looking at him. He needed a better answer. "Unless . . . What do you wanna do?"

Then Ryan, not sure he wanted to know the answer but a little too curious, asked, "What do you guys do around here?"

Seth walked with Ryan down and around the house and out to the beach. There below the Cohens' house and Marissa's, Seth readied his sailboat. Ryan tried to help but he was just getting in the way. He was lost when it came to boats.

The only boat he'd ever been around was the toy one he used to sail in his bathtub as a child and that was a distant memory. Everything on this beach awed him. He'd never lived somewhere where you could walk to the beach and your very own boat. The coolest thing he ever walked to from his house was the Slip and Slide Theresa's mom had brought home one day when they were kids. And she had found it at a garage sale in Irvine on her way back from work. That was also the closest Ryan had ever gotten to a large body of water.

"Ready?" Seth asked as he pushed the boat slowly into the water.

Ryan looked out at the expanse of ocean in front of him. He couldn't believe he was going to do this. "Sure," he said as he helped Seth push the rest of the boat into the water.

Seth sat high up on the back of the boat, steering with the rudder, making sure to catch the wind just right. Ryan could tell that this was something Seth did often. He was impressed. Most of the kids he knew only knew how to ditch school and hide from the police, or, like his brother, steal cars. He'd never known anyone his age who was passionate about anything, but he could see that Seth really enjoyed this.

"You been doing this long?" Ryan asked.

"My grandpa taught me when I was six. He sails a lot. He has a yacht too. Sometimes I get to drive that. Not too often, though."

Ryan nodded. Then —

"Come about." Ryan looked at him. What? "Switch!" Then all of a sudden Ryan saw the boom swinging right at his head. He understood.

"Switching."

Ryan ducked and leaped to the other side of the boat. This wasn't so fun after all. He was freaked. Seth saw his uneasiness.

"Relax. Worst-case scenario — you fall in."

But that didn't calm Ryan. "I can't swim!"

Now Seth felt bad. First he'd offended Ryan when he assumed he didn't know what the new PlayStation was and then he'd talked about stealing cars, and now he had Ryan in the middle of the ocean and he couldn't swim. By the time he got back he'd have one less friend than he had before. *Was it possible to have negative friends?* he wondered. *What if Ryan drowned? Was that worse?*

"I very rarely capsize. But just in case — you should wear this," Seth said as he handed Ryan a life vest and tried to play it cool.

Ryan grabbed it and stared. Embarrassed. But Seth understood. "I should wear one too . . ."

The boys floated in silence as Seth sailed them farther away from shore. From here, Ryan could see the beautiful coastal expanse that was Newport. And though he was still frightened of the open water, he was too in awe of the mansions that lined the cliffs and the beaches to care. One house here was bigger than an entire block of houses in Chino stuck together. Ryan thought about home. What would happen to him here? Would he ever go back to Chino? When would he see Theresa again? What would his mom say when he returned? Was he really kicked out forever?

Seth felt awkward in the silence. He could see Ryan's eyes move fast like he was thinking and Seth got nervous. This guy must think I'm a complete dork, Seth thought. He was probably bored out of his mind. This wasn't like stealing a car. This paled in comparison. He felt lame. But he had to think of something to say. The silence was killing him and he needed to redeem himself for taking Ryan on such a boring ride. There weren't any whitecaps and the wind was starting to settle. This really wasn't sailing, but maybe Ryan wouldn't notice. Seth fished for something, anything to start a conversation.

"So . . . first time sailing. You like it?" Ryan

didn't reply. Couldn't. His mind was still in Chino. But Seth was being so nice. He nodded. Seth nodded back. "I love it."

But Seth's plan hadn't worked. There was silence again. Now what? he thought. Ryan stared at the shore. At the houses. At Marissa's. Seth fidgeted. Could he tell him about Summer? His plan. Maybe Ryan would like it. Find it charming. But gross, why did he want Ryan to find him charming? He didn't but he needed something to say. Something to talk about. Something that could carry them all the way back to shore.

Ryan continued to think about Chino, about how he had left Theresa all alone. About his brother in a damp, dark cell, and he felt guilty for being here in the middle of the ocean, for thinking about Marissa. And he felt guilty for not paying attention to Seth.

He turned back to Seth as he continued to talk. Seth had decided. He was going to tell him.

"I have this . . . plan. Or, I dunno. You might think it's —" He couldn't believe he was doing this. "Whatever — maybe — but . . ." This was not like telling Captain Oats. "Next July. The trade winds shift west. And I . . . well . . . . I wanna sail to Tahiti. I can do it in forty-four days. Maybe even forty-two."

Ryan was unsure how to respond; he'd never met anyone with such big plans. "Wow. That sounds really —" And he wanted to say it sounded amazing. Like one of the best plans he'd ever

70

heard, but he couldn't do it. He didn't want Seth to think he was soft.

But Seth finished the sentence for him. "Awesome?" Did Ryan really understand him? He was in shock. He'd never shared this plan with anyone real before. He got gutsy and decided to continue. "No rules. No map. Except the sun and the stars. And maybe a sextant. Catch fresh fish off the side of the boat, grill 'em right there. Total quiet. Solitude."

Ryan was still in awe. Seth had dreams. And he believed in them too. It was amazing to him. He wanted to know more. "You won't get lonely?"

Without even thinking Seth answered, "I'll have Summer with me." Seth choked on his words. He'd blown it.

Ryan glanced at the side of the boat. It was labeled *Summer Breeze*. "You're going to take this to Tahiti?"

And then Seth knew it was over. Negative one friend. He was about to sound incredibly pathetic. "No. The girl the boat's named after."

Ryan thought she must be some girl. He had never done anything that sweet for Theresa and they'd known each other since he was five. But maybe that was how relationships worked here. "She must be pretty stoked."

Seth dreaded the next few words that were about to come out of his mouth. "Yeah . . . she has no idea. I've never talked to her before."

Now Ryan felt bad for bringing it up. He could tell it was a sore spot for Seth and he could tell he was embarrassed. They headed back to shore in silence. The wind blew hard again. Ryan gripped the side of the boat. His knuckles turned white as they picked up speed and landed on the soft sand.

Sandy came down the hill to join the boys as they derigged the boat.

"So. Seth. I thought we'd head over to the fashion show around seven?"

Great, Seth thought. The trials and tribulations of the school year would begin early. "Have fun," Seth retorted.

Ryan wondered why Seth didn't want to go. He looked back up at the Cooper house and wondered about Marissa. Was that her standing in the window? He couldn't get her image out of his head from the night before. Her tan skin, her dirty-blond hair. And the lucky cigarette she had smoked. He had to find her. He needed that luck.

Seth and his father continued to bicker about the fashion show, but all Ryan could think about was Marissa. There was something about her that intrigued him. Made him feel alive in this lost world.

"Well, Ryan has to go. Marissa invited him." Even Sandy knew it. Seth looked up surprised.

"She did?" Seth started. "I've lived next to Marissa forever — my mom and her dad almost got married — and she's never even invited me to her birthday."

Now Ryan understood Seth's situation. And he empathized. Right now he felt like an outsider too.

Ryan came to Seth's rescue. "Maybe Summer will be there?"

"She is best friends with Marissa. . . . Interesting . . . Seven?" Seth was in.

Ryan smiled on the inside. He was glad to have done something for someone else for a change. That was more his style. He liked Seth and he felt for him.

Seth headed up to the house, leaving Sandy and Ryan all alone. He felt like the day was a mild success. Operation Criminal Friend might work out all right. He just might have exposed a little too much about Summer, but other than that, things weren't looking so bad.

Sandy waited until Seth was out of earshot. "So who is this Summer girl?"

"I wouldn't worry about it," Ryan said as he remembered Seth's dream out on the boat. Sandy patted him on the back as they set off up the hill to get ready for the fashion show.

High above, Marissa stood on her balcony. Watching. Eyeing Ryan as he walked with Sandy. His tank top. Muscles rippling. She hadn't been able to get him off her mind since the night before. There was something different about him. He intrigued her. He made her forget about the monotony of Newport. Her mundane life. He was her Pucci dress. Her escape. And she wanted more.

She stood watching as he went inside. Pondering. Plotting. She would see him later.

6

Marissa stood in front of her mirror in her bra and underwear, inspecting her hips. Would Ryan notice how big they were? She didn't want to go to the fashion show. In the next room over, she could hear her mother helping Kaitlin get dressed. Criticizing. Encouraging perfection. She was next.

Julie knocked on the door.

"Marissa, dear, you're not even dressed. Come on. Here." Julie handed her daughter the black Donna Karan she had tried on the other day. Plain and perfect. Marissa slipped the dress over her head. "And your hair. Are you going to straighten it?"

"Sure," she replied, but she kind of liked her hair the way it was, down and wavy. Marissa turned on her straightening iron.

"There, now I have to go finish getting ready. See you downstairs in fifteen."

Marissa nodded okay. But she could care less. She hadn't been less enthusiastic about a National Charity League event since her fish, Ziggy, had died the morning before the Sail for a Cure annual yacht race. She had given it a proper burial flushing and the thought of having to go out in the ocean where thousands of fish got to roam free and alive had made her upset. Her dad had let her stay home and watch cartoons with him. As Marissa started straightening her hair, she thought about how easy life was when she was ten. No pressure. No boys. No vanity. And no Newport monotony. She almost had her hair completely straight and smooth when her cell phone rang.

Marissa picked it up. It was Summer. Panicked. Almost in tears.

"Oh my god, it's horrible. Coop, I need help."

"Okay. Calm down. What is it?"

"My dress. It was totally low budge and now the zipper is ripped off. Why didn't I buy another dress at Neiman's? Marissa — help."

"Can you fix it?"

"No. My tailor left this morning for Hawaii. And the stepmonster is helpless. Coop, what do I do?"

But Marissa didn't know what to do. She didn't know how to sew.

"Don't worry, we'll figure something out," Marissa said as she ran the iron through her hair once more. It was perfect. Too perfect. And she hated it. The image in the mirror was immaculate. Plain. Perfect. And horrible. She pulled it back and up off her face. She couldn't help thinking about the Cohens' mysterious cousin. There was something about him that intrigued her and made her believe that she could escape Newport with just one look at him. With him she didn't need a trip to Neiman's or a Pucci dress.

"Coop . . . ?" Summer cried again.

"Don't worry. I have a dress for you," Marissa began as she pulled the Pucci dress out of the closet. "I bought that dress the other day. It's not really my style. It'll look good on you. I'll bring it for you."

"Coop, I love you. You just saved me," Summer said as she hung up the phone.

Marissa gave the dress one last look. It really wasn't her style. She didn't need it. She had Ryan. And he would be her escape even if all she ever did was look at him.

Next door, Ryan stood in front of the mirror in the pool house trying to figure out how to tie a tie. He was competely lost. Now he knew why Seth hadn't wanted to go to this thing. He felt hopeless as he looked at himself in a suit that probably cost more than his entire wardrobe. The only glimmer of hope he had was the image of Marissa's smile. There was something about it that made his heart jump. Whatever luck that cigarette had brought, he was ready for it. This strange place had his stomach all tied in knots, but her smile made him feel at ease. Now, if he could only figure out how to tie the tie, he might be able to make it through the night.

He fumbled for a few more seconds when Sandy entered. He tried to cover up his inability, but Sandy caught on.

"I didn't know how to tie a tie until I was twenty-five."

Ryan felt uncomfortable. He was caught. He handed over the tie. And Sandy stood behind him.

"Now it's important that the skinny side be shorter than the fat side," Sandy began as he placed the tie over Ryan. "And then we loop it up — watch —"

Ryan watched as Sandy completed his tie. He was uncomfortable, but in a good way. He had never had an adult take this much interest in him ever. It felt strangely nice.

"And *voilà.*" Sandy stood behind Ryan and admired his handiwork in the mirror. Ryan smiled. *Maybe this was what having a father around was like.*

"So you got to spend some time with Seth. Was he — how did it — was it —" Sandy began then stopped.

Ryan waited — unsure how to respond to Sandy. He liked Seth. A little odd, but he liked him.

"He's an interesting kid if you just get to know him," Sandy finally said.

"He's cool," Ryan answered nonchalantly, unsure of the response Sandy was expecting.

Sandy nodded, really? But Ryan just smiled back. His image in the mirror was impressive. Maybe he could fit into this world. If only Theresa could see him now . . . or Marissa.

*   *   *

77

Upstairs, Seth hadn't even showered. His so-so experience with Operation Criminal Friend had left him a little scared. He never wanted to go into anything again without a tight plan.

In front of him sat all of his charts and maps for his sail to Tahiti. He had realized now that he was going to need much more than a good route. He needed things to talk about, entertainment, provisions, all the things he lacked on his one-hour sail with Ryan. But at least now, he had time. At least a full year. But he'd have to work hard. No distractions.

Sandy stood outside the door, knocking. A distraction. Seth quickly hid his maps in a drawer.

"Hey. What are you doing?"

"SAT prep. Working on my vocab," Seth said quickly to cover.

"Uh-huh. Well, come on. You gotta shower. Get dressed."

Seth nodded and turned back to the papers in front of him. Sandy stood for a beat, then walked away. "Yeah, Dad, can't wait. I'll be dressed in a jiffy," Seth muttered to himself. As much as he wanted to see Summer, he really wasn't in the mood for the fashion show.

Twenty minutes later, everyone was ready to go. Seth and Ryan followed Kirsten out to the car. The air cooled as the sun began to set. Ryan felt the chill.

Marissa looked out her window and watched as the Cohen family got into their car. She would see Ryan after all. A smile painted her face as she put her Pucci dress in a bag for Summer and headed downstairs.

"Oh, Marissa. You look so —" Julie gave Marissa a once-over. "I thought you were gonna wear your hair down. Pulled back like that — it's a little harsh. On your angles."

Marissa forced a smile.

"Welcome to the dark side," Seth said to Ryan as they headed toward the reception.

Two giant glass doors opened to reveal the back patio of the St. Regis Hotel. It was more elaborate than anything Ryan had ever seen in his entire life. There was a pool with a bridge over it. An ocean view. Hundreds of Newporters covered in silver and gold. Waiters with hors d'oeuvres. An open bar. A display of wealth straight off the pages of *The Great Gatsby*.

Ryan took it all in. Completely amazed. He felt lost and out of place. A waiter approached him.

"Mushroom leek crescent? Crab and brie filo?" This really could be the dark side, he thought as he looked at the foreign foods on the tray. He turned to Seth for solace, but found himself alone.

Seth had wandered off to find some real food.

Ryan grabbed a crescent thing off the waiter's tray and walked over the marble bridge. Taking in the light of the sun setting over the ocean below, he'd only made it a few steps when a beautiful older woman approached him.

"So you're the cousin from Boston, mm? I could

never live there. I just hate the cold. . . ." Ryan nodded, unsure what to say. But she was oblivious. She kissed his cheek and made her way around him. Leaving him alone again in this strange world.

Ryan continued walking, but it seemed word traveled fast in Newport. As he attempted to move through the reception, he was bounced around like a pinball, bombarded by a barrage of questions. Everyone seemed to have heard a different story. Ryan was tossed from one person to the next, no one really quite knowing who he was. Everyone curious. Was he from Canada? Seattle? Boston?

Across the way, Marissa spotted Ryan trying to escape the mayhem. She smiled but turned the other way when he looked over at her.

I need you — he thought. *I need your luck to save me.*

But Marissa kept her back to him. He went to the bar and ordered a drink, and just as soon as he had it in his hands Kirsten showed up. Disapproving. She took the drink away from him and said quietly, "I want my husband to be right about you." Ryan was a little taken aback by the comment, but he understood. And he wanted to prove to her that Sandy was right about him. That he was a good kid, a smart kid with a future — now all he needed to do was believe that himself. Ryan was about to respond politely to Kirsten when Mrs. Milano approached.

"Hey, Kirsten. I was wondering if I could steal

your nephew for a moment. There's someone I want him to meet."

Mrs. Milano took Ryan's arm in hers and steered him right to Marissa. Her beauty stunned him again, for the second time. He pressed his toes against the inside of his shoes. Fighting the emotion.

"Marissa, sweetie. I want you to meet somebody. This is Ryan."

Marissa turned around and gave Ryan a once-over. He looked even better than yesterday. Even more intriguing, she thought.

"Hi, Ryan. So nice to meet you." She wasn't about to let him know that she was interested.

And Ryan got it. She wanted to play. "Uh-huh. You too . . ."

There was a beat of silence between them. An awkward beat.

Ryan looked around at the absurdity that was Newport society. Women with made-up faces so taut and leathery. Men with tanned skin and Rolex watches. Girls pretending they were best friends.

"So. What do you think of Newport?" Marissa asked as a group of Newpsie women passed.

Ryan wanted to answer her. Tell her he felt lost. Out of place. That when she was around he felt lucky. Like things might just work out fine. But Marissa's dad interrupted them and she was pulled away before he had a chance to respond.

Ryan watched as she walked off. So graceful and elegant, perfect and at ease. This all seemed easy for her and he admired that. If he had grown up here he wasn't sure how he'd act in this sort of situation. The money. The presence of adults. The kids acting like adults. It was all so new to him.

Seth came up behind Ryan and handed him a water. As they stood there taking it all in, Luke stepped beside them and grabbed a drink from the bar. This is my chance, Seth thought, deciding to make an attempt to talk to Luke. They were coming up on a new school year, they were older, more mature — maybe things had changed.

"Hey, Luke," he said timidly.

Luke sipped his drink and walked right past Seth. "Suck it, queer."

I guess some things never change. Seth cowered, embarrassed. But Ryan stepped up. Locked eyes with Luke and stared him down. Understanding fully how Seth fit into this world. And not liking it.

"My vacation was great too, Luke. Thanks for asking," Seth said as he tried to cover and play it off like he didn't care. Ryan just nodded, trying not to make Seth feel any more uncomfortable than he already did.

When Ryan turned back to Seth his eyes were wide. What now? Ryan thought.

"Summer. There. Look. Don't look. I mean, look. But don't look like you're looking."

Ryan looked across the pool and saw Summer standing next to Marissa. She was every bit as gorgeous as Marissa, but not quite as sophisticated.

Across the way, Summer was checking out Ryan.

"Who is that?" she asked.

"The cousin. The pool boy. I don't know," Marissa responded as she wondered who he really was. She liked the mystery, but why did it have to be clouded by Cohen, she thought as she saw Seth cowering next to him.

"Well. I'm gonna find out. . . ." Summer whispered sexily.

Back across the pool, Sandy walked up beside the boys and noticed them staring.

"Is that Summer?" Sandy asked as he pointed obliviously at her. Summer turned away.

Seth was horror-stricken and left to go inside and find a seat.

"Way to salt his game, Mr. Cohen," Ryan said before following Seth.

Inside the hotel, the ballroom was packed. Kids and parents everywhere. A zoo of couture and champagne.

Ryan made his way through the crowds of people and finally caught up with Seth.

"Hey," Ryan said. "Where do we sit?"

Seth didn't respond.

There were no seats left. Luke and his crew had taken over their own table and Sandy and Kirsten's table was full. And everyone else seemed to be saving places for their friends. Ryan felt a little lost and Seth was embarrassed that he hadn't planned this out better. Then he saw two empty seats next to Chester, his sailing student. This couldn't be that bad, Seth thought. Chester wouldn't mind; Seth was sure he looked up to him. After all, he was his teacher, and he was older.

"Hey, Chester. This seat available?" Seth asked as he sat in the chair next to him. But Chester didn't respond. "Great. So are you looking forward to your next sailing lesson? You're really making great strides." Chester again said nothing, his face blank. "Okay, Chester. I'm glad we had this chance to catch up."

Ryan sat down next to Seth. A little uncomfortable. This was the kids' table. And Ryan and Seth looked completely out of place. The kids stared at the two guys as they tried to get settled in their seats.

Seth felt like a complete loser and thought that any chance he had of making friends with Ryan up until this point was now blown. No one wanted to sit at the kids' table. And no one wanted to be friends with someone who —

But Seth's thoughts were interrupted by applause. Marissa took the stage and everyone's attention was drawn to her. The crowd quieted.

"Thank you all so much for coming. Every year we put on a fashion show to raise money for the battered-women's shelter. We couldn't do it without your support and the support of Fashion Island . . ." Marissa continued and the crowd listened. Once again, Ryan was enraptured. He couldn't keep his eyes off of her. ". . . Enjoy the show."

As Marissa turned and walked backstage she

caught a glimpse of Ryan looking at her. She smiled and her smile grew as she stepped behind the curtain where Summer stood in her Pucci dress. It looked amazing on her. *Go show the world your beauty. I've got Ryan now*. And she slapped Summer a high five as she took the stage.

The music pumped and the crowd cheered.

Summer's personality bounced on the catwalk — bubbly and fun and overflowing. She owned the room. The crowd loved her and so did Seth. He couldn't stop staring. She was gorgeous in her brightly colored dress with its swirled patterns.

"She's got Tahiti written all over her. . . ." Seth said in awe as he watched her strut down the catwalk. In just a few months, he thought, it would be time to talk to her, get himself on her radar. The Summer plan was coming along nicely. Just as he had planned.

Backstage looked like a Victoria's Secret show. Girls running everywhere — frantically changing in and out of dresses, painting on makeup and straightening their hair. Stick-thin girls in push-up bras. A parade of vanity and designer dresses.

In the bathroom, Marissa had just finished applying a coat of lip gloss when Summer came busting in. "Look what I stole. . . ." She laughed as she held up two glasses of champagne.

But Marissa had something better as she opened her bag and offered up a bottle of vodka. "Look what I stole."

The girls giggled as they downed the champagne. This was turning out to be an all right night, Marissa thought. Ryan was there, the show was a success, and Summer looked great in the Pucci dress.

Everyone applauded as Marissa took the stage. The crowd was even more responsive to Marissa than they were with Summer. She had such charm and grace — everyone loved her. Ryan couldn't keep his eyes off of her. Marissa noticed and when they locked eyes, time seemed to stand still. This girl really was lucky, he thought. Lucky to be here — with the world at her disposal. Ryan wondered if some of that luck would rub off on him. What was it about this girl?

But his fantasy ended when Luke and his crew stood up and started hollering. Their husky voices and catcalls filled the room like fans cheering for the winning touchdown. Ryan was a bit appalled. For kids with so much money, they had so little class. Luke caught Ryan looking at Marissa and gave him the stare-down. Ryan stared back. Two Alpha males sizing each other up.

Ryan stood from his table; he couldn't sit any longer. Things were just too perfect in there and he needed a breath of reality. An escape. Marissa caught it all — Ryan's and Luke's looks, but most of all she noticed her dad's uneasiness.

At the table full of adults, Marissa saw her dad crouching in his seat. Uncomfortable and upset. She wondered what was wrong. Had he seen Summer in her dress? Was he mad? Now she felt bad, but she'd always let Summer borrow her clothes. Was there something else? Marissa thought about the two SEC guys who had showed up again this afternoon. And she wondered what was happening to her father.

In the bathroom, Ryan had just begun toweling off his hands when Jimmy entered and stumbled into a stall, slamming the door behind him.

Ryan stood quietly as a commotion erupted behind the door. Then sobbing. Was this grown man really crying? Ryan had never heard a father cry before, not even his own — and he was in prison. Maybe life wasn't so perfect here, Ryan thought. Maybe these people had the same problems as everyone else. Maybe he was just sad or maybe he felt out of place too. Whatever it was, Ryan knew that there was nothing he could do. He felt helpless and wanted to burst in and save him, just like he'd been rescued, but he couldn't. It wasn't his place. Ryan left Jimmy alone and headed back to his table.

When he returned, the show had just ended and everyone was clearing out. Ryan spotted Seth and followed him out the front door. Summer intercepted.

"Hey. Where you going?" she said as she grabbed his arm gently. Ryan stood speechless. "My friend Holly — well, her parents are letting us use their beach house. As a gift. You know, 'cause of all our hard work for charity. . . ." Summer smiled at him flirtatiously. "If you need a ride. Or anything . . . I'm Summer." And she walked away to a car full of giggling girls.

Ryan was in awe. A beach house? This really was a world apart from Chino. And he was curious. Marissa would probably be there. Seth came back to claim him.

"We should go to that party. At this girl Holly's —" Ryan said, hoping Seth would want to go.

"Uh-huh. No. That's not for us," Seth answered quickly. He couldn't take any more humiliation in front of Ryan and he knew he didn't belong at that party.

Ryan thought for a moment. What was the best way to handle this? "Summer just invited me."

"She did? She invited . . . you?" Seth asked. Crushed. This was even worse. The love of his life was interested in Ryan.

Bad way to handle it, Ryan thought. "Us. She asked for you specifically," he covered.

"Really? She did? That makes no sense. But. . . ." And Seth agreed to go as he looked over and saw Summer hopping into the back of a convertible Range Rover. He couldn't resist her.

The girls hollered for the boys to get in and Seth was there in an instant.

Ryan followed close behind and just as he shut the door behind them, he caught Marissa's eye as she climbed into Luke's Yukon. Luke noticed. But this time he wasn't buying the whole "neighbor's relative" thing.

"Who is that?" Luke asked.

"How would I know?" Marissa responded.

"Maybe 'cause you keep staring at him."

"I'm not. Besides, I'm with you," Marissa said as she leaned over and kissed Luke on the cheek.

"Keep that up and I'll forgive you," Luke responded as he pulled away. Marissa kissed him again, but she kept her eyes open and watched as Ryan disappeared in the distance.

In the other car, Ryan shrugged and looked at Seth, who was grinning from ear to ear. Newport wasn't turning out to be so bad after all.

7

"Come on, Marissa," Luke said as he gently pulled her shirt up. But Marissa placed a discouraging hand on top of his.

"Luke, no," she giggled. Trying to make light of the situation.

"Six years. Are we ever . . . ?"

"Yes. But not here. Not now," Marissa said as she looked around the bed of Luke's truck. They had pulled onto the beach at the gap between the houses at Fifty-first Street and climbed in the back to make out. As always, things had gotten heated between them and Luke wanted to go further. But Marissa still wasn't ready to have sex with him, especially not now. She didn't want her first time to be in the back of a truck.

"You always say that. When, Marissa? When's it going to be?"

"Let's go to Holly's. Everyone's probably already there," Marissa said, ducking the question and hopping off the back of the truck.

Luke sat for a moment. He was growing impatient. When, he thought, when was this going to happen? He wasn't sure how much longer he could last without having sex with her. Part of him wanted to wait and make it special, but the other part of him was just a horny teenage boy.

Marissa sat in the passenger seat waiting for Luke to come around and get in. Why did all their make-out sessions always have to end with Luke getting upset because she wouldn't sleep with him? Didn't he understand that she just wasn't ready? As much as she wanted things to be different in Newport, she wasn't ready to take that step. Besides, she had Ryan to look at now, and he was all the escape she needed.

Luke got in the truck and slammed the door behind him. Marissa tried to give him a kiss, but he pulled away and stepped on the gas, angrily reversing off the sand.

"Welcome to the dark side," Ryan said to Seth as they walked into Holly's beach house.

The place was complete chaos. Kids freely pouring alcohol into plastic cups. Kegs. Lines of coke — mirrors on the table. Beer bongs and bongs for smoking. Girls grinding on guys' laps. Condoms in jars. Music blasting.

Ryan was in awe. This was a Chino party with a large budget. There'd be no tattooed bald man charging him a dollar for beer here.

Seth and Ryan continued to walk through the party, passing by girls dancing in bikini tops and miniskirts, making their way out to the back patio.

"Yo. Fresh keg, bro. You bros need a drink?" a drunk guy in a colorful spooner, who'd deemed himself the Keg Bro, shouted to the party.

"Yeah," Ryan said as he held out a cup.

"Yeah? Yeah. Yes," Seth wavered. He'd never had a drink before in his entire life.

Ryan held his cup under the tap and tilted it to the side to avoid foam as the Keg Bro pumped the tap. Seth took note and did the same when it was his turn, but something went wrong and he ended up with half a cup of foam and a little beer.

"Sorry about the foam, bro. Check it. If you just swipe some oil off your nose and swirl it in the beer — no more foam!" the Keg Bro said as he stuck his oiled finger in Seth's beer.

"Why would I want to drink oil from my nose?" Seth asked, slightly disgusted that the guy had stuck his own nose oil in his beer.

"Bro, I don't know," the Keg Bro responded, a little thrown off. No one had ever questioned the theory before — to him it was the drinker's law. Unchangeable.

Seth and Ryan took their beers and headed back inside, both feeling out of place.

When Marissa arrived, Summer and Holly immediately swarmed her with kisses and "Oh, Marissa"s like they hadn't seen her in years. Luke stood behind her but quickly got the hint and headed off to find Nordlund and Saunders out on the beach.

The girls gathered in the kitchen and began pouring themselves drinks.

"Is that a new purse?" Summer asked as Marissa dripped vodka in her drink.

"So cute," Holly responded as she held it up.

"Does your dad ever say no?"

Marissa was about to respond yes. But then she remembered the Pucci dress that he'd given her money for. *I guess he never really does.* Then she thought about her dad crouching in his seat at the fashion show and how she was sure she'd done something wrong. She sipped her drink and smiled weakly at the girls, but they were too busy checking out the guys at the party. She poured more vodka in her drink, took a sip, then added some more.

"Hey. Look who I brought," Summer began as she looked around the party.

"He's cute." Holly smiled.

Marissa brought her cup to her mouth and sipped as she turned her head to see who the girls were eyeing. It was Ryan, with Seth in tow. Awkwardly navigating these new social waters. Marissa watched him carefully. He was cute. And mysterious. She gazed at him but turned her head just as their eyes were about to meet. She didn't want him to see her. She wanted to be mysterious too. She took a sip of her drink. It was strong, but it would have to do.

"I'm going to play him hot and cold," Summer

started as she eyed Ryan up and down, then turned to the girls. "You wanna pee? I gotta pee."

The girls turned around and disappeared to the bathroom together. This was Newport and no girl peed alone. It was tradition and there was no straying from tradition in this town. So Marissa grabbed her drink, even though she hated tradition, and followed behind the girls.

Ryan watched as they disappeared. He couldn't keep his eyes off Marissa. He was drawn to her. He sipped his beer and smiled.

Luke wandered back inside and stood just a few feet away from Ryan, watching as Marissa closed the door to the bathroom. When he was positive she was out of sight, he turned to a cute freshman, Nikki, standing next to him.

She felt his eyes upon her and spoke to him. "Isn't it, like, so beautiful — the sand. And the water."

Luke looked at her cute dimpled face and thought, maybe this could be all right. He turned back and looked at the bathroom door. Still closed.

"Yeah. You wanna go check it out?" he asked.

Nikki turned to where she had seen Marissa standing before with Summer and Holly. "But what about —"

He looked back and saw Ryan staring at him. The bathroom door still closed. "No worries . . ."

Nikki grabbed Luke's arm and followed him out to the beach. There was no way she was saying no to him. Ryan watched as they walked out together.

Eyeing them, wondering, Why would Luke leave Marissa?

Inside the bathroom, the girls were giggling as they downed most of their drinks. They had been talking about Ryan and the other cute boys at the party.

"He's so cute, don't you think, Coop?" Summer asked. Marissa smiled, *sure*, but Holly noticed her less-than-enthusiastic response.

"He's not Luke, obviously. We know. No one compares. But he's still hot."

Marissa laughed at Holly's comment. "Funny."

"Speaking of Luke, you guys took a long time getting here tonight. Did you guys do . . . ?"

"Summer! No," Marissa responded quickly as she pulled open the bathroom door. She knew what Summer was asking and she didn't really feel like telling the girls all of the details. That Luke wanted to do her in the bed of his truck right at the beach on Fifty-first Street. "Come on, I need another drink."

The girls followed Marissa back to the kitchen.

Outside, Seth had made his way back to the keg for another beer. He was starting to get tipsy. So this is what being drunk is like, he thought as he fumbled with the tap. Keg Bro came along and helped him pour another beer. He grabbed one for Ryan and found him inside.

"Here, buddy," Seth said as he handed Ryan another beer. "I got you a brewski."

"Thanks," Ryan said as he took the beer from Seth's trembling hand.

Seth was nervous. He'd just called Ryan "buddy." They hadn't even crossed the friend line. And now he was calling him "buddy." This was awful, he thought. This was like calling a girl "baby" after the second date. Oh, he'd killed it. Operation Criminal Friend was over. Seth immediately turned and went back outside.

Ryan stood alone sipping his beer. Watching the chaos that was this Newport party. Couples hooking up out in the open. Surfers taking hits off a bong. A couple of guys doing lines off the table. Not your typical teenage party, but very entertaining. Ryan made his way over to the bar in an attempt to blend in. He chugged his beer and had just finished pouring another when Marissa approached.

"So. You never told me. What do you think of Newport?" she asked with a smile.

Ryan looked at the party around him. Then at Marissa's gorgeous eyes.

"I think I can get in less trouble where I'm from."

"You have no idea. . . ." she replied as she grabbed his cup and took a sip from it. Then she poured herself another stiff drink and stirred it as she licked a drop off her lips. The two held gazes for a second, both entranced by the other.

"Coop, it's your turn to deal," Holly yelled from the kitchen table, interrupting their connection.

Marissa smiled at Ryan. *Got to go.* And walked off unsteadily.

Ryan stood alone. Wondering if Marissa knew Luke was outside with Nikki, as he watched her join in her friends' card game. He felt bad for her, but more than that he was mad at Luke for jeopardizing his relationship with such a beautiful girl. She deserved better.

On the back patio, Seth had discovered the keg. He had a good buzz going. He felt loose and almost cool. He poured himself another beer. It filled with foam. Great, he thought, but there was no way he was going to swipe his nose and put the oil in his drink.

"Do you mind?" Seth asked Keg Bro as he nodded to the keg. Keg Bro chugged his beer, poured another, and stepped back, giving Seth the floor.

Seth sipped his beer and then sat down next to the keg, tipping it in his direction. He pulled on the hose and unscrewed the tap. Inspecting.

"I see how this works" — Seth began mostly to himself — "the carbon dioxide from the tank is used to pressurize the keg." Interesting, he thought. "Interesting — and then you use the regulator to lower the pressure and . . . *voilà.*"

Some kids had gathered around to see what he was doing.

Seth stood the keg upright and poured himself

another cup full. Foamless. He pounded it and poured another.

The kids clapped.

"See. No need for the nose oil." He turned to Keg Bro. But the Bro was passed out. Kids drew obscenities on his face with permanent marker. More for me, Seth thought as he chugged some more beer and filled up his cup yet again — stumbling off to check out more of the party.

Ryan poured himself another drink from the bar in the kitchen and made his way through the crowd. He couldn't believe that these kids' parents had allowed them to throw such an outrageous party here. Drinks were spilled all over the floor and every fifteen minutes or so he heard a loud crash and a big "uh-oh." A girl in a bikini slipped by. Newport wasn't turning out to be so bad, he thought. But still, he felt completely out of place. He'd seen his share of drugs and alcohol and sex, but never so openly. He'd always imagined that rich kids had everything — that they didn't need drugs or alcohol. Where he was from, kids did drugs and drank because they had nothing else to do. Because they had no future. No one there had dreams of becoming doctors or lawyers, or even had parents who had great careers. Where he came from, guys were lucky if they got promoted to foreman or site manager at a local factory. But now Ryan stood among a sea of wealth and wondered — was this the future?

The wealthy — doctors and lawyers and real estate moguls? If so, how did he fit in?

Ryan made his way to the patio to get a breath of fresh air.

Inside, Marissa poured herself another drink. Summer, who was a bit more than tipsy, noticed Ryan standing outside all alone.

She staggered out to the patio as Marissa watched from afar — adding more vodka to her drink.

"Look who I found," Summer slurred as a bit of her drink spilled onto Ryan. "Oops. Hi," she finished as she clumsily tried to dry him off.

"Hi."

"Hi," she said as she moved closer. "I'm wasted."

Ryan nodded, a little uncomfortable as she moved in on him.

"So what's your name anyway?" She threw her arms around his neck flirtatiously.

"Ryan," he responded, even more uncomfortable as he thought about Seth.

"I'm so wasted, Ryan. I need someone to take care of me. Mmm-kay?" She pinned him against the railing.

Ryan stumbled. Unsure what to do. Laugh? Go for it? But then he thought of Seth and tried to move away. Summer had him cornered. He was going nowhere.

Just inside, Seth made his way through the

party and was heading out to the patio to get another beer.

Summer threw herself on Ryan, going in for the kiss. Seth pushed back the curtain. He heard Ryan's voice.

"You gotta check the keg. I totally fixed it and —" Seth stopped dead in his tracks, seeing Summer all over Ryan.

"What — what are you —"

"Seth. Hey," Ryan said as he finally wriggled free from Summer.

But Summer followed after him. "Excuse me!"

"What are you doing? I mean, I named my boat after her," Seth said, devastated and drunk.

"What? Eww. Who are you?" Summer said as she moved closer to Ryan.

Ryan turned to Seth, trying to make the situation right. "It's not what you think. She's just drunk."

"C'mon, Ry-Ry," Summer said as she draped herself over Ryan.

"I don't believe you!" Seth shouted as he shoved Ryan against the glass door. Now the party was quieting down. Curious, Marissa got up from the table and made her way over to see what was going on. Seth wasn't letting up. "Why don't you go back to Chino? I'm sure you can find a nice car in the parking lot to steal." The crowd was silent and still. Seth stumbled off to the beach.

"Chino? Ew . . ." Summer gasped.

Ryan stood alone. Marissa caught his eye. Even

in her drunken state, she realized everything he had told her last night was true. He was a thief. And he wasn't the Cohens' cousin. Maybe he wasn't as good as she thought. He was generic. A Pucci knockoff. She stumbled back to her friends and grabbed her drink as Ryan ran past her. He was embarrassed and ashamed. He hadn't wanted the night to turn out like this.

He had to leave. Go back to Chino. Go anywhere but here.

On the beach, Seth tried to make his way past the bonfire but was stopped by Nordlund and Saunders and some of their crew.

"Go home, geek," Nordlund shouted.

"Who invited you, suckass?" Saunders chimed in.

The truth was that all Seth *wanted* to do was go home. He didn't want trouble. He just needed a ride, or some directions. The beer was really starting to hit him and Operation Criminal Friend was over.

But Nordlund and Saunders weren't done with him.

As Ryan approached the front door, he heard shouting coming from the beach. *Seth*, he thought. And charged back through the house.

"You don't belong here, Cohen," Nordlund grunted as he grabbed Seth's leg.

"I know. . . ." The guys picked up Seth's other leg and arms and held him above the sand. "And if you ever let me go I promise I'll never come back again."

"Too late," Saunders said as the guys dragged Seth toward the water. Seth tried to break free but it was no use.

Ryan stood on the patio. He saw Seth suspended in the air. "Hey. Hey!" he shouted as he ran out to the beach.

Luke heard the commotion too and came running with a disheveled Nikki close behind.

"Put him down," Ryan yelled as he eyed Luke and Nikki.

"What's up, dude? You gotta problem?"

"You tell me," Ryan responded as he pulled back his fist and nailed Luke across the face. *That's for Marissa. And Seth.*

The other guys dropped Seth, reprioritizing, and charged Ryan. Ryan ducked but got hit by another guy. Then Luke jumped in and dropped him into the sand. Everyone jumped on him. Seth stood back, but knew he couldn't wait much longer. He pulled one of the guys off of Ryan, and was shocked at his strength.

He stood in awe, but was quickly clocked and laid out on the sand as well. Luke and his crew continued to punch and kick Ryan. Seth lay motionless. Both guys down for the count, just waiting for the beating to end.

Luke gave Ryan one last punch and kicked sand in his face. "Welcome to the O.C., bitch. This is how it's done in Orange County. I ever see you here again you're dead. You hear me? Dead!"

Luke and his crew walked off, leaving Ryan and Seth in the sand.

Marissa, Summer, and Holly stood on the patio with the rest of the crowd and watched as the fight dispersed. Marissa and Summer returned to drinking. Ryan was not who they thought he was. But Holly was slow to follow. She stood alone for a beat and watched as Luke and Nikki headed back to his truck. She shook her head in dismay — *she could never tell Marissa.*

Ryan and Seth slowly rose from the sand. The pain radiated. Silently they stumbled along the beach and began the long walk home.

Out on the beach, Luke and Nikki lay in the back bed of his truck.

"Now where did we leave off?" he asked as he kissed her.

Inside, Marissa finished the drink she had left on the table.

Ryan and Seth walked in silence.

Nikki leaned into Luke, giggling. He unbuttoned her top. She smiled and encouraged him. He smiled back, kissed her soft skin as she ran her hands through his hair. He took off his shirt, let her run her hands over his chest.

Marissa took a shot. This night was turning out to be a disaster. Ryan was a fake.

Ryan wiped the sand from his face. Seth stumbled.

Luke whispered in Nikki's ear. She nodded yes.

Marissa poured another drink. Extra vodka. She had to escape. Where was Luke?

Seth led the way as they trudged through the city. Both in pain.

Nikki kissed Luke.

Marissa let half the drink slip through her mouth, entering her bloodstream. She stumbled. Fell into her seat. What had she done to her father?

Ryan felt guilty and selfish. Did Seth hate him?

Luke almost felt guilty. Then Nikki kissed him again.

Marissa's eyes fluttered open and closed. Summer and Holly saw their friend drift away.

Seth couldn't speak. He'd blown the plan. Negative one friend.

Luke couldn't wait.

Summer searched for Luke. Holly gave Marissa some water. She knew Summer would not return with him.

Ryan looked to Seth. His glimpse at a family was fleeting.

Luke and Nikki lay still — barely touching.

Summer and Holly led Marissa to the car. The girls slammed the door and sped away.

Seth pointed at the hill above. They were close.

Ryan thought the walk would never end. He hadn't realized Newport was so big. They had walked in silence. Both unsure what the other was thinking.

They entered the pool house and collapsed onto the floor. Buzzed, bruised, and battered. There was a long silent beat and then Seth just couldn't take it any longer.

"I don't know what to say. Except. Tonight was unbelievable. You totally had my back. You were like . . . straight outta *Fight Club*." Seth sat up and kicked his legs in the air, pretending to fight. "If you taught me a few moves I think we could take 'em next time."

For the first time since he'd arrived in Newport,

Ryan really smiled. Seth was all right, maybe he didn't hate him.

"And no, that wasn't exactly how I planned to first talk to Summer. But. I am on her radar. Think I should tell her about Tahiti?" Seth asked. Maybe the night hadn't turned out so bad after all. He felt comfortable around Ryan. Maybe that's what friends did. Maybe Operation Criminal Friend had turned out just fine.

"Not yet," Ryan said as he smiled again.

"That's what I thought. What a night. I'll never forget it. It was so . . . so . . ."

Ryan turned to look at Seth, but he was out. Unconscious and snoring. Again Ryan smiled. This night was unforgettable. He was wired. He couldn't sleep. Everything that had happened this weekend kept going through his head. Trey. Theresa. A.J. His mom. Sandy. Marissa. He had to get outside, take a walk.

As he stepped out into the lush grass, Ryan discovered a balcony on the side of the yard that overlooked the Coopers' driveway. He stood on it and gazed out at the ocean as it sparkled under the moonlight. It was peaceful and serene. He heard a car approaching. He looked down and saw a Mercedes pull into the Cooper driveway.

Summer and Holly got out of the car and went around back to pull Marissa out. The girls were still fairly drunk as they tried to gently carry Marissa to her home.

"I can't believe her. . . ." Summer whispered as she stumbled.

"I swear to God. She's so retarded sometimes."

The girls carried Marissa to the front door and dropped her on the cement.

"Coop — where are your keys? How are we gonna find her keys?" Summer asked as she fumbled through Marissa's purse.

"If her parents see us they'll kill us."

"Shouldn't her boyfriend be doing this? He's so worthless." Summer stumbled back.

Holly wanted to say something about Luke, how he had left with Nikki, but didn't. "I can't find her keys."

"We can't wake her parents. Her dad'll freak out."

A silent beat as the girls contemplated their decision. They couldn't ring the doorbell. And they couldn't take her with them. Then they decided — an unspoken consensus. They had to leave.

"Bye, Coop."

"Call us!" Holly added as they ran back to the car and drove away.

High above, Ryan watched Marissa lying there alone. He'd seen his mother like that countless times before. He couldn't leave her in the chilly summer night.

He walked around the house and down to her. Shook her, whispered her name, but couldn't wake her. He couldn't leave her.

He gathered her in his arms and carried her up the hill to the pool house and placed her in his bed. Her soft skin passing by his face. Was this luck? he wondered as he pulled the sheets over her and went to lie down on a cushion next to Seth.

He watched as she breathed gently — her chest moving up and down, her eyes fluttering. And he wanted to save her from whatever it was that made her so numb, so dead to the world. The way his mom had been. Was it Luke?

He thought about his family. Wondered what they would think if they saw him here, in these clothes, with this beauty in his bed. Would they approve?

8

Ryan dreamed of Marissa. That when he awoke she would be lying next to him. That they were together.

But when the sun beat through the glass of the pool house she was gone. And he was alone.

Kirsten came pounding on the door.

"Seth? Seth — are you in there?"

Seth sat upright on the cushion where he had passed out. His head ached. He was dizzy. He lay back down.

Kirsten came bursting through the door.

"Thank God," she said as she found her son. But then she noticed his black eye. "What happened to your face?"

Seth touched his face and remembered the fight last night. He probably had a shiner. How cool, he thought. "I got into a fight. It happens."

But that was not what Kirsten wanted to hear. Ryan could see she was angry, and he blamed himself.

"What? With who? Why?"

"I don't really know. I was drunk." Seth sat up. Even more dizzy. "I think I still am."

Kirsten grabbed him by the arm, unsure whether to yell or cry. Her baby was drunk and in a fight.

"Let's go. House. Now." And she pulled him out the door, shooting Ryan a cold look. Ryan knew he was doomed. That this was the end of his stay at the Cohen house.

Seth waved goodbye. Ryan forced a smile.

As Ryan lay alone in the pool house, he thought about home. He was returning. He knew it. He looked at the empty bed where Marissa had slept and thought about Theresa. Now he knew what it must've been like for her when he'd disappeared. That would be the one good thing about returning home. At least he could apologize for leaving her in the middle of the night.

Ryan gathered his things and went inside the house. He stood alone in the kitchen. Waiting for his ride home. He looked at the empty table and thought at least he could do something nice to re-pay the Cohens for their hospitality. So he began to cook them breakfast. It was the one thing he had learned to do in all his life that made people happy. It was the one thing he'd learned that got rid of his mom's hangover and made her quiet, if only for a second.

He had just finished cooking the eggs when Kirsten entered. Pissed off. Ready to throw Ryan

110

out. But when she saw him, and the bacon and the eggs . . . she couldn't yell.

"Look, Ryan. I don't mean to play bad cop —" She looked over at the table. A complete breakfast ready to be eaten. Ryan saw her looking.

"I made it. I usually make breakfast at my house. My mom's not really a cook so . . ."

Now she really couldn't yell. "I'm sorry. You seem like a nice kid —"

"It's okay. I get it." Ryan understood. He knew this was coming. He picked up his bag. "You have a really nice family," he said as he walked out. And he meant it too.

Upstairs, Ryan looked for Seth. He had to say good-bye. He knocked on the bedroom door and a groggy Seth sat up in bed.

"Hey, man. So. I gotta jet."

"You're leaving?" Seth got out of bed. "Oh. My head. My first hangover . . . Interesting . . . What's up?"

"I — uh. I gotta go back. Try to figure things out back home," Ryan said quietly. This was harder than he thought.

"Cool." Seth quickly caught himself. "Not cool. But. Well."

Ryan extended his hand. Ready to say goodbye. But Seth, overcome with emotion, threw his arms around Ryan, pulling him into a giant hug. Ryan patted his back, unsure what to do. This was awkward, but nice. He hadn't been hugged much in his life.

"I'll come down to Chino. And visit you. You can show me your world."

Ryan thought about the trouble they had gotten into last night and the kind of life he lived in Chino. The two would not mix.

"Uh-huh . . ." he said, trying not to sound offensive.

But Seth wasn't listening. He quickly moved to his desk and opened a drawer. Inside he found a map and brought it back to Ryan.

"Maybe there's some place you wanna go. It's good for ideas."

Ryan smiled at Seth. *Thanks.* And walked off. *Seth was all right.*

Seth stood alone in his room. Captain Oats looked at him, *so?*

Seth picked him up. "Operation Criminal Friend was a success."

Outside, Ryan waited in the car. As Sandy gave Kirsten a kiss goodbye, Ryan wondered if his family was even home right now. What would he say when he returned?

Sandy started the car and backed out of the driveway, right past Marissa, who had just left her house. She stood alone, waiting. Ryan looked at her and they locked eyes for the last time. *Who would save her now?* She watched as they drove away, thinking she would never see him again. After last night, she didn't care that he was a fake. He was her escape. Her life vest in this sea of turmoil. Her Pucci dress. She would never forget him.

The gates of the community closed behind them. They rode in silence as the golden beaches of Newport slowly returned to the cold concrete of Chino.

As Ryan watched the gold turn to gray, he thought about his life, about everything that had ever happened to him. He felt abandoned and alone. His father was in prison, his brother was too, and his mom wanted nothing to do with him. And now he had screwed up the one good thing that had come his way in a long time. He looked at Sandy, who tried to force a smile. This was the end, he thought. Where would he go from here? He'd had his chance at life and he'd blown it.

Sandy turned off the freeway and into Chino.

The graffiti-covered buildings screamed desolation. This was home. A city full of the abandoned — wandering aimlessly through life. Ryan pushed his toes against the sole of his shoe. His throat choked him and he felt dead to the world as they approached his house.

Sandy stopped the car out front and unloaded Ryan's bike from the back. They stood there, awkward silence growing as neither knew what to say. Then Ryan stepped forward.

"So. Thanks. For everything."

"I'm gonna make sure everything works out, Ryan. I promise."

Ryan nodded thanks and turned to walk up to the door. Sandy started to follow. But Ryan didn't want him to see the misery that was his family.

"It's okay. I can take it from here." Then he remembered Sandy's line to him when they had first arrived at the Cohens'. "I've got a lotta esplainin' to do."

Sandy nodded and backed away.

Ryan took a deep breath and began what seemed like a long walk up to his house. With every step he took, the knot in his stomach got tighter. He was afraid and nervous. Would things just be like they always were? Could he go straight to his room and say nothing to anyone?

He got to the door and pulled out his keys. His hands shook. He placed the key in the lock and turned, ready for the worst, but the door swung right open.

It wasn't locked.

Ryan cautiously pushed the door open wider and walked inside. He was not ready for what he saw.

The entire place was empty. Abandoned. There was no trace of his family.

He walked inside. Taking in the emptiness.

On the counter he found a note. *Ryan, I'm sorry. I can't.*

He crumpled the note and pressed his toes against the inside of his shoe. He felt his sock rip. The hole tightened around his toe.

This was the end.

Outside, Sandy saw the door wide open. He knew something was wrong and walked up to the house.

Ryan stood alone.

Sandy entered and saw the empty home. He had no choice.

"Come on, let's go."

And Ryan turned and followed him back out to the car.

He was all alone without family. He would not apologize to Theresa. He would never see his bed or her couch. Mr. Ramirez and his two daughters. The ghetto birds. Trey. His family. They were gone.

He got in the car.

His mind was quiet.

They drove in silence. Ryan with his head against the window. Watching.

The graffiti screamed at him, but he said nothing. He had no answers.

The gray turned to gold, the concrete to sand. And they continued to drive.

All Ryan could hear or feel were the few tears that ran down his cheek. He was not ready to return to the Cohens', but he knew he had no choice. He had nowhere else to go. And no one else to turn to.

9

Ryan had been staying with the Cohens for a few days. In limbo. Waiting. All alone. Quietly going about the days. Unsure of where he stood.

Now he was in the kitchen with a contract in his hands.

Sandy hovered behind him as he flipped through the papers.

"As your attorney I'll cosign these forms. It just basically states that you don't have a legal parent or guardian available."

Sandy handed Ryan a pen to sign on the dotted line. Essentially, Ryan thought, he was declaring that he had no family. That he was all alone in the world.

He signed the paper. From here on out the world would know him as 038-29-65. A number. Without family he had no identity. Maybe his decision to ride back to Newport with Sandy was not the best one. Maybe he should have stayed in Chino. Lived in his abandoned home until someone took it over. Or gone back to Theresa's and stayed on her couch.

Ryan handed over the papers, his face sullen. A number for a name. Sandy noticed and tried to ease the situation.

"We'll meet with your social worker in the morning. She'll take you to the . . ." Sandy hesitated. Ryan knew this wouldn't be good. "Group home. My Child Services contact got you a room with only two other kids. Sometimes they can get crowded. . . ."

And Ryan was right. This wasn't getting better. Things were getting worse. A group home? That sounded horrible. All he could picture was the girl in *White Oleander* — stranded, being tossed from one awful home to the next. Theresa'd made him see the movie with her. The image disturbed him. Staying in Chino alone would have been better. But Ryan tried to appear happy — after all, the Cohens had given him more than he could ever imagine, and he'd only been there a few days.

Sandy could tell that Ryan was not happy. "You should know — they do find foster homes for kids . . . your age."

Seth overheard the conversation and chimed in, "Yes. 'Cause who doesn't want a sixteen-year-old? We're an underappreciated species." Sandy and Kirsten both stared at him. *Seth?!* But Seth didn't care. He was upset. He'd finally made a friend and now his parents were kicking him out.

And he'd probably never see him again. "I'm sorry if I'm the only one who won't say the obvious —"

"Seth," Kirsten exclaimed, trying to get him to quiet down.

"We have all this extra room and a pool house, and instead you wanna ship him off to a group home?" Seth paused. Everyone's attention on him. "Am I the only one who gets how much this sucks?"

Ryan was shocked. No one had ever stood up for him like that in his entire life.

"It's okay." He turned to Seth graciously. "Really."

Ryan slid the papers next to the model home that sat on the counter. Kirsten had brought the model home from work.

Ryan looked at it closely. The model was nicer than any home he had ever lived in even though it was made out of cardboard. He imagined what it would be like to live in a nice home, with a complete family, with people who cared, parents who took an interest in him. And he wanted to find one himself. "Can you build me one?" he had asked her earlier, trying to lighten the situation, but she hadn't really responded.

He turned to her now. "Good luck with it. Looks perfect." And he walked outside. " 'Night."

Seth stood alone with his parents in the kitchen, but he had nothing to say to them except the same, "'Night." And he headed upstairs to his room.

*   *   *

Outside in the pool house, Ryan lay silent in his bed, his mind racing. Tomorrow he would go to Child Services and his future would be handed to him. Family or no family? Brother, sister, group home? Everything was completely uncertain and he hated it.

He grabbed the leather band around his neck, pulling it taut against his skin. He wanted to rip it off and scream at the world. Throw it at the window and watch the window shatter. His family had left him. And now he was a number. A boy without a dream, a family, or a name. To the world he was nothing. He didn't want to live in a group home. He didn't want to be placed in some other family's home. If he couldn't live at the Cohens', he was leaving. He wanted stability and the only way he knew how to get it was to take matters into his own hands. He had to leave.

Ryan got out of bed and threw on his T-shirt. He was determined. He picked up his backpack and ran out the door and right into Seth. His plan halted.

Seth stood there in his pajamas.

"Hey. I saw your light on. And I thought — a little PlayStation perhaps?" Seth paused. He saw Ryan's backpack. Ryan tried to hide it. "You're running away?"

"Go back in the house, Seth." Ryan didn't want Seth involved. He took a step forward. Determined to leave.

But Seth wouldn't move.

119

"You can't run away. What about Child Services? And my dad. And — I'll come with you." Seth didn't want to lose the only friend he'd ever truly had. He pulled out all the stops, thought about days before when he was devising Operation Criminal Friend. "You know what I've always wanted to do?" Ryan looked at him. *What now?* "Besides sailing to Tahiti? The whole Kerouac thing. Hit the road, drive from diner to diner. The pancake tour of North America."

"No," Ryan responded. He had to do this on his own.

"Fair enough." But Seth would not let up. "Where you going?"

"I don't know. Leave town. Get a job somewhere. Save some money."

"Great plan, dude. You've really given it a lot of thought."

"You got a better idea?" Ryan asked as he started to walk off. But Seth grabbed his backpack and stopped him in his tracks.

"Actually? I do."

Ryan looked at him. *Really?* And they stood there in silence for a beat, both thinking. Seth wanted him to say yes. Ryan contemplated the decision. It was true — his plan really wasn't that great. Seth's plan couldn't be any worse than his. He nodded yes and Seth headed up to his room to get provisions.

Upstairs, Seth changed into a black turtleneck and dark pants and began frantically stuffing a duffel bag full of stuff — flashlight, sleeping bag, clothes. . . . But there was a knock at the door.

"Seth. Hey, Seth?" Sandy called from the hallway.

Seth panicked and hid the bag under his bed before he climbed on top of it and pulled the sheets up over his head.

Sandy entered the room. Seth lay still, pretending to be asleep.

"Dad? Is it morning?" Seth asked groggily.

"You're asleep?" Sandy sat on the end of the bed.

"Was. So, what's up?"

"Well. I just wanted to talk to you about Ryan."

Seth squirmed a bit. *Did he know?* "It's cool. We don't need to discuss it."

"I think we do." Great, Seth thought as Sandy continued. "I know you're upset." *That's what he thinks?* Seth breathed a sigh of relief. "Your mom and I are upset too. But our responsibility is to our family."

"Look, Dad. I get it. This is a person's life we're talking about — we need to leave it in the hands of the authorities."

"There's no need for sarcasm."

Seth wasn't being sarcastic. He just really wanted his dad to leave. Ryan was waiting. "Look, Dad. Really. It's okay."

"Okay. But when you want to talk about it —"

"You're the guy to talk to. Good night," Seth replied quickly, trying to get his dad to leave.

Sandy backed out of the bedroom, "Good night."

And as soon as the door closed behind him, Seth leaped out of his bed, quietly scurrying back into action.

Outside, Ryan waited at the end of the Cohen driveway. *Come on, Seth.* He was starting to get anxious. What if someone saw him? He would never be able to escape then. There was no sign of Seth. Nothing. Behind him, he heard the chirp of a car alarm being deactivated and turned around to see Marissa walking up her driveway.

He stood still, in shock. He didn't know if he should hide or run. He took a step into the bushes, but Marissa spotted him.

She stared at Ryan. Stunned to see him. Hadn't he left for good? Their eyes locked — just like they had before.

"Hey," Ryan said as he stepped out from the bushes. He couldn't hide forever.

"Hey." Marissa paused, gathering her thoughts. "I didn't think I'd see you again." She wanted to say so much, but she couldn't. "I wanted to say thanks. For the other night."

But Ryan didn't need the thank-you, he wanted to know: "You always drink like that?"

She avoided the question, just like he knew she would, just like his mother always had.

"I thought you left."

"I did. I am," he started. "This whole Newport scene. It's not really for me."

"I know what you mean," she responded as she thought about Luke and her friends and the monotony of her life. And she looked at him. But you, she thought, you are different. She wanted him to stay.

"Uh-huh," Ryan began. "So why do you keep hanging out with them?"

He had a good point, but would he have the answers? "You got any better ideas?"

Ryan was about to answer. Tell her he could help her, save her from this world, but Seth came skating down the driveway.

"We're all set. You ready to —" And he froze when he saw Marissa. "Oh. Hello, Marissa."

Why is this geek here? she thought as she eyed his bag and black turtleneck. "What are you doing?"

"Nothing. We're just . . ."

"You guys are up to something." She wanted to know what they were doing. It was intriguing. Geek or no geek.

Ryan and Seth hesitated for a second about whether to tell Marissa their plan. But neither would fess up. Instead Ryan turned and smiled at her. "So you should probably be off. The Newport social scene awaits."

But Marissa wasn't leaving. Now she was curious. And Ryan had challenged her, questioned her lifestyle. She wanted to be part of their plan. Whatever they were up to, and she knew just how to do it: She had a car.

The three had been driving for quite a while. Ryan sat in the passenger seat and Seth sat in the back, leaning forward, so as not to be left out of anything.

"This is pretty far away," Marissa said as she continued driving.

Seth stuck his head between the two front seats. "Complaining. That's interesting — seeing how no one invited you."

Marissa turned up the radio, ignoring Seth. The Libertines played. She turned to Ryan. "You like them?"

Ryan wasn't really paying attention. He was too caught up in Marissa's nearness and the fact that he was running away. "Yeah. I guess."

"What do you like?" Marissa was trying to get to know him.

"Everything. I don't know. I don't really listen to music."

Marissa looked at him. Surprised. This guy really was mysterious. Who didn't listen to music? Even Seth thought it was a weird answer.

Ryan realized all eyes were on him and turned to Marissa. "What do you like?"

"Right now? Punk."

"Mmmm . . . no. Avril Lavigne does not count as punk," Seth said to her.

"What about The Cramps? Stiff Little Fingers? The Clash? Sex Pistols?"

Seth was defeated. She had him there. "I listen to the same music as Marissa Cooper." He fell back into his seat. "I may have to kill myself."

Now Ryan was intrigued by her. "Punk?"

She smiled back at him and answered, "I'm angry."

He liked that.

They pulled up in front of an unfinished house. Ryan stepped out of the car and took it all in. He studied the layout and realized this was the model home. The same cardboard layout he had seen in the Cohens' kitchen. The same home he had asked Kirsten for earlier in the night. He wondered how long he would stay here as he walked toward the front door.

Seth and Marissa followed close behind.

Out here in the dark, Newport was kind of mysterious. There were no nosy neighbors, no fashion shows, and no parents. Just the quiet stillness of the California night. Marissa was intrigued. She liked it here. She grabbed a flashlight from Seth and walked into the house. Lighting the way for Ryan, who stood in front of her. Seth joined them.

The place was empty. Tarps and dust covered everything. Tools were scattered about. Their flashlight beams bounced around the room. Seth pulled a couple of tarps off the windows, letting in the moonlight, giving them a better view.

Marissa looked around the room. There was no carpet, marble tile, no furniture, no lights. How could anyone live here? she thought. "You want him to stay here?"

Seth looked around at the dust and the plywood floors. "So this place needs some sprucing up. Did I say sprucing?" Marissa looked at him. *Geek.* "Never mind." He turned to Ryan, ignoring Marissa. "But you can stay as long as you want. Until we come up with a real plan."

Ryan walked around the room, taking it all in. This was nicer than any place he had ever lived, even if it wasn't finished.

"Wait till you see the best part," Seth exclaimed as he led them to the double doors that opened out onto the backyard. There was nothing there.

Marissa and Ryan stood, staring.

"It's an empty pool," Ryan stated.

"To some people," Seth responded as he headed back into the house, leaving Ryan and Marissa alone.

They both looked at each other quizzically. *Where's he going?* But they shrugged their shoulders and headed outside.

Ryan sat down at the edge of the pool and gestured for Marissa to sit next to him.

They sat awkwardly for a moment. Neither quite sure what to say.

He wanted to ask her what it was that made her get so drunk and numb. What he could do to help her ease the pain. He wanted to tell her she was lucky, that the world lay in front of her. That she could have anything she wanted.

She wanted to ask him the truth. Discover the real Ryan. What·had made him return? And she wanted to tell him that he was her escape, even if he had never done anything for her.

But they were both left without words, waiting for the other to make the first move.

"So," Ryan started.

"So," Marissa replied.

Silence floated between them. An awkward beat.

Then Marissa couldn't hold back. She wanted to know. "How come you're back in Newport? I thought you —"

"Left. I did."

"Then why . . . ?"

"Why am I back? Let's see. . . ." And Ryan wasn't sure she would believe him, but he thought he'd try. "My mom kicked me out. Sandy took me in. I came to Newport. Got in a fight. Seth got a black eye. Kirsten kicked me out. Went back home to Chino." Ryan paused, pushed his toes against his shoes. "But no one was home."

"And Sandy wouldn't let you stay alone?" Marissa asked, unclear.

"No. The house was empty."

"You mean . . ."

"Yeah. My mom moved out."

"Really?"

Really. Now I'm just a number in a system. Ryan put his head down and nodded. Marissa felt uneasy. Bad that she'd even asked. She couldn't imagine how it would be if her parents ever moved out. Either one of them.

The silence returned.

They gazed at each other. Each wanting to touch the other, absorb the pain.

Seth interrupted the silence when he returned with his skateboard.

"Did you miss me?" Seth asked as he placed his board against the lip of the pool.

Ryan just smiled at Seth. Always so optimistic. Marissa laughed.

Seth ollied off the lip of the pool and skated back and forth. Leaving Ryan and Marissa to themselves.

Marissa looked at Ryan. She had to break the silence.

"So. Your mom. She has to come back, right?" Marissa asked, hoping. But she didn't know the kind of life Ryan had.

"I don't know. My mom is kind of a train wreck," Ryan responded. He wanted to say more. Tell Marissa how she drank a lot, had an abusive boyfriend — warn Marissa of that path. But he couldn't. He barely knew her.

"So's mine," Marissa confessed. She thought about her own parents. How Julie criticized her and how she was daddy's little girl. "Well . . . what about your dad? Can you call him?"

"My dad's in jail. Armed robbery. Impressive, huh?"

Marissa was shocked, but she kept her cool. Her dad wasn't in jail, but her life was troubled too. Maybe that was the connection she felt with Ryan.

"My dad. He's, like, a financial planner. I think he's in trouble."

"I don't have any stock tips," Ryan said, trying to make a joke. But Marissa was serious.

"He stopped going to the office. And these guys keep showing up. Like, cops. But he won't answer the door." Ryan looked at her. *Is that what makes you numb?* "I haven't told anybody that. . . ."

And now Ryan understood. She was alone with everyone around her. An outsider in a sea of friends. "I can keep a secret."

They sat for a beat. Each absorbing the other. Both intrigued.

Marissa's cell phone rang and interrupted the moment.

She looked at the screen and saw that it was Luke. Ryan saw too. Marissa walked away for privacy.

"Where you at, girl?" Luke was at Holly's beach house waiting for Marissa. He had already been there for an hour or so drinking with his buddies Nordlund and Saunders.

Ryan sat alone as Marissa talked to Luke. Seth continued to skate by. He wanted to tell her a secret. Tell her what he knew. Tell her that Luke was cheating on her. Save her from him. But he couldn't. Even though he felt the connection, he barely knew her, and he didn't want to complicate things.

Marissa hung up her phone. Seth stopped skating.

"How long you been with him?" Ryan asked, trying not to pry too much.

"Luke? I'm not sure really —" She didn't want to tell Ryan the truth, but Seth filled Ryan in.

"Only since, like, fifth grade, when you guys got your mack on during our class trip to the Museum of Tolerance. Back of the bus. Classy."

Marissa smiled at Ryan, then turned to Seth. "What is your problem, Cohen? What did I ever do to you?"

"Nothing." Seth smiled. "I've lived next door to you forever and you've never done or said anything to me."

"Omigod. You're the one who never talks to me. You think you're so much better than everyone."

Seth was stunned. He'd never looked at it that way. *Me ignoring Marissa?* But he covered his surprise. "Well, if by everyone you're including Luke — then, yes. The guy shaves his chest. That's all I'm saying."

"He plays water polo," Marissa answered quickly, so Ryan wouldn't think she was dating a freak.

"We know. Half the team tried to kill us the other night," Seth told her.

She looked at Ryan. *Is this true?*

Ryan nodded yes. "I'm not too popular around here. And your boyfriend? A little angry."

Now Marissa was really intrigued by Ryan. No one in this town had ever stood up to Luke. "You're telling me you didn't hit him back?"

"Actually? I hit him first." She was even more impressed.

"Hard to believe you're not more popular."

Ryan smiled at her. Seth hopped out of the pool and headed into the house. Marissa and Ryan stood up and followed close behind.

Upstairs, Seth led the way into a giant bedroom. Ryan hesitated.

"I still don't know if it's a good idea for me to stick around or —"

But there was no way Marissa was going to let him leave that easily again. "You should stay," she said as she smiled at him.

"Okay. For a little while." Ryan couldn't resist her smile.

"Oh. So when she says it — you listen."

Before Seth had a chance to say anything more, Marissa's cell phone rang.

It was Summer. Seth got excited at the mention of her name.

Marissa hung up the phone and turned to the guys. "I gotta go meet my friends." She paused a beat, realizing that Seth and Ryan were slowly becoming her friends as well. "My other friends . . ."

Seth found her gesture endearing. *Seth Cohen*

and Marissa Cooper as friends? This could be good. Seth got up to leave too. "Now, we all need to promise. No telling anyone about this place. Ryan won't. Obviously. And I could get grounded. So that leaves . . . Marissa." He glared at her.

"I can keep a secret," she said. Ryan smiled at her, recalling their conversation earlier out by the pool.

"Okay. So. I'll see you tomorrow," Seth said to Ryan, oblivious of the connection happening between Marissa and Ryan.

"Me too. We'll fix this place up," Marissa added. Seth was surprised that she planned on returning, but he let it go as all three of them stood silent for a moment. In just one night, they had somehow become friends.

Seth snuck quietly back into his house. Slowly tiptoeing up the stairs. When he got inside his room, he fell onto his bed, relieved. He had snuck out, hidden Ryan, and not gotten caught. This was the first time in his life he had done something his parents wouldn't approve of — well, besides Holly's party. And he'd gotten away with it. Usually he would have ratted himself out to them by now. But there was something different about Ryan. Something that made him feel stronger. Something that made him feel invincible.

And as he climbed under the sheets he knew what that something was. It was the feeling of true friendship. And he liked it. He smiled at Captain Oats. *All that worrying and planning was worth it.* He smiled again and closed his eyes. If he felt this good now, he couldn't wait until his plan with Summer came to fruition.

Marissa arrived at Holly's completely sober. The margs were flowing, but she wasn't really interested. Ryan was back. She didn't need the escape.

She stood to one side, gazing around the room. She was starting to realize that she only enjoyed these people when she was buzzed or drunk or better yet, passed out. They always did the *same* thing and gossiped about the *same* people. Every night. The monotony was killing her.

She couldn't deal with Luke tonight. Sometimes he was just too much for her, or maybe he wasn't enough. She felt empty around him. She decided to leave.

She drove back to her house and climbed the stairs to her room. She couldn't believe she was thinking these things. Was it because of Ryan? Was she doubting her relationship with Luke? She shook her head. No, she couldn't be — they'd been together forever. Even so, she couldn't get Ryan out of her head.

She fell onto her bed and started thinking about Ryan. What it would be like to kiss him, to hold him, her mind kept wandering. He intrigued her. And after tonight she felt even more for him.

They had shared secrets. There was something about him that made her feel safe in Newport, in her crazy monotonous life.

At the model home, Ryan lay on the hardwood floor wrapped in his sleeping bag. This was no pool house, but it was not his house in Chino.

Marissa turned on the music. But it didn't help. Every song reminded her of Ryan. She let the music play and thought of him.

He couldn't sleep. His mind raced. The picture of Marissa smiled in his head. But he worried . . .

She would see him again. She'd make a CD of "Ryan" songs and call it "the model home mix." She'd give it to him tomorrow.

Would he be homeless and family-less forever?

10

"Come on. Trust me," Ryan said as he rode over to Marissa. She looked him in the eyes and thought about all he had done for her so far. And decided to trust him.

She climbed up onto the pegs on the back of his bike and gripped his shoulders as he started pedaling. Seth followed close behind as they rode down through Newport Shores, past all the beach houses, and out onto the boardwalk that led to the pier.

As they passed by lifeguard stand fifty-four, Marissa made Ryan speed up, pretending she liked the thrill. But really she was trying to avoid Luke and his crew. She could see him out in the water and wanted to move by quickly so that he wouldn't notice her with Ryan. She felt guilty. Like she had cheated. But part of her didn't care. When she was with Ryan she felt free and she liked it.

They rode down the beach as the sun grew bright overhead. Seth and Ryan raced toward the pier, laughing. Marissa held on tight as they sped ahead of Seth. Local grommet kids watched as they raced by, dodging them as they held their tiny surf-boards under their arms.

By the time they got to the pier, all three were laughing hysterically; none of them had had this much fun in a long time. Marissa held on to Ryan as they drifted down the pier, occasionally placing her warm hands over his eyes, joking with him as he swayed back and forth trying to keep his balance. Seth skated ahead of them and stopped once he reached the diner at the pier's end.

Ryan and Marissa came to a giggling halt. Flirt-ing as they got off the bike.

"Thanks for the ride." Marissa laughed.

And he smiled. *Anytime.* "Thanks for the CD."

"Think of it as the beginning of your education in surviving Newport."

"Thanks," he said as he placed his hand on the small of her back, guiding her into the restaurant.

At the booth, Seth shoveled syrupy bites of pancakes into his mouth as Ryan and Marissa sat eating their meals.

"See, this could be the first stop on our pan-cake tour of the country," Seth said to Marissa, but more for Ryan's benefit. Since he had turned down the plan the night before.

"Like in *On the Road*? That's my favorite book."

"Mine too . . ." Seth told her uneasily. What is this world coming to? Seth thought. First Marissa Cooper listens to the same music, and now the same favorite book. Seth was not prepared for this. He and

Marissa weren't supposed to have anything in common. They had labels. And the labels said this wasn't supposed to happen.

Ryan sensed Seth's uneasiness. "So I was thinking. About the plan? My mom had this boyfriend. He hired me to work construction last summer. But then they broke up. He moved away." He paused a beat before continuing. He couldn't believe he was saying this about someone his mother had dated. But then again, he didn't have many options and the ex was the nicest man his mom had ever been with. "To Austin."

"Texas?" Marissa asked, not too excited about the prospect of Ryan going that far.

"That's pretty far away. I was thinking like, Long Beach. So we could still hang," Seth added.

This was hard for all of them. But Ryan tried to stay strong. He knew he had no other option and he couldn't live in the model home forever. Eventually, someone would buy the house and he'd have to leave. He might as well go now before he couldn't leave. Before he became too attached.

Seth thought about what it would be like not to have Ryan around, not to have a friend again, and he didn't like it. For the first time since the night Ryan had come to stay with them, he thought about boarding school. He wanted to go so badly and start over — to be someone other than Seth Cohen. And he realized that maybe now Ryan would have that chance.

"In a way you're lucky. You get to go to a whole new place. Start over. Be whoever you want to be."

Ryan nodded. Seth was right. This could be a great opportunity. But then he looked at Marissa and thought how hard it would be to leave. The bell above the diner door chimed, breaking the moment.

Ryan glanced over, his whole body suddenly tightening, as Luke, Nordlund, and Saunders entered. Marissa and Seth saw them too. This was not good.

"Okay. I'll handle this." Marissa jumped up.

"I can handle it," Ryan stated.

"And ruin your popularity? You sneak out the back before anyone sees you. . . ."

Seth and Ryan quickly got up and headed through the kitchen to the back door.

Marissa slid out of the booth and made her way over to where Luke and his crew were sitting. She sat down next to Luke and he placed his arm around her. Ryan watched as Luke touched her. He wanted to run back in there and punch him. Tell him that he didn't deserve Marissa. But he didn't. He just watched as he followed Seth to the emergency exit. The only other door out. They stopped.

They were trapped. The alarm would go off. They had to go out the front.

Ryan put his hood up and quietly walked toward the front door. Seth followed, but didn't make it very far, as a busboy came bustling toward them and ran right into Ryan. A bucket full of dishes came crashing down around them.

Seth leaped in front of Ryan, trying to create a distraction.

"Hey, Luke. Fellas. You guys like the food here? It's pretty tasty."

"Shut up, queer." Luke laughed at him. Marissa looked away, embarrassed that she was with Luke.

"At least I don't shave my chest," Seth muttered under his breath.

Luke stood up and bumped Seth. "What'd you say?"

Marissa tried to stop him, but he ignored her.

"You want me to break you, Cohen?"

Suddenly, Ryan turned and looked Luke in the eyes. "Your food's getting cold."

Luke was caught off guard. "No way. Look who's back." He flicked Ryan's hood off his head. "You're a little far from 8 Mile."

Ryan looked at Marissa. He needed the strength. A reason not to hit Luke.

"Luke. C'mon," Marissa pleaded.

But he turned around and snapped at her. "What are you? Like, spokesman for Geeks of America?"

That was not the reason Ryan was looking for.

"You know what I like about rich kids?" Ryan asked as he turned and punched Luke in the gut, sending him sprawling. "Nothing."

And Seth and Ryan took off running. A team escaping. Seth used his skateboard to hold the door shut against Luke and his crew and Ryan unlocked his bike and started pedaling. Seth ran after him and jumped on the pegs. Leaving Luke and his crew behind.

Marissa sat in the diner alone with her head in her hands. Disappointed in herself and Luke. Why was she with him? And why was she so worried about Ryan?

Luke returned to the booth.

"What's wrong?" he asked her.

"Nothing," Marissa said as she lifted her head out of her hands.

"Good," he said, kissing her. "For a moment I thought you were upset about the geek and the *8 Mile* kid."

Marissa shook her head no and pulled away.

"Dude, though, he like totally got you, man. Right in the gut," Saunders said as he reenacted Ryan's punch on Nordlund. "You gonna go after him later?"

Luke pounded his fist in his hand and smiled at the guys. "He shows up again, he's dead."

"Didn't you, like, say that last time you fought him?" Nordlund asked.

"Who asked you?" Luke blurted as he saw Marissa become disinterested in the conversation.

She tried to slip out of the booth, but Luke stopped her. "Where you going?"

"Uh, I have to go and . . ." But she had no good excuse. And she couldn't tell him that she wanted to go back and see Ryan.

"Stay," Luke said as he put his arm around her. "I

got to tell you about the waves we caught today. I ruled it. And Nordlund" — he laughed — "got barreled. I almost had to call the lifeguard on his ass."

The guys continued to tell their stories as Marissa sat in silence, thinking of Ryan.

Ryan and Seth rode back to the model home, Seth on the pegs of the bike.

"I was thinking, Ryan. We make a pretty good team. And if you want to, say, stick around awhile we could learn a few moves. Get a good strategy going. Take down Luke and his crew one at a time. Until we rule Newport."

Ryan laughed.

"So, what do you say?"

But Ryan had no answer. He wanted to say yes. Say that he would stay here forever, but he knew that could never happen. He had seen the police cars arriving earlier as they rode away from the diner. Sooner or later he would get caught and then instead of a foster home he'd be in jail. If he didn't leave now and take matters into his own hands, he didn't know where he'd end up.

"Okay, well, you think about it. And I'll just be upstairs putting," Seth said as he hopped off the bike and entered the model home.

Ryan was going to miss Seth, but more than that he was going to miss Marissa.

Upstairs, Ryan and Seth started a little game of "horse" with the putting green. Ryan was awful. He had never golfed before in his life. The ball was everywhere. Seth kept laughing whenever it was Ryan's turn.

"It's not that funny."

"Come on, Ryan. Relax. This isn't the LPGA. No reason to hate the stick or the ball."

"Thanks for the mental picture."

"Anytime."

Seth grabbed the putter and sank another shot. He started celebrating, running around the room, but stopped when Marissa entered.

"You didn't have to hit him."

"Yes he did."

But Ryan felt bad. "Sorry . . ."

"I don't know why he did that . . . does that. He's just . . ."

"An ass?" Seth asked.

"Protective."

Before she could explain anymore, the sound of a car pulling up outside the house grabbed all their attention.

It was Jimmy and Kirsten.

The three of them hid, trying to hear the conversation.

Seth's mind was racing. Was his mom having an affair? That wasn't possible, he thought. She was in love with his dad.

Marissa stood still. She knew this wasn't good.

She heard her father asking for money. $100,000. Her heart sank. She knew that her dad was having problems, but she didn't know they were this big — or this expensive.

Ryan looked at Marissa. Felt her pain.

But things only got worse. The contractors were coming tomorrow. The house would be occupied. Ryan had to go.

He knew this was coming. He looked at Marissa again. They held each other's pain.

Marissa's eyes welled up as her dad left. Ryan held her in his eyes. Realized that maybe having a family didn't mean that life was perfect. That maybe what appeared perfect on the outside was flawed inside.

Seth and Marissa left. Tomorrow they'd come and say their last goodbye.

"They found Ryan," Sandy said as he entered Seth's bedroom. Seth quickly hid the bus ticket he had just printed out. *Did he know?* "Or spotted someone who meets his description. I guess he got into a fight down by the pier."

Just play it cool. "Oh. Huh. Really." Seth turned off his computer monitor.

"Which means he's probably in the area. We should try and find him before the authorities do. Before he gets in any more trouble."

"Now? Do you need me or —" Seth didn't want to go. He knew Ryan was okay and he wasn't about to rat him out.

"Seth. I thought he was your friend."

Seth nodded. He knew his dad wasn't giving up. If he didn't go now, he'd get suspicious.

"So what's up? You've been all weird-acting lately," Summer asked Marissa as she poured herself a drink.

Holly was having another party.

"Yeah?" Marissa asked, contemplating whether or not she should tell Summer about Ryan. "You ever wonder what your life looks like through someone else's eyes?"

"This is what I'm talking about. What's up with you?" Summer asked as she sipped her drink. She wasn't used to Marissa being so philosophical.

"It's just . . . well . . ." And she wanted to tell Summer everything. Her Pucci dress. Her dad. Luke. Life in Newport. The monotony. The loneliness. But she knew Summer would never understand.

No one did.

Except Ryan.

And she wanted to tell her about him. But she couldn't.

She was sworn to secrecy.

11

The soft picking of the guitar echoed through the empty house. Jeff Buckley's "Hallelujah." Ryan hit pause and held the CD case Marissa had made him. Looked at it. The tiny little home on the cover suggested the perfect family. The family Ryan knew he would never have.

"Seriously, dawg. Let's find that piece of white trash's trailer park and burn it to the ground," Nordlund said to Luke and Saunders as Holly poured them all some fresh margaritas. Summer joined them.

"Who dat?" she asked.

"That freak from Chino. The guy was all up in Luke's grille."

"Maybe he's on Oxycontin. Oxycontin is gnarly," she said as she twirled her hair and sipped her drink.

"I heard he's, like, a total psycho," Holly added.

"If I see that kid again I'm gonna beat his ass." Luke was pumped with adrenaline and tequila.

"Run him out of Newport fo' sho'," Nordlund added as everyone laughed. Marissa came up behind them. She had heard it all. And she was glad she hadn't told Summer the truth about anything.

"I got to go. . . ." she said as she ran for the door. Disgusted.

Luke ran after her. Grabbed her.

"Wait up. Where're you going?"

"I can't be here right now," she said. *I can't be a part of this.*

"What's the matter?"

"You don't know him. You don't know anything about him." She broke free from Luke's grip and got in her car.

Luke watched as she drove away. *What was that all about?*

Ryan folded up his tent. Began to pack his things. All around him, candles flickered. He pressed play. The guitar returned. Whispered. *Hallelujah.*

"Promise me right now — that you'll never do this. That you will never run away. No matter how bad things might seem to you — your mom and I will always be there."

Seth nodded okay. He felt guilty for dragging his dad around the city. Searching for Ryan. But he had a friend. And a secret. He tried to convince Sandy to return home. Stop looking. But Sandy wasn't giving up.

"I'm warning you. You run away? I'm coming with you."

Seth was touched. He liked his dad's persistence and his caring nature. "I guess we could look a little longer. . . ."

Hallelujah. Hallelujah. The song continued. Echoed. Ryan rolled his sleeping bag. Felt a presence in the room.

He looked up to see Marissa. *Hallelujah.*

"This song reminds me of you." She stepped toward him.

He stood still. "I thought you were with Luke."

"I was."

They both stood quiet. Awkward. *Hallelujah.*

"I don't know why I'm here. . . ." Marissa's hands shook. Ryan pressed his toes against his shoes. "I just . . ." She stepped forward. Hesitated. "Wanted to see you." He stepped back. Paused. Wanted to run to her. "I mean. You're leaving tomorrow. And what if I never . . ." She couldn't say it. "We never . . ." He knew what she was saying. Felt it in her eyes. Wanted to hold her. "Maybe I could spend the night." Caress her. "Just hang out . . ." Make her whole.

But her body trembled. So small and fragile and scared. He couldn't involve her. She would never survive. He'd crush her with his uncertainty.

"You can't stay," he began. Marissa's lip quivered. "If you stay . . ." He wanted to kiss it. Make it still. ". . . if we spend the night?" Hope glimmered in her eyes. "I don't know that I could leave."

"Then don't," she pleaded.

But he couldn't do it. It wasn't how the world worked. "You go back to school in the fall. And I'll just — what? Live like some ghost? Hiding from house to house until the cops find me? And I have to disappear again?" He hated to say it. "We're from different worlds." He couldn't bring her down with him.

"That's not true," she answered.

"I'm not like you. You can't help me." Marissa reached out for him. Wanted to grab his pain. "No one can." He pulled away.

"Please." And he turned his back on her. "Just. Go."

Her eyes welled with tears. *Hallelujah.*

And the song slowed. *Hallelujah.*

She ran out the door and into her car. Tears streamed down her cheeks. She gasped for breath. For safety. For hope. *Hallelujah.*

And she drove away.

Ryan ran after her. But it was too late. The last . . . *Hallelujah.*

Luke and his crew watched from the car. They had followed Marissa. And now, Ryan.

"Yo, that's Chino. What are you going to do?" Saunders asked.

"What do you think I'm going to do?" Luke said as he pounded his fist into his hand.

"Really? But is it worth it, man? The cops came earlier today."

"Yeah. Let's go back to Holly's," Nordlund

added. "Besides, you cheat on her. What's the big deal?"

Luke stared at Nordlund. This *was* a big deal. And he was ready to fight.

Seth and Sandy continued the search for Ryan. Driving up and down Newport. Combing through neighborhoods, gated communities, the resorts, golf courses. Searching. Seth was starting to feel guilty. Leading his dad on such a wild-goose chase. But the image of Ryan living in a group home kept his mouth shut and they continued searching.

"Seth, I'm up here. You get the bus ticket?" Ryan yelled toward the door as he heard someone approaching. He continued to pack his things.

The candlelight flickered.

But it wasn't Seth.

It was Luke, with Nordlund and Saunders in tow.

"Bus ticket?" Luke asked as he entered the room. "You're not going anywhere."

Nordlund and Saunders stood on either side of Luke. His support. Still. Powerful.

Ryan stood tall. Bracing himself. Ready for a fight.

A standoff. Three against one. Each waiting for the other to make the first move.

Luke took a step forward. . . .

Marissa's eyes burned with tears.

"Hey, Marissa," Jimmy said as she passed by

the study. But she didn't answer. "Marissa?" Still no response.

She continued to her room and flung herself on the bed. Her small body bounced on the down comforter. Heaving sighs of pain. Her eyes welled. She cried.

Jimmy knocked on the door and entered to find his daughter gasping, crying.

"Hey. What's the matter?"

She wiped her eyes and shook her head. *Nothing.* But she wanted to tell him everything.

"You can tell me." He sat on the edge of her bed. It sank with his weight.

Marissa looked at him. *She couldn't tell him.*

"We tell each other everything." He reached out for her.

Marissa fell into his arms. Her body collapsing up and down with each new sob. Ryan. Luke. Newport. The monotony. The pain. And now. Jimmy.

"Do we?" she asked as she held him tighter. They used to tell each other everything. But she remembered today. The money. Kirsten. And she knew her dad was holding something back.

The room was quiet. The calm before a storm. As Luke and his crew circled, hovered, ready to pounce, Ryan stood tough.

"What are you doing here, man? What are you doing with my girlfriend?"

"Nothing," Ryan answered. He thought about Marissa and knew this wouldn't end well.

Luke pushed him. Ryan stumbled back. "It didn't look like nothing."

Saunders stepped up. Looked around the room. "Is he squatting here?"

Luke grabbed Ryan by the shirt collar. Held him up to his face. Almost spat in it. "Tell me, or I'll kill you."

But Ryan didn't care. He was all alone. "Kill me. And quit talking about it."

Luke slammed him against the wall. Ryan's head dented the drywall. A cloud of dust floated in the candlelight.

Ryan got his bearings and kneed Luke right in the groin. Luke doubled over in pain. Coughing. Choking. Ryan stepped back and tried to catch his breath, but Saunders wouldn't give him a break.

He drove his shoulder straight into Ryan's chest, sending him sprawling. All over the floor. Everything went flying.

Candles fell. Wax dripped.

And in the darkness no one saw as the sleeping bag began to burn.

Ryan stood up, entangled with Saunders. Punching, kicking, he finally freed himself.

But found himself face-to-face with Luke again. Punches flew. Blood dripped from their faces. Their eyes swelled. Their hate grew.

The flames doubled.

Luke threw Ryan across the room. The windows shook. Almost shattered.

"What were you doing with my girlfriend?"

Luke asked as he picked the beaten Ryan off the floor.

Ryan's mouth was swelling. He couldn't answer. He had no answer.

Luke punched him hard in the gut.

The fire spread.

Ryan doubled over and fell to the floor. Luke kicked him. Then jumped on top of him in a fit of rage.

"What were you doing here?!! Tell me! Tell me!" He kicked Ryan again. Then pulled his head back and slammed it to the floor.

Ryan was out. Completely unconscious. All around them the fire continued to burn. Grow.

"Dude — the place is on fire!! We gotta go!" Nordlund screamed as he ran out the door and down the stairs. Luke and Saunders took off after him.

But Luke paused.

Ryan lay still on the floor as the flames grew closer.

The smoke billowed. And the heat from the fire intensified.

He couldn't do it. As much as he hated Ryan, he wasn't a killer.

He ran back into the room. The smoke filled his lungs, choking him. He grabbed Ryan and dragged him down the stairs and out the front door.

His limp body lay on the dusty ground.

"Let's go, man!" Nordlund screamed from Luke's truck.

Welcome to the O.C.

Ryan Atwood realizes that he's not in Chino anymore.

Seth Cohen — geeky-cute, he's not like the rest of the O.C. crowd.

Ryan with his new family, the Cohens: Sandy, Kirsten, and Seth.

Marissa Cooper, the girl next door — she's got it all.

Marissa finds herself drawn to Ryan.

Marissa's boyfriend, Luke, is BMOC.

And he's very jealous of her feelings for Ryan.

Summer Roberts has always been Seth's secret crush.

Seth became Summer's good luck charm at Casino Night.

Ryan and Marissa share a dance at Cotillion.

And Seth dances with Anna.

Ryan comforts Marissa as Luke looks on.

Seth persuades Ryan that a road trip is in order.

What happens in Mexico, stays in Mexico.

Ryan and Marissa look for Luke — and find him.

Luke looked at his friend, then back at Ryan. His beaten face twisted. His eyes closed. He lay on the dusty ground unmoving, but as Luke watched his chest fought to rise and fall.

Luke took one last look at Ryan's beaten body and ran to the truck, driving away.

Dust stirred.

After they had disappeared, Ryan came to, gathered the last bits of strength he had left, and pulled himself up off the ground. Slowly. Almost crawling. As he moved away from the house, he looked back and found it engulfed in flames. Burning. Everything he had ever owned burning. Destroyed.

Kirsten phoned Sandy. The model home was burning down. Her work destroyed. And Seth felt even more guilty. Like this was all his fault.

They drove silently to the house and arrived to find the remains a pile of smoking embers. A shell of a home.

Fire trucks, firemen all around the wreckage and Kirsten stood in the middle. Pacing. Upset.

Sandy went to her and wrapped his arm around her. Gave her comfort.

And when an investigator approached Kirsten and told her that someone was living in the home, Seth fessed up.

"It's my fault," Seth said quietly. "Ryan was living here." And he hung his head low. He knew he had lost his friend.

*　　*　　*

"Dude. That kid was f'ed up," Nordlund whispered to Luke as they made their way through Holly's party.

Luke was hoping to find Marissa, but she was nowhere to be found. The image of Ryan popped in his head. His bloody face. His chest rising and falling.

"He was breathing . . ." Luke said in his defense.

But Nordlund didn't look so convinced. "I hope so."

Luke's mind raced. He couldn't find Marissa. And he found himself in a situation he wasn't used to. He felt guilty. He had to go.

Ryan walked down the dark street. Alone. Trying to hitch a ride to anywhere. This was the second time in one week he had found himself homeless and without anyone. Abandoned.

He grabbed the leather band around his neck and ripped it off. Angry. Hurt. He threw the band over the side of the road and watched as it floated down to the sands below. The darkness hiding his pain. The brown leather melting into the golden sand. The warm tide drinking up his past. His family. Drifting into the sea.

Luke found Ryan on the side of the road and pulled up next to him.

Ryan heard the car approach but didn't want to look. He watched as the waves carried the band

154

away. The white foam masking all that was wrong. Hiding the disaster that was his family.

He turned around and found Luke staring at him.

"You're alive," Luke said as he saw the sad look on Ryan's face and the bruise that was forming over his eye.

"Disappointed?" Ryan asked, thinking Luke had come to finish what he had started.

But Luke was actually relieved. "Where you going?" he asked. For once, he was curious. He truly wanted to know. What was it about this kid from Chino that had Marissa running to him?

Ryan took one last look at the ocean waves below. The band was gone. "Don't know . . ."

"If we keep our mouths shut — they might never know it was us," Luke suggested — an offer to make peace. He hated Ryan, but he couldn't just leave him. Ryan thought for a moment, then got in Luke's car. He knew what he had to do and Luke knew it too. They wouldn't get away with this.

They drove in silence back to the Cohens'. Both thinking about the night. Feeling guilty and angry. Hating each other. Hoping the others would forgive them.

And when they arrived at the Cohens', Ryan got out of the truck first. He thought about Trey and he knew how this worked. He held out his hands and allowed himself to be cuffed. The cop shoved him

155

against the squad car. Out of the corner of his eye he saw Luke.

But this was not like when he and Trey were arrested. This time he was the one who knew what he was doing. Luke slowly emerged from the truck, hesitated. Marissa glared at him and looked to Ryan, who nodded at her that it would be okay. And he looked to Luke and did the same. Luke came forward and joined Ryan in the back of the police car.

As they drove away, they both watched Marissa. Luke turned his head in shame when she looked at him. But Ryan and Marissa locked eyes. Said goodbye. Perhaps forever.

12

"We can't keep jerking this kid around. Pulling him out of Juvie to send him to foster care. Giving him hope and taking it away," Sandy said to Kirsten as Seth and Ryan played PlayStation in the other room.

After the model home burned to the ground, Ryan had found himself in Juvie again with Sandy as his attorney. But earlier that day, Kirsten and Seth, who was eager to see his friend, had gone to visit Ryan and returned with him.

"They were going to kill him in that place, Sandy. He couldn't stay there." Sandy glared at her. "But he can't stay here," she continued. "We have to find his mother."

But Sandy was reluctant, remembering how quickly Ryan had run away last time. "He doesn't want to find her."

Ryan stood in the doorway listening. Kirsten and Sandy were oblivious to his presence.

"He's a kid. He doesn't know what he wants."

"So I guess I won't unpack," Ryan said softly.

He understood. He was starting to get used to this life. Being tossed from one place to the next, only to find himself alone.

Ryan left the kitchen and went to the pool house. Sandy and Kirsten stood speechless. What would they do?

Ryan couldn't sleep. This was worse than his second time in Juvie. The pool house was not his home. It was only a reminder of what he didn't have. He wondered if he was ever going to have a family, a place to stay permanently. Ryan looked out the window.

Outside, the moonlight reflected off the pool and bounced the water over the side, into the ocean.

He stepped onto the patio and stood at the edge of the yard, thinking. Wondering. Would he ever find a home? He thought about his own family and wondered what they were doing at that very moment. He reached for the leather band around his neck, his only reminder of his father, his family. But his neck was bare. And he thought about the events of two nights before.

Marissa. Luke. And the fire.

Maybe Sandy was right. He needed something to ground him in this world. They couldn't keep pulling him back and forth like this. No one could.

Seth was observing his morning ritual: a bagel, coffee, and the Arts and Leisure section when Ryan entered.

"Hey, man," Ryan said, barely looking at Seth,

meandering through the kitchen aimlessly. This too was not his home.

"Bowls are to the left. A wide variety of breakfast cereals in the pantry."

Ryan nodded thanks and poured himself a bowl of Cap'n Crunch.

Seth took note. *Good choice.*

He sat quietly, but wanted to say so much. Ask a million questions. He wanted to know about Juvie. Did he shower? Use soap? He already knew it was rough. That's why Kirsten had brought him home. But he wanted to know what it was like to have to sleep next to criminals. Live in a dingy cell. Wear a jumpsuit. Life outside of Newport.

Ryan sat at the table eating his cereal in silence. He didn't feel like talking.

Seth was still full of questions. He wanted to know about Marissa and Luke and the night the house burned down. He looked at Ryan. Still quiet.

But he couldn't hold back. "So. What happened that night?" Ryan took another bite of his cereal. Seth kept prodding. "With Marissa? Before Luke showed up."

Ryan stopped chewing and swallowed. "She came to see me . . ."

This was good, Seth thought. "And?"

"And I told her to leave." He took another bite of his cereal.

"You told her to leave?" Seth was shocked. "That's it? You two are all alone up there and you expect me to believe —"

159

"I thought I was taking off the next morning. It didn't seem right. . . ." Ryan thought about Marissa. She seemed so fragile. He wanted to see her, but he knew it was better this way. He would crush her. They had already said goodbye. If it wasn't good for him to be bounced from place to place, it certainly wouldn't be good for her to have to keep saying goodbye.

Seth nodded, impressed by Ryan's restraint. But he was curious. What now? "You're still here. She lives next door. . . ."

Ryan thought about the possibility of seeing her again. "I dunno. I said some things that —" But he knew — it was probably best if he didn't see her — things were just too complicated, and the way things were going for him right now — nothing seemed to last — why would he start something that was just going to end as soon as it started?

"Well. Now you can take it back."

No, I can't. Sometimes goodbyes needed to stay forever. Marissa needed stability, a constant. He thought about it for a moment and it pained him — maybe Luke was right for that part.

Next door, Marissa was thinking just the opposite. She couldn't get Ryan out of her head. The image of him riding away in a cop car, staring back at her, nodding that it would be okay. But she was worried. She knew things weren't going to be okay. That Ryan was probably in a dark cell, locked away, alone. Seth had come over the day before and asked her to go visit Ryan with him, but she had refused. She didn't want to complicate things and she blamed herself for everything. If she hadn't gone over there that night, Luke never would have followed her and discovered Ryan and they wouldn't have fought. She and Ryan would have parted on good terms. Friends. But now she didn't know if she'd ever see him again. If she'd ever get the chance to apologize.

"Marissa — honey — enough moping. It's very sweet that you're so concerned about this boy. But he's in the system now. He's being taken care of." Marissa had been trying on dresses for her mom all morning. The Casino Night charity event was the following night and her mom wanted her to look perfect. But Marissa was tired and didn't care. All she could think about was Ryan. "And he's not your responsibility just because he's in love with you."

"He's not . . ." Marissa paused. *Could he be?* ". . . in love with me."

"Why not?" Julie asked naively. What guy wouldn't fall in love with her daughter? "He thinks he's too good for you?"

Marissa thought about it for a minute, about his comment that night. *They were from two different worlds.* "He thinks I'm too good for him," she realized.

"Well, he's right. But no matter. That's the past. And you need to focus on the future. Which means Luke."

Ryan's image popped in her head. She would

161

never see him again. Her mom was right. She'd had her chance, her opportunity to escape. And it had passed. She had Luke and Newport and she needed to learn to deal with it.

"You've invested so much with Luke. And your relationship has too much potential to be squandered on some misunderstanding." Julie looked at Marissa. "So finish with your hair. Put on a nice top. And meet me at the club."

"Okay, Mom." She looked at her image in the mirror. She'd go see Luke. "Thanks."

"That's what I'm here for."

". . . and this is Ryan," Kirsten said as she introduced him to the women of Newport. She had taken Ryan and Seth to help the Newpsies set up Casino Night at the ballroom of the Hyatt Newporter.

But the Newpsie women weren't so excited to meet Ryan. Word traveled fast in Newport and they knew his reputation. They knew about Luke, about the model home, and about his past.

Julie Cooper was quick to introduce herself. "I've heard so much about you," she said to Ryan sarcastically.

Ryan felt the tension, the sarcasm, and knew there wasn't much love in the room for him. He wondered if Marissa had told her about him. "Nice to meet you too," Ryan said as he offered his hand, trying to make peace, but Julie ignored him.

Luke had just arrived.

"There he is!" Julie exclaimed as adoring moms and Newpsie women swarmed him. Luke knew how to work the ladies. Somehow he had come out of this whole ordeal as a saint. Ryan was furious, as he watched the women surround him. Luke was the cause of all this, yet no one seemed to care.

"Thanks for coming, Luke," Kirsten said.

"Anything I can do to help make amends for what happened." Luke smiled, kissing ass. Then he turned and glared at Ryan. *We could have kept this all to ourselves.* But Ryan just stared right back. *You'll get what you deserve.* The room chilled. Seth and Kirsten felt it.

She pulled Ryan aside. "I forgot he was coming. If you want to leave, you can —"

But Ryan wasn't going to let Luke get the better of him. "No. I'm here. How can I help?"

"Well. Now that we have our big, strong, strapping men — time for the heavy lifting!" Julie interrupted.

The ballroom was empty and there was a lot of moving to be done before the event.

Marissa made her way through the chaos of the ballroom. Her mom was right, she needed to make things right with Luke.

She found him standing in the doorway holding one end of a table.

"Hey. Your dad said you were here. . . ." she began as she approached him. But he ignored her. "And I thought maybe we could talk."

163

Luke continued walking forward, ignoring her, maneuvering the table through the doorway. Marissa followed but when they got inside the room she realized why Luke wasn't talking. Ryan was holding the other end of the table.

Marissa and Ryan looked at each other. Locked eyes. Both surprised. Marissa was shocked and speechless. He wasn't supposed to be here. She was coming to make things right with Luke. Not apologize to Ryan. She felt angry. Every time she thought Ryan was gone, and she had gotten him out of her mind — gone back to Luke — he seemed to show up again.

Ryan didn't know what to say, but Luke did. He'd seen Ryan and Marissa staring at each other.

"Which one of us do you want to talk to?" he asked, bluntly.

"Luke. C'mon," Marissa pleaded, but it was too late. Luke dropped his end of the table with a giant thud and headed out the door. Marissa paused. Watched him go and looked at Ryan. He couldn't keep doing this to her. Pulling her back and forth. She had to go after Luke.

She took a step toward the door, but Ryan stopped her.

"Wait," he started. Marissa turned, reluctant. "I'm sorry. I feel like since I got here — I've just messed up your life."

Yes, you have. She looked out the door through which Luke had just gone. She was torn. On the one hand she wanted to run after Luke, go back to her stable and monotonous life. Please her mom. On the other, she wanted to run into Ryan's arms, stay with him, be different and intriguing. Allow herself to be swept away into his crazy lifestyle. Escape Newport. Wear the Pucci dress.

But now, as she stood in front of Ryan, she knew what she had to do.

"I'm sorry," she began. "It's my fault too. I . . . never should've left Luke to see you that night . . . And those things you said —"

Now Ryan felt bad. "I didn't — what I said, I —"

Marissa looked at Ryan. This was hard for her. "You were right." And she didn't want to admit this, let alone accept it as truth. "We're from two different worlds." *This will never work.* Then she looked at him, thought about the last time she saw him, driving away in a cop car. "I'm glad you're okay."

Thanks, Ryan thought as he watched Marissa walk away. *I guess that's it.* He and Marissa had ended whatever it was they had, their connection, just as quickly as it had begun.

Seth soon found Ryan and Kirsten and they left the ballroom.

Marissa went home and sat in her room, thinking about Ryan and Luke. Thinking that suddenly she had no one. She picked up her phone and called Summer. She needed her dress. Her escape.

On the ride back to the Cohens', Kirsten and Ryan bonded. Ryan was starting to feel like he belonged.

That maybe Kirsten would let him into her family, even if it was only for a few more days.

But when they entered the house everything changed.

Ryan was in shock. He walked into the living room and discovered his mother sitting there next to Sandy, waiting.

"Hey, Ry," she said nervously.

Ryan was speechless. Every ounce of pain he had felt over the last week and a half boiled to the surface. All that had happened with Marissa paled in comparison. He pushed his toes against the inside of his shoes, trying to fight the tears and the rage.

He had nothing to say.

He walked off, unsure how to react. On the one hand she was his mother, on the other, she had abandoned him.

Seth stood silent. Caught in the mess. Should he follow Ryan? Stay with the adults? Or leave altogether?

Seth chose the latter and went to his room.

Upstairs, Seth could hear his parents talking to Dawn through the vent on his wall. But he wasn't interested. Outside his window, he watched as Ryan disappeared into the pool house.

Seth could feel the anger and the hurt from all the way up here and he wanted to run down and help his friend. But he knew he couldn't. That somehow, some way, Ryan would have to figure this one out on his own.

*   *   *

Later that evening, the Cohen and Atwood families had dinner. Awkwardness filled the air.

"So. Dawn," Sandy began, trying to break the tension. "How long have you worked at the laundromat?"

"Not long. Just a couple weeks," Dawn answered as she took a bite of her food.

Ryan became uncomfortable. "What happened to the restaurant?"

"They were making . . . cutbacks," Dawn replied uneasily.

But Ryan knew the truth. He hadn't been there to call in sick for her. "You got fired."

Seth took a bite of his food. Felt the temperature rising.

Kirsten and Sandy looked at each other. What had they gotten themselves into?

"Have you seen Trey?" Ryan asked, ready to fire a million more questions.

"I went to the prison to visit him. He wouldn't see me."

I'm sure he wouldn't. Ryan took a bite of his food and thought about Trey. Alone, eating prison food.

Kirsten tried to change the subject, move on to brighter things, but everything she tried just circled back to the disaster that was Ryan's family. Even A.J.

"I broke up with him. We're through. No more. I put up with too much. He laid his hands on me — on Ryan — too many times."

167

Ryan was embarrassed. Dawn noticed.

"What? I'm saying, he was a bad influence. With his drinking."

" 'Cause A.J. was the problem," Ryan snapped.

Seth became uncomfortable with the stories Ryan and Dawn told back and forth — the alcohol, the drugs, the abuse — and he tuned out. He couldn't even begin to imagine what a life like that would be like. Vacations? Birthdays? Holidays? *They must be so sad and lonely.* Seth thought about his favorite holiday — Chrismukkah. Maybe Ryan could come visit them this year — it'd be nice to have someone his age to share the holidays with. Seth's mind continued to wander and he missed the end of the verbal fight between Ryan and his mom. It was only the clanging of silverware on expensive china that brought him out of his daydream.

Ryan stood up abruptly and left the room. Silence encased the dining room. Dawn nodded politely at the Cohens and got up to follow her son.

Inside the pool house, Dawn found Ryan with his back to her.

"Will you at least talk to me?" Dawn shouted at him.

Ryan turned suddenly. "What are you even doing here?"

"I came for you."

He didn't believe her. "Why? What do you want with me?" He couldn't hold back any longer. "You left a note! You couldn't take the time to call?!! But you took the time to write a note!"

"Ryan — let me explain —" She took a step toward him.

But Ryan didn't want an explanation. "You abandoned me! You threw me out and then you just took off!" He wanted to yell. He had to yell.

"I know, honey. I was . . . And A.J. . . . And the drinking, and —" Ryan looked at her. He'd had enough of her excuses. She felt it. "It's gonna be different now, Ryan."

"That's what you said when we moved from Fresno. After Dad got arrested." Ryan reached for his neck. The band. His hand trembled.

"I'm gonna be different. We have a chance to start over, babe. We never had people like them before —" She nodded to the Cohen house — "who wanted to help us."

Still, Ryan was defensive. *You left me.* "Right. So someone offers you a nice place to stay, and suddenly you're all about the mom thing."

Now Dawn felt bad. "I didn't know what I was doing when I married your dad. I was too young when I had your brother. But with you . . . you were always the smart one. The good one." Ryan looked at her. *You never said that before. You never cared.* "So when you got arrested? I knew I'd failed. You were my last hope." *I was? Why?* Ryan softened. "I should just go," Dawn said, turning away.

Ryan was torn. He wanted to hate his mom. Send her off for good. Never see her again. But there was a part of him that just couldn't do it. She headed for the door.

"Wait."

Dawn stopped and looked at him. He wanted to resist her, like he had with Marissa. Tell her to go. But he couldn't. She was family. And he reached out to her. *Prove me wrong.*

"Will you ever forgive me, kiddo?"

"Let's just go slow," he said, trying to resist her. But she hugged him tighter.

"Whatever you want. I'm not gonna lose you again. . . ."

And they held each other tight. Each wanting to believe the other's promises. Each wanting to believe they had a chance at a family. A new life.

13

"So where did they go anyway?" Seth asked Kirsten as he scooped leaves out of their pool.

"I don't know. Out."

"You just let him leave with her?" After last night's dinner, Seth was concerned.

"She's Ryan's mother."

"Oh. Okay. So we'll just wait for happy hour to end. . . ." Seth replied sarcastically.

"Seth," Kirsten scolded. "We have to be supportive. It seems like she's really trying. This is how it's supposed to be."

"How do you know?" Seth asked, unconvinced. "This woman abandoned him. And now all she has to do is show up, and you're gonna let her take him away? She should be the one on probation. Not Ryan."

Ryan and Dawn walked the sites of Newport. Through the Back Bay and all around Balboa Island, out to the boardwalk and the pier.

Together they explored this new world. And for

the first time since he set foot in Newport, Ryan didn't feel alone.

He smiled at his mom.

"This is fun," she said.

"Yeah," he said as he nodded. *This wasn't so bad.*

Ryan looked around at all the young families, the tiny kids building castles, the parents being buried in the sand, and smiled. This was what having a family was like, he thought. And he wondered if everything would be okay. If one day he would have a family again.

Dawn ran ahead of him, the warm summer sand sliding through her toes. Ryan hesitated, watched as she walked out to the ocean. The waves lapped at her feet. And she laughed as she ran from the tide.

Ryan smiled at his mom running in the wet sand and thought about Trey and his dad, remembering when it was just the four of them. When there was no A.J., no tequila bottle, no prison cell, and no anger. Just the four of them. A family.

He sat down at the top of the hill that sloped into the water and watched as his mother continued to play in the ocean waves.

She made him smile. And not just because she was entertaining at the moment, but because he felt like he was part of a family again. At least half of one.

His mom had abandoned him, he knew this, but she had returned and today was going well. He wondered if maybe she would stay. If maybe they could rent an apartment here. Maybe the warm golden sun could dissolve all the gray from their lives and they could live happily ever after.

Dawn came up the tiny hill and sat down next to Ryan, her feet dripping salt water and sand. She was out of breath. Ryan gave her his smile, that turn of his head that let her know he was deep in thought.

"So, what do you think?" she asked him.

"About what?" he asked. Unsure where she was going with this.

"Us. Starting over. A fresh start." *To what?* Ryan cocked his head. "I want to be a mom. Do this right. Do what I shoulda done from the beginning."

Ryan nodded. He understood, but he was still skeptical.

"I don't know. . . ." Ryan started.

"Just think about it."

Ryan nodded okay.

They sat in silence and watched the tide drift out to sea.

The waves got farther and farther away as the sun began to set in front of them. Ryan wondered what to say to his mom. Should he answer her? Tell her he was ready to let her back in his life as his mom? Give her the opportunity to prove herself. Or was he just setting himself up to be let down again?

Dawn held up a pack of cigarettes. *You want one?*

Ryan grabbed the pack and was about to take one when he realized there was no lucky one. No cigarette flipped the other direction, begging to shout his luck to the world. He thought about Theresa and her belief in luck and how he had abandoned her, and he thought about Marissa and how she had taken the luck and how they'd abandoned each other. Maybe he shouldn't test fate, just let things play out as planned, he thought as he handed the pack back to his mom.

He wasn't going to smoke. He didn't need to.

His mom was back.

Seth and Kirsten were still on the back porch when Ryan and Dawn returned to the Cohen house, laughing. Kirsten was surprised to hear them so happy. She'd never heard Ryan laugh, or seen him smile like that, and she was surprised.

Ryan and Dawn approached them. Seth stood next to his friend.

"Well. We should probably head out soon. I told my friend Marianne we'd be crashing at her place."

Seth glared at Kirsten. He didn't want them to go.

"Actually, I was thinking —" she started. "You just got here. You don't have anywhere to stay. We're all just getting to know one another —" Kirsten looked to Seth. He smiled at her. *Thanks.*

"And we're having a party tonight," Seth added.

"Right," Kirsten said a little reluctantly. Ryan noticed. *Is that such a good idea?* The images of Luke and Marissa popped in his head.

Dawn hesitated. "Not for me. Thanks, though."

"Vegas Night?" Kirsten tempted.

"Vegas? Huh," Dawn began. But Ryan looked at her. He didn't want anything to ruin this day and from what he'd learned so far, a Newport party screamed disaster. Dawn noticed Ryan's unease. "It's very nice of you to offer. But . . . I don't have anything to wear."

"I think we could find something." Kirsten wasn't giving up.

Seth hung out in the pool house on Ryan's bed while Ryan finished getting dressed.

"Summer's probably going to be there. Actually, Newport charity event? She will be there. And I was thinking, Ryan, tonight might be the night. Tell her about Tahiti." Ryan looked at Seth with hesitation. Seth felt it. "Okay, maybe not all of Tahiti. Just a few details, some hints. Play a little game. Girls like games. Right? Right."

Ryan stood back and looked at his image in the mirror. He still wasn't used to wearing a suit. Seth continued talking. "So, what do you think? I'll drop a few hints tonight. Leave a sextant in her purse. Perhaps a ransom letter. Cut words out of magazines. Jumble them up. She'd never know it was me. . . ." Seth continued, but Ryan tuned him out. He was too worried about the night. About his mom and Marissa and Luke.

Seth finished his rambling as Ryan straightened his tie for the tenth time.

"Maybe we should just lay low," he said as he thought about Marissa.

Seth looked defeated. Ryan covered, "At least I should. I think I've caused enough trouble here."

Seth understood and nodded okay. "I see where you're going with this, Ryan, and I like it. The elusive approach. I never thought about that, but it's good."

The Newporter ballroom had been transformed into one of the best casinos in Vegas. Lights, chips, money, girls, and booze all done Newport style.

Ryan and his mom entered together.

"Are all their parties like this?" Dawn asked, in awe of her surroundings.

Ryan thought about it for a second. The fashion show. Holly's beach house. *Yeah.* "Pretty much."

"Well. Let's clean 'em out. Huh?" Dawn said enthusiastically as she dragged Ryan over to a black-jack table.

Ryan looked around the room and saw Marissa with Luke, but he quickly turned back to his mom. He didn't want to start any trouble.

"Betting kind of big, Mom?" Ryan asked, concerned, as he noticed the giant stack of chips displayed in front of his mother.

"It's for charity," she said. "Besides, the count's way positive."

A smile spread across Ryan's face. This was the mom he remembered. The one who had a bright outlook on life. The one who believed that things were going her way. That the count was positive.

"Honey, if I teach you anything in this world? The count goes way higher with multiple decks," she whispered to Ryan. "Hit me."

The dealer screamed, "Blackjack!" and the crowd around the table went crazy.

"See? Our luck is turning around already." Dawn turned to Ryan. He grinned. She was right. For the first time since the night he had been cuffed with Trey, he felt lucky.

Across the room, at a craps table, Seth had been roped in by Summer. His elusive approach had worked. He had become her lucky rabbit's foot.

"Do it again," she said as she held out the dice for Seth to blow on.

He blew and she rolled. Another win.

"You're not going anywhere, Syd," Summer said as she grabbed Seth's arm playfully.

"Seth," he corrected her.

But she wasn't listening. To her, it didn't matter. She held out the dice. "Blow."

And she won again. *Keep this up*, Seth said to himself, *and we'll be in Tahiti in no time.*

Marissa sat near the slot machines watching her mother and father argue. She wondered if Julie knew about the money he had borrowed from Kirsten. And she wondered what she had done to make her father

177

so quiet and secretive. She wanted to be a part of his life again, but she felt like she was living on the outside. Away from all she had ever known.

She looked up and her eyes met Ryan's. Away from all she would ever know.

"Go. Have fun with your friends," Dawn said as she noticed Marissa staring at them. Ryan hesitated. "I'll be fine. You don't have to babysit me."

Reluctantly he left the table and approached Marissa.

Dawn smiled as she watched her son go, but her hand trembled with insecurity.

"Hey," Ryan said uneasily as he got close to Marissa.

"Hi . . ." She looked over at the blackjack table. "Is that your mom?"

Ryan paused. He had never admitted this before. He had always been too embarrassed. "Yeah."

Marissa paused, remembering the night they had sat around the pool at the model home. "She came back. So I guess . . ." And it pained her to say this. ". . . that means . . . you're going home?"

Ryan looked at his mom. "Yeah. I guess."

"Well — good luck with everything," she said, recalling their last night together. They were from two different worlds. *This would never work.*

"Yeah. You too. Have a nice life." *I'm sorry. I'll never see you again.* Ryan looked away. This was too hard. He'd already done this once before.

But he saw Luke staring at them and he knew he was making the right decision.

"You should go."

Marissa nodded reluctantly. And she went off to join Luke.

Seth and Summer continued to win at craps. He liked being her lucky charm, even if she didn't know his name.

Marissa confronted Luke. "You can't just not talk to me."

"Watch me," he said as he turned away.

"It's not like you're totally innocent in all this. You didn't have to attack him."

"What was I supposed to do? You left me to go up there. With him."

All the pent-up emotion and anger from the night at the model home exploded.

"It wasn't like that," Marissa replied. But she knew it was more. And she knew — "It was a mistake." Ryan was leaving. They would never work.

Luke felt her insincerity, the doubt in her voice, and blew right past her. Marissa sat alone. Upset. She had lost Ryan *and* Luke and wanted to be with both.

Ryan looked over and saw Marissa. He knew what he had to do.

He walked after Luke.

"Hey."

"What do you want?" Luke asked, whipping around.

"Nothing happened." Luke glared at him, but Ryan continued, "With me and Marissa."

"I'm not talking about it." Luke turned to go.

But Ryan couldn't give up. He couldn't bear the burden. He had to do right. "Then listen. She chose you. You're the one she wants." And with that he walked away. The goodbye was better forever.

Dawn's hands continued to tremble at the blackjack table. But it wasn't nerves. As hard as she had tried, she couldn't do this. She couldn't be the perfect mom.

She ordered a drink.

"You rock, Stanley!" Summer said as she threw her arms around Seth.

He drank her in, absorbing every ounce of her tiny body. *Tahiti was just around the corner.* He smiled.

Luke found Marissa sitting at a slot machine. Unamused. He approached, grabbed her, and kissed her — an apologetic hello. Ryan had done right.

Dawn ordered another drink.

Ryan walked alone through the party. Trying to fit in. Everyone was having fun except him. Even his mom was busy winning. Seth approached him.

"Greatest night ever. Like, one of those moments when, like, the stars and the skies and the cosmos align and like . . . Wow." Ryan smiled for him. Then Seth remembered. "How's your mom doing?"

Ryan looked over to the blackjack tables. Her hands went up in the air. Another win. "She's high-rolling. It's like she was made for this place."

"Maybe this could work," Seth said.

"Yeah?" Ryan paused, looked over at his mom. "Maybe." And he genuinely believed it. Maybe she had changed. Maybe he could go home.

"Rabbit's foot! *Vámonos!*" Summer called to Seth.

"Duty calls. . . ." he said to Ryan as he took off running.

Ryan smiled and grabbed a soda. Maybe this could work out. Maybe he would have a family. A life. A mom.

But his thoughts were interrupted by a crash of glasses.

He looked over to see what all heads were turning toward and his dreams shattered.

"Mom!"

He ran over to find her sprawled on her back. Laughing. Soaked. Surrounded by broken glass.

Everyone gathered around.

Ryan filled with embarrassment and hurt and anger as he knelt down beside his mother. All eyes seemed to be upon him.

"Quit staring and get me up."

Ryan hesitated.

"Help. Me. Up!" she screamed belligerently.

But Ryan froze. He couldn't do it. All his hopes

181

were shattered in just one moment. All his dreams of a family, broken. He couldn't.

Seth and Luke arrived and helped Dawn up.

Ryan took a step back. Still hesitant. Afraid that if he touched her, admitted she was with him, that it would all be real. That there would be no escape.

Sandy stepped in for Seth.

Marissa made her way to the front of the crowd, saw the pain in Ryan's eyes.

"What are you lookin' at?" Dawn asked drunkenly, realizing everyone in Newport was staring at her. "Where's Ryan? Ryan!"

Then it was over. There was no escape. It was real. Ryan took a deep breath, looked over at Marissa, and accepted it. His fate. He moved toward his mom and got under her other arm. Luke stepped away.

"I'm so sorry, Ryan. I ruined it, huh? I ruined everything. I did. You hate me."

And Ryan wanted to scream, *Yes, I hate you. You abandoned me. Promised me. And left me again. Yes. I hate you.* But he couldn't do it.

"No, Mom." He paused. He wanted a family. "I love you. . . ."

Ryan sat on his bed and watched his mother sleep. His mind raced. He wondered what happened to the family they once had. When it was just the four of them. When there was no one and nothing else.

He wondered what went wrong. What had he done?

He was alone. His hopes and dreams shattered. Trey was right. Dreams didn't come true. He should have listened.

He watched as his mom breathed deeply. Oblivious and numb to the world.

And the sight of her passed out on his bed reminded him of Marissa.

He lay down on the floor next to the bed and fell asleep thinking — how long can I keep on like this — taking care of everyone, but no one taking care of me? When can I pass out in someone's arms? And wake up with everything okay . . .

The sunlight broke through the pool house window.

Ryan woke to find his bed empty. Abandoned.

He stepped outside and stopped dead in his tracks.

Dawn stood next to Kirsten. Her bag in hand. And he knew.

She was trying to leave without saying goodbye. But he couldn't go to her. Tell her goodbye.

He didn't have the strength. And he held up his hand. A silent truce. *This would never work.*

A wave. Goodbye.

And she walked away.

He went to the balcony where he had watched Marissa lay numb on her front porch and saw his mother get into a cab.

When he turned back to the house, Kirsten's eyes held him. He knew — the goodbye was forever.

14

"Dude. You're a Cohen! Welcome to a life of insecurity and paralyzing self-doubt," Seth said, raising his hand for a high five.

Ryan smiled.

After some legal maneuvering, Sandy and Kirsten had decided to assume legal responsibility for him.

He had spent the last week or so wandering aimlessly through the days. Playing video games with Seth and lying around the pool house. Avoiding Marissa and much of Newport, staying away from any more uncertainties. The only thing that had been certain through it all was that his mom was gone. That he had no family and no place to go or stay forever. But now there was certainty.

Ryan Atwood was now a Cohen, and Newport would be his home.

Ryan sat in the pool house pondering his new position. He smiled to himself. He'd made it through. He had a name, no government-issued number, a family, Sandy, Kirsten, and Seth, and a place to live, Newport.

Upstairs, Seth sat in his room with Captain Oats.

"We did it," he exclaimed. "Operation Criminal Friend was a bigger success than expected. He's a Cohen now."

Captain Oats sat still, smiling at Seth. Seth smiled back and remembered all that he'd been through in the past couple weeks. He'd made a friend, Ryan, gotten on Summer's radar, Casino Night, and now he had a brother, a friend forever.

It was time, he thought, thinking back to the first night Ryan had arrived at his house and the inception of his plan. He rummaged through his bookshelves and found his copy of *Kavalier and Clay*. They were brothers now.

"Hey," Seth said as he entered the pool house, the book hidden behind his back.

"Hey," Ryan replied.

"How's it feel?" Seth asked.

"What?"

"Being a Cohen, you know the —" Seth sneezed. "That. You got the allergies yet? Runny nose, itchy eyes." Ryan looked at Seth quizzically. "Right. No. Of course not."

Ryan pulled the sheets on his bed tight, trying to make his bed. If he was going to stay here permanently, he wanted to show he respected and understood his luck.

Seth plopped himself on the bed. All the sheets

wrinkled. Ryan cringed. "It's okay. Rosa comes to-day. Sit."

Ryan sat down next to Seth.

"Now that you're a Cohen, Ryan, there's a few things you need to know. Mom, Kirsten, can't cook. Not allowed near the stove. You catch her — tell me." Ryan nodded. "Dad, Sandy, avoid mentions of *Grease*. Unless of course you enjoy musicals." Ryan smiled and thought of Theresa. He'd actually done a few musicals when he was younger. "In that case, I say go for it. *Oklahoma!*, *South Pacific*, *Guys and Dolls*. He'll sing them all for you. And finally . . ." Seth pulled the book out from behind his back. . . . "the essential."

He handed the book to Ryan.

Ryan held it in his hands as Seth continued talking. "A sort of Cohen brotherhood bonding offering. An emblem of our friendship. Of course, you'll have to read it first."

Ryan looked at the book, then turned to Seth. "So you're saying we can't be friends until I read this?"

Seth thought for a minute. "Yes, Ryan, that's what I'm saying."

Both guys stared at each other. *Are you serious?* Then started to laugh uncontrollably. Not that anything either had said was that funny, but for some reason neither could stop laughing. It was contagious and they kept passing it back and forth.

Kirsten knocked on the door and they stopped to catch their breath for a second.

"What's so funny?" she asked as she stepped inside the pool house.

The guys looked at each other. This was between them.

Kirsten couldn't help but smile too. The boys continued laughing.

"Okay, okay," she said, walking around the room. Inspecting. Figuring out ways to make this a bedroom. A home.

"We'll have to clear all this out so you have someplace to put your —" The boys quieted. Ryan looked at her. She paused, realizing. "Right. You don't have any stuff. Which is why we need to take you shopping. You need clothes. Shoes. Underpants."

"Mom. You can't say underpants," Seth gasped.

"Look. I've already got everything I need. Really," Ryan said. He didn't need anything else from the Cohens. They had given him a home. A family. More than enough.

Kirsten thought for a minute. "Do you have a tuxedo? Because you're going to need one."

"For what?"

"For Cotillion," Kirsten replied matter-of-factly.

"What's Cotillion?"

"Dude, don't ask," Seth said.

Pelican Hill Country Club sat on the cliffs above the Newport shore. The rolling green grass melted into the ocean and the California sun rose high over the clubhouse. Kirsten pulled up in her Range Rover and escorted the guys inside.

"Cotillion is one of Newport's biggest events," she said, walking alongside them. "It's when the young girls make their debut into society."

Ryan nodded and continued walking.

The clubhouse was immaculate. Marble floors, wood detailings, and expensive paintings on the walls. Ryan took it all in and thought aloud, "Maybe I should skip it." Bad things always seemed to happen whenever he entered one of these rich Newport locations.

"You can't. It's a family tradition, and now you're part of the family." Kirsten paused. "And if I have to go, you have to go."

Ryan smiled. At least he wasn't the only one who felt out of place here.

"Come on, boys. It'll be fun."

The boys followed Kirsten back into the men's grill, which had temporarily been converted into a fitting area full of racks of white gowns and designer tuxedos. The boys were immediately ushered away by the fashion coordinator.

Ryan and Seth joked around in the fitting area as they tried on tuxedo pants. Laughing at their images in the mirror as they pulled on pairs of pants that were too small and others that were too big. Finally, Ryan found a pair that fit and went out into the main room to see if they would get approved by the fashion coordinator. This wasn't so bad, he thought, looking around at all the beautiful girls in their long white gowns. He could get used to life in Newport.

But he had temporarily forgotten that he already had a past in Newport.

Ryan turned around and saw that past standing behind him — Marissa. "Hey."

"Hey. What are you doing here?" she asked.

"I had an appointment with my personal shopper," he said, hoping she wouldn't ask again.

"But I thought — a couple of days ago," she started. This was what he didn't want her to say. "You said you were leaving with your mom."

Ryan stepped back, embarrassed. How would he explain? She had left him for good. Said goodbye forever. "It didn't really work out. So — I'm kind of living with the Cohens."

Ryan dreaded her response. Would she tell him to hide in the pool house forever? Never step foot on the driveway, lest their paths cross?

Was he really here? Marissa wondered. Would he stay? "For good?"

Ryan nodded. "If I can stay out of trouble."

Marissa took it all in. Thought about Luke, the Pucci dress Summer had returned, and now Ryan standing in front of her. Unsure how to react. She was with Luke. But now the unknown stood in front of her. She stared at Ryan.

"Wow. So we're — neighbors," she finally said.

"Is that . . . gonna be okay?" *Here it comes.*

"No," Marissa started. *This is it.* "It's great."

Great? "That means you and I can be — friends. Right?"

Ryan hesitated. He wasn't expecting that. He was expecting an all-or-nothing answer and knew the answer would have been nothing. But now, friends? He could accept that. It wasn't everything but it was better than nothing. He smiled at her and she smiled back.

They would be friends. But they held each other's gaze, both wanting more. Both wishing things had turned out differently.

"What are you still doing here? I thought you went back to Chino," Luke said, interrupting their gaze.

"Had a change of plans," Ryan answered defensively.

"Ryan's living here now," Marissa said as she stepped between the boys.

"He's what?"

"Look — I'm not here to cause problems," Ryan said as he took a step away from Marissa and Luke. He didn't want to cause any trouble. He'd made a promise to the Cohens. He couldn't cause any trouble. They had an agreement.

But Luke wasn't about to let up. "Then you'd better stay the hell away from me. And stay away from Marissa," he said as he stormed off.

Kirsten returned to see if the guys had found tuxes and breeched the awkwardness between Marissa and Ryan.

"I was going to call you, Marissa. Since you're

the lead deb, I'm pleased to present you with a couple of White Knights." She indicated Seth and Ryan. "In case any of your girls needs a last-minute escort."

Summer approached and recognized Ryan. "Every girl needs a White Knight," she said, eyeing him up and down.

But Seth was oblivious. His mind glassed over by the image of Summer. "Seth Cohen. White Knight," he said, offering himself up as her escort.

But she ignored him and continued to stare at Ryan. "So you'll be at the rehearsal?"

"Absolutely," Seth answered.

Summer stood in her bra and panties, holding up gown after gown in front of her body.

"That Chino guy's back. He's kind of cute," Summer said as she slipped a dress over her head. "And lonely. And since you're the head deb and all, I was thinking . . ."

"You want me to fix you up with Ryan? I thought you said he was a psycho."

Summer took the dress off and looked at her figure in the mirror. "That was before I got to know him."

"When did you get to know him?" Marissa asked, skeptically and a little hurt. She thought she was the only who knew him. Who felt his pain. Who knew his secrets.

"Just now. Plus, I'm into that whole brooding, bad boy thing. He's wounded. I can save him." Summer pulled on her jeans.

"Have you ever talked to him? He's not really a bad boy."

"He will be by the time I get through with him," Summer smirked as she pushed her breasts up in her bra.

Marissa smiled weakly. She wanted to be the girl to save Ryan. Change him. Make him her own.

"What? You're not, like, into him, are you? I mean, you're with Luke. Right?"

"Right," Marissa replied. She didn't like this idea, but Summer was right. She was with Luke. "I'll see what I can do."

In the pool house, Ryan unpacked his tux and hung it up in the closet. A lone outfit. The only piece of clothing on a hanger besides his hooded sweatshirt and a pair of jeans. A reminder of Ryan's lonely past. As he stood looking at the tux in the bare closet, doubt surfaced within him. Luke, Marissa — a complicated past. All foreshadowing trouble. Maybe he wasn't ready to live in Newport, be a part of this society. He turned to Seth, who was reading a comic book on his bed.

"So. I think I'm not going to Cotillion."

"Okay. Except. You are," Seth replied without even looking up from his book.

"I made a promise — to your parents — that I would stay out of trouble."

"It's a debutante ball. What kind of trouble could you get into?" Seth said, putting down his comic book.

"I dunno. Why don't you ask Luke?" Ryan said as he walked over to the window and looked out at Marissa's house.

Seth considered this for a moment. Luke was the source of all their trouble and he didn't want to lose Ryan, but Summer was Marissa's friend and if Ryan didn't go Summer probably wouldn't even notice him.

"Dude. We're White Knights. Marissa's probably already got a sad, lonely deb all lined up for you to escort. You can't just call and cancel at the last minute."

"You're right," Ryan replied. He couldn't call and cancel on Marissa. They were friends. He picked up the phone and handed it to Seth. Too scared to do anything. "Will you call her?"

But Seth wasn't buying it. "No. If you're gonna bail on Marissa and some, like, poor, pathetic, dateless girl — you're gonna have to do it yourself."

Ryan sighed. He knew Seth was right, but he wasn't sure seeing Marissa right now was the best idea.

Marissa was trying to zip up her gown at home and model it for her dad when the doorbell rang.

"Coming," she yelled as she held the dress tight to her body and ran to the door, opening it to reveal Ryan.

"Hey. You're at my house," she said, surprised, almost forgetting that he now lived next door.

"Yeah. I. Well," Ryan stuttered. The sight of

Marissa in her gown made him speechless. "Wanted to talk to you about the Cotillion."

"Oh. Okay," Marissa replied as she fidgeted with her dress, trying to zip it tight to her body. "I was just — trying this on — and I can't seem to reach the —" Marissa reached behind for the zipper but it was no use.

"Do you want me to . . . ?" he asked.

"You mind?" she answered, turning so her back was toward him.

Ryan leaned in and held the tiny zipper in his hand, breathing in the beauty of Marissa. The way her hair fell against her neck. The smell of her soft skin. His mind raced as he pulled the zipper up.

He couldn't tell her that he wasn't going to Cotillion. He had to go. He couldn't resist her.

The rehearsal the following morning got off to a shaky start because, as Ryan said, "I really . . . don't . . . dance."

But Seth convinced him to enter the ballroom. They were in this together. Brothers. Cohens.

"So, guys? Can I introduce you to your debs?" Marissa said as she walked over to them. Everything bad about dancing melted away upon seeing Marissa. Ryan was ready.

Summer entered the ballroom, thinking that Ryan was her partner, but Seth knew otherwise. It was written in the cosmos. They would be together. Even when she stepped up and said to Ryan,

"We've already met," assuming that Marissa had done her duty as a friend.

"Actually, Summer, Ryan's already been promised to someone else."

"What?" Summer gasped. "I can't believe this. You gave him to someone else? Who? Who is pathetic enough not to have a date the day before Cotillion?"

"At this point, that would be you," a sweet raspy voice said from behind her.

Summer looked around at all the debutantes. Everyone was paired up already. The voice was right. But who was this girl?

Behind Summer stood Anna Stern, a brown-eyed, blond beauty with an East Coast charm and style all her own. Her short funky hair and her daring clothes made her stand out from all the couture-wearing Newport debs.

"Anna Stern, this is Ryan Atwood. Anna just moved here from Pittsburgh," Marissa said as she introduced the two of them. They shook hands.

Summer took one look at Anna and cringed. "Pittsburgh? Ew."

But Anna didn't let Summer's comment bother her. "Can we just get this over with?" she asked as she grabbed Ryan and walked off.

"So, like, what am I supposed to do?" Summer asked, still standing with Marissa.

Behind her Seth stood quietly, waiting to be noticed.

Finally, Summer turned to him and sighed. "Just. Don't. Talk to me."

All in the cosmos. Seth smiled. "Right. Totally. Because our connection is deeper than words," he said sarcastically. Summer glared at him. "That was it for me. I'm done. Chock-full o' quiet."

On the dance floor Marissa attempted to teach Ryan and Anna how to waltz. But her attempt was failing. Ryan looked to her for help as Anna weakly placed her hand on Ryan's shoulder.

"Not like that. Here, watch," Marissa said, stepping into Anna's position, her slender arms resting on Ryan.

They looked at each other and the room seemed to go silent. Both lost in the touch of the other. There was something between them — something real, palpable, heart-wrenching. *Friends.* Ryan sighed.

"I'd be jealous if Chino wasn't gay." Before Ryan even turned around, he knew it was Luke. All good things were always ruined by Luke. But he didn't say anything. Just stepped away from Marissa and gave her space. He had a pact with the Cohens and he wasn't about to lose his chance at a family over Luke. He went back to Anna.

"So, you're into her, huh?" Anna asked. Ryan was taken aback. No one in Newport had been so up front with him. "Man, are you in trouble."

"I know," Ryan said as he looked over at Marissa with Luke. This could never end well.

*   *   *

When Seth and Ryan returned home, Seth was ecstatic.

"Ryan, did you see my moves?" Seth said as he pretended to twirl a girl into the pool house. He couldn't get Summer off his mind. They had spent the afternoon dancing and she had told him he didn't suck, which was better than the usual "ew" he got from her or the no acknowledgment at all.

Ryan looked at him and laughed. "Yeah," he replied unsympathetically, giving Seth one of his cocked-head, eyebrows-raised glances.

Seth stopped twirling and sat down in the chair across from Ryan's bed.

"Dude, you got to get rid of those looks. You're a Cohen now. Guys like Luke? Not really into our clan. But it's okay, because I've got an idea."

What now? Ryan thought. He didn't like the sound of this. He wanted to stay in the pool house. Hang out with the Cohens. Get used to having a home and a family. He didn't want to get into any more trouble.

"Okay, here's the plan," Seth started. "I've got Summer in the bag. Well, at least she's been assigned to me. So, I figure I'll work that. Give her a little Seth Cohen charm she can't resist. Then the news of Tahiti will sound like a godsend to her. What do you think?"

"Sounds good," Ryan responded, still not so into the idea. He couldn't get the image of Marissa and Luke out of his head. He wanted to go rescue her. Save her from Luke. But he couldn't.

197

Seth hesitated. Why wasn't Ryan into his plan? And then he remembered. How selfish of him. "Right. You need a plan too. Well." Seth started trying to think of a comparable plan to his. "You've got Anna. She seems pretty cool, spunky. And much like yourself, new to Newport." Ryan nodded, *and?* "I don't know. Maybe you two will hit it off. Or make Marissa jealous."

"Right." Ryan nodded. Seth's plan wasn't all that convincing. He didn't want to make Marissa jealous. He didn't even know if he could. After all that had happened, she still returned to Luke. And they had agreed to be friends.

Seth got up to leave. "Oh, and, Ryan, one more thing. We have to go to Holly's barbecue. See you in an hour."

"No," Ryan said quickly, but Seth was already out the door. This could only mean one thing. . . .

"Kids getting drunk. Puking. I can't get in any trouble here." Ryan smiled at Seth as they entered Holly's beach house and drifted into a sea of kids. A party in full effect.

"Ten minutes," Seth assured Ryan. "I'm just gonna find Summer. Lock things down for tomorrow. See where the night takes me." And Seth disappeared into the expanse of drunken teens.

Ryan made his way over to a couch and settled down, trying to blend in. But it was obvious he was not part of this scene. His clothes and his demeanor set him apart from the rest of the crowd.

And then he saw Marissa. Standing with Luke and his water polo buddies, looking so bored and pained. And he wanted to run over to her and take her away from them, but he couldn't. The sight of Luke made him hold back. He turned his head. Ten minutes and he'd be gone.

But Marissa looked at Ryan and motioned for him to join her. He nodded no thanks. She waved again. Still, he shook his head no. But she wasn't taking no for an answer and she headed toward him.

Outside, Summer was trying to trade Cotillion escorts with Holly, which Seth was oblivious to as he approached.

"Hello, Summer," he said as he joined the two girls around the grill.

"What'd I say about talking to me?" she snapped and quickly turned her body to shut him out from her conversation with Holly.

"No, right, I know," Seth said as he stepped back. But he had a plan. A mission. "I was just checking to make sure we were still on for —"

Summer scanned the party, looking to be any-where but here. "I guess . . ." she said, defeated.

But Seth wasn't going to let her get away that easy. "Could you at least pretend to be a little bit stoked?" She glared at him. "Fair enough," he said as he walked off. *Soon you'll be in Tahiti and none of this will matter.*

Back inside, Marissa sat down next to Ryan on the couch.

But Ryan was hesitant as he looked over at Luke and his crew downing a round of shots. "You sure you want to be seen with me?"

"I'm glad you came."

Really?

"I mean how could you miss all this?" she said sarcastically, looking around the room.

Ryan nodded, *right*. But got up to leave as soon as he saw Luke approaching. He knew this would be trouble.

But Luke stopped him. "Now that you've moved in — I see you're making yourself right at home," Luke said to Ryan as the rest of his crew followed close behind.

Ryan said nothing. He wasn't about to start a fight. Marissa tried to hold Luke back, make him understand that she and Ryan were just friends.

"I am trying to understand why there's all these people here" — Luke looked right at Ryan — "and you only want to talk to her."

"I wanted to talk to him," Marissa said, surprised at herself. She had never talked back to Luke like this.

"Look, babe, why don't you go over there and talk to Summer? She looks lonely."

But Marissa didn't want to go. She wanted to finish talking to Ryan. She didn't care what Luke wanted. For once in her life, she had the courage to stand up for herself. Ryan could feel the tension rising.

"That's okay. We're done talking. I'm just gonna go." Ryan took a step back.

"No. Stay," Marissa said as she reached out for Ryan.

Luke stepped between them. "What are you doing? Don't tell him he can stay."

"Don't tell her what to do," Ryan said as he took a step toward Luke. Family or no family, he couldn't let Marissa be treated this way.

Luke turned to Ryan and grabbed him by the arm. "I thought you were leaving. Here, lemme help you out," he said as he pulled him toward the door. But Ryan broke free from his grip.

"I'm not going to fight you," he said, trying to walk away before anything happened.

Seth saw what was going on and immediately walked over.

"Oh, yeah? Even if I do this?" Luke asked as he swung at Ryan and connected with his gut. Ryan doubled over in pain, but he couldn't fight back. He wouldn't fight back. He had a family.

Seth came to his side as Marissa and Luke continued to argue. Marissa stormed off and Luke followed.

"Dude. You got your butt kicked and didn't fight back. You really are a Cohen," Seth said as he put his arm around Ryan, helping him off the ground.

Ryan just looked at him. He was in no mood to smile. He had a home and a family, but he hadn't realized it would be this hard. He'd left Theresa behind, and now he couldn't even be friends with Marissa. He couldn't go to Cotillion.

He looked at Seth and for the first time completely understood. He was a Cohen — an outsider.

15

Marissa sat on her bed staring at her white gown. Cotillion was in two hours, but she couldn't bring herself to get dressed. The white dress was too perfect. Too controlling. Too much unlike the Marissa she knew she was. She didn't want to debut into Newport society. How could she become one of Newport's elite if she didn't even want to be here? She felt like an outsider in a city that was all hers and she just couldn't bring herself to put on the dress.

Ryan sat on his bed reading a stack of comic books. His tux sitting all alone in the closet. He couldn't go to Cotillion. How could he escort one of Newport's debutantes into society if he wasn't even allowed in? He was an outsider who would never get the key.

Seth entered the room, fully dressed in his tux.

"Why aren't you dressed?"

"I'm not going," Ryan said matter-of-factly. He had a family now and that was all he needed. He didn't need to be a part of this society. "Could you let Anna know? She'll probably be relieved."

Julie knocked on Marissa's door to find her still undressed, but she failed to notice her daughter's sad face. She grabbed the gown off the bed and held it in front of her as she gazed at her own image in the mirror.

"I love this dress," she said as she smoothed the white satin against her own body.

"Maybe *you* should wear it," Marissa said shortly.

But Julie was oblivious to her daughter's concerns. "That's sweet, but I think we both know I'm not a size zero anymore."

Marissa looked at Julie as she continued to gaze at her own image and summoned all her courage.

"I don't think I want to go."

"What?"

"Luke and I got into a fight last night, okay?"

"So, you got into a fight. You've had fights before. You guys have been together forever."

Marissa thought about it, realizing that it wasn't just Newport that made her feel alone, it was Luke too. "Maybe. That's the problem." And she thought of Ryan. "What if there's someone else out there?"

Julie put the dress down and turned to Marissa. "Like who? That boy from Chino?" Marissa didn't answer. "You want to end up like your aunt Cindy? With four kids in a trailer park?" But Marissa didn't say no. Maybe Aunt Cindy was happy. She didn't care where she lived. "She broke my mother's heart. I will not let you break mine."

"Oh, so this is all about you?" Marissa asked furiously. Sometimes her mom was so selfish.

"No, it's about *you*. What kind of a future do you think you're gonna have with him?"

But she didn't care. She wanted to enjoy the present. "Mom, I'm sixteen."

"And the choices you make when you're sixteen can affect your entire future. Luke comes from a good family. If you stay with him, you will always be comfortable."

That's what Marissa was afraid of. She didn't want to be comfortable and plain and perfect. She wanted to break free and try new things. She was tired of the monotony.

"Nothing in life is certain. . . ." Julie snapped at her a little too angrily.

"What does that mean?" Marissa asked, sensing that her mom was talking about more than just her relationship with Luke.

Julie quickly covered. "It means you're going to put on that dress, do your hair the way I showed you, and make your debut into society with Luke."

"No," Marissa said defiantly. She didn't care what her mom was talking about, she knew in her heart that she could not debut into Newport society with Luke. She knew that if she did, it would forever be Marissa and Luke, and she wasn't sure that was what she wanted. She knew she didn't want those things today, and she wondered if she ever would.

"I'm sorry," she said to Julie.

But Julie was irate. "No, you're not. But you will be." And she stormed out of the room, leaving Marissa all alone with her dress.

"Anna! Anna? Has anyone seen —" Seth shouted as he searched through a crowd of girls all wearing long white gowns.

"Seth. Behind you," Anna said as she emerged from the sea of white.

Seth turned around to find Anna in her Cotillion gown. He was almost speechless. She was stunning.

"Wow," he said as she stepped toward him.

"You think?" she asked, a little skeptical.

Seth nodded yes. No other girl besides Summer had taken his breath away like she just had.

"Which makes this even more difficult for me to say. But just know that, in life, there are peaks and —"

"Ryan's not coming," she said quickly.

"Kinda took the wind out of my sails, but yes. Are you okay?" he asked, genuinely concerned.

"I think I'll survive," she said as she kicked her shoes off in relief.

And Seth watched her walk away, still in awe of her beauty.

Marissa sat at home, still staring at her white dress. She didn't care what her mother said, she wasn't going. She picked up the dress and went to hang it in the closet, but paused when she saw her Pucci dress hanging there in the light.

She hung her white dress next to it. The color and the white juxtaposed against each other — two sides of her life. And she thought about Ryan — how he had said goodbye only to return again. And she wondered when she would see him again. Thinking about . . .

Her thoughts were interrupted by the ringing of her cell phone.

It was Summer trying to get her to come to Cotillion, but the answer was still no. She wasn't going. But when she told Summer that it was because of Ryan and Luke, Summer told her that Ryan wasn't even there. Her mind raced and she hung up the phone. She looked in her closet. The white against the color. She knew where he was and she had to see him.

Next door, Sandy and Ryan were playing PlayStation, enjoying each other's company. Ryan was laughing as he showed Sandy all the controls and options on the game. He was glad he hadn't gone to Cotillion.

"You didn't feel like going, huh?" Sandy asked as they continued to play.

"Yeah — no — not really for me," Ryan answered as he thought about Marissa, who probably looked amazing in her dress.

"What? Waltzing and orchids? What could be more you?"

Ryan smiled at the image of him in Newport. "I guess I don't really fit in, huh?"

"I got news for you. No one does. I guarantee you, every single person at that Cotillion feels like a fraud. They've all got secrets, and they're all terrified the guy next door is gonna find them out."

"Sounds like fun," Ryan said, thinking about all the secrets he already knew. Luke and Nikki. Marissa's dad.

"They've taken one of the most beautiful places on earth and turned it into a prison."

Ryan couldn't agree more, but he was curious. "So, what's your secret?"

Sandy paused for a beat before he answered. "Sometimes? When the sun's coming up, and the surf's good — and I haven't pissed off my wife quite as much as I have today — I kinda like this place."

Ryan smiled at Sandy. He kind of liked this place too. For the first time in a long time, he felt like he belonged. He felt home.

Backstage, Seth and Anna talked as debs and escorts raced around them trying to get ready.

"I mean, whatever you think of the whole superhero movie genre, at least it's getting people to read the original source material," Anna said.

Seth had finally found his match. Someone who understood him, who knew what he liked. He had finally found the female version of himself.

"I cannot believe you read comic books," Seth answered. Almost shocked. "I mean — you're a girl."

"What is that supposed to mean? And I call them graphic novels. In fact, if more people did, maybe the form wouldn't be so marginalized."

Seth was stunned. Not only had he met someone who liked the same things he did, but she was smart too.

"I couldn't agree more." *Who is this girl?* he wondered, gazing at Anna, who smiled back at him.

There was a knock at the Cohens' front door. Ryan got up from his game with Sandy and answered it.

"Hey," he said, surprised to see Marissa standing there. "You're not at Cotillion."

"Neither are you." She smiled. And then she thought about it for a moment. "I hope you didn't not go because of last night. Because of me." Her mind raced. Was this a mistake? She thought about running out the door and back to her bedroom, but Ryan led her inside.

"How come you didn't go?" he asked her.

Marissa just shrugged her shoulders, not wanting to answer. All the reasons jumbling in her head, but she was afraid to tell Ryan. Afraid that if she told him, he might not understand. Or worse, he actually might understand. And if he did, she would have to choose. Luke or Ryan?

She followed him into the kitchen, still not answering his question.

"So, you think just staying home and hiding out is gonna make everything better?" he asked as he stopped and turned to face her.

"Seems to be working for you," she answered quickly, turning the tables. Ryan smiled a tiny smile.

Marissa looked at him. She had to make a leap. A change.

"I'll go if you go," Marissa offered.

Ryan considered the possibility for a moment and it felt right. He couldn't hide in the pool house forever. At some point he'd have to step into Newport society, and he might as well do it now.

"I don't believe it," Julie shouted as Marissa and Ryan entered the backstage area together. She rushed over to her daughter and immediately starting twirling her hair up and getting her ready for the event.

But Luke was not happy.

"You told Summer you weren't coming. And now you're here with him?" Luke asked as Julie took a step away from Marissa.

"I'm not — Ryan and I aren't —" Marissa pleaded.

"I'm not an idiot," Luke said as he looked at Ryan.

But Ryan wasn't about to just sit back and let Marissa take all the blame. "Then listen to her and stop acting like one," he said.

"What'd you say?" Luke asked, shoving Ryan.

But Ryan wouldn't answer. He didn't want any trouble.

"What'd you say to me?" Luke shoved Ryan again. Harder. But Ryan still wouldn't answer.

Marissa stepped between the guys and pushed Luke away. "Luke. Stop it," she screamed.

And Luke took a step back. Marissa had never stood up to him like this before and he didn't like it. He couldn't share his girlfriend with another guy.

"I'm over this. We're done," he snapped at Marissa as he stormed off.

Ryan backed away and left Julie and Marissa alone, regretting, once again, that he had ever come here.

Who was he fooling? He wasn't part of Newport society. He might never be.

He watched from the corner as Marissa argued with her mother. Hearing bits and pieces of the conversation, but mostly just trying to figure out what to do next.

". . . you want me to have Daddy go find him?" Ryan heard Julie ask as Marissa shook her head no. "Well, you can't make your debut without an escort." And Ryan took that as his cue. He couldn't stand back and watch Marissa end up alone.

He walked over to them.

"I hear there's a White Knight available," Ryan

said as he approached, offering himself as Marissa's escort.

"It's nice of you to offer, but I don't think that's appropriate," Julie said quickly.

But Ryan wasn't asking her. He looked to Marissa, who smiled at him. "I'll get dressed."

"Could you be any more pathetic?" Anna asked as she approached Seth, who was sitting alone on the floor of the hallway. "Lone figure, sitting on the floor, wondering if you're gonna be alone for the rest of your life . . ."

Seth turned to Anna, a dry tear in the corner of his eye. Summer had found another escort. "Oh, hey. Your sensitivity is really — nonexistent."

Anna sat down next to him. "You know what your problem is? You're not a man."

"Again, not appreciating the brutal honesty."

But Anna wasn't trying to be mean. She liked Seth and she wanted to help him. "You know what girls find sexy?"

"Dudes who play water polo?" Seth questioned, not sure where she was going.

"You know what else?" she asked. Seth shook his head no. "Confidence. Watch this," she began as she got in close to Seth. "Hey, Seth, I don't have a date for Cotillion. Want to be my escort?"

Suddenly Seth was flustered. No girl had ever asked him out before. Most girls had only ignored him.

She moved in closer. Seth could feel her breath on his cheek. "Confidence, Cohen."

And Seth got to his feet, standing tall. He liked her. She made him feel like a new man. Confident. They walked off together.

When they got backstage, Summer approached Seth to be her escort again. But he looked at Anna and smiled. He said no. He already had a date.

He didn't need Summer. He had Anna.

"Good evening. Welcome to the forty-seventh annual Newport Beach Debutante Cotillion," the announcer said over the loudspeaker as the families of the elite took their seats.

Backstage everyone rushed into their places.

Marissa and Ryan emerged from their dressing rooms. They smiled at each other, each amazed at the other's appearance.

"Are you ready to make your debut into Newport society?" Marissa asked Ryan.

He looked at her beauty. *Yes.* And he took her arm in his and escorted her to the stage. With Marissa on his arm he was ready to face anything. He was ready to be let in to Newport.

With the same amount of fanfare as the introduction of royalty, the Newport girls were debuted into society. The elegant ballroom was filled with white flowers. Soft music played as each girl was introduced and then handed to her escort by her father.

When all the girls had made their debut, the

first dance began. Ryan wrapped his arm around Marissa and they danced.

Next to them, Seth spun Anna around in glory.

The unlikely brothers had found their matches. Ryan and Seth nodded to each other. A congratulations.

Ryan looked into Marissa's eyes and held her close as they swayed to the music. Maybe someday we could be much more than friends, he thought, breathing her in.

She looked at Ryan and the Newport society that surrounded them and thought how she would be okay, how she could claim Newport as her city, as long as he was hers.

Marissa couldn't have asked for a more perfect debut into society, into her new life. She was finally taking charge of the woman she was becoming. She had stood up for herself — to her mother and Luke. And even though Luke had left her, she was okay. She knew there was much more out there. That there was a world beyond Newport and a man waiting to be her one. She looked at Ryan and smiled, *maybe*.

The music continued to play but as the songs changed over and the adults started to join the debs and escorts there was a commotion.

Holly's dad, Greg Fisher, was yelling at Jimmy.

Heads began to turn. A crowd gathered.

And just as Marissa was enjoying the evening, she turned around to see her father get clocked in the face.

Jimmy was out cold. Sprawled on the floor. Sandy held Greg back as Ryan rushed to his aid.

Marissa gasped and ran to her dad. She knelt down next to him and held his head. *Daddy.*

She knew. This was what he had been hiding. That whatever it was, it was bigger than she could imagine. And she wanted to help him, hold him, go back to when she was a little girl.

A tear ran down her cheek and fell onto Jimmy's forehead. She wiped it away and kissed him. The paramedics arrived and pushed her away.

She looked at her father once more and ran off.

Ryan stood back and watched as Marissa disappeared. He wanted to follow her and hold her, but he knew what it was like to watch your family fall apart in front of you. And he knew that she needed time alone.

Seth approached.

"Hey. You don't mind if I . . . walk your date home, do you?" Seth asked as he motioned to Anna, who smiled at him from across the room.

Ryan shook his head no. "I'll see you at home." And walked toward the door.

"See you at home," Seth said, liking the sound of that.

Seth went over to Anna and offered his arm to her, escorting her out of the ballroom.

"So. You think I'll see you again?" he asked with hope. He still had his plan for Tahiti, but he liked

Anna. She was special. Another person he could call his friend and he didn't want to lose her.

"No," she replied quickly.

"Oh. Okay," Seth said, caught off guard. He thought the night had gone well.

"I know this sounds really — like — whatever. But. I'm kinda going on a sailing trip for the rest of the summer. To Tahiti."

And now Seth was really caught off guard. *Tahiti?* This girl was perfect — and they walked out, both smiling.

Ryan found Marissa outside, shivering, her eyes red from tears. He held out his jacket and placed it on her shoulders.

"Are you okay?" he asked.

Marissa shook her head no. A tear fell down her cheek.

"What happened in there?"

"I don't know," he replied, wishing he had the answer.

"What's gonna happen now?"

"I don't know," he answered again and put his arms around her. Though he had no answers to her questions, Ryan knew what it was like to feel alone in this world, to feel like everything was falling down around you, and he held her tight. Words couldn't heal the pain she felt.

She fell into his embrace.

"C'mon. Let's go," Ryan said, her small body shivering in his arms. She nodded okay and they started to walk toward the clubhouse. She felt comforted. And tried the best she could to smile at Ryan.

But she couldn't. The pain was too much and now Luke stood in front of them. Imposing. Hoping to help her. But she didn't want to listen to him. She couldn't choose.

She needed to be alone. She handed Ryan his jacket and walked off, leaving Ryan and Luke together.

She walked onto the green golf course and gazed up at the sky before taking off her shoes and beginning to run. The dewy green grass of the perfectly groomed fairways slipped beneath her toes and Marissa remembered the very first time she felt safe in the world.

It was Fourth of July, she was five, and her dad let her run through the sprinklers and the sand traps. Defying the rules. And when the groundskeeper came out to yell at them, her father got the man to let her continue playing. In her mind he was perfect.

The image of her father unconscious on the ballroom floor flashed through her head and she fell into the sand of a bunker. Her white gown brushed with brown.

The tears fell down her cheeks. Her hands dug into the bunker. Searching. Trying to go back. Where was the groundskeeper and her dad to save her?

Her breath shortened. She wondered if he would ever be perfect again.

16

"There and gone," Seth said to Captain Oats as he sat at his desk downloading songs to his iTunes collection, the summer sun rising outside his window. "Just you and me again." He patted the horse on the head, leaning back in his chair.

What to do, Seth thought as he bought another Death Cab for Cutie song. He'd downloaded twenty songs this morning and already he was bored. Ten minutes had passed since he'd said goodbye to Ryan.

It was Ryan's first day on the job as a busboy at the Crab Shack down by the harbor and Seth had been reluctant to let him take the job. He'd tried to convince him that parents worked for them. That Ryan didn't need to get a job. That Sandy and Kirsten had taken legal responsibility for him, and therefore assumed all financial responsibility as well. But Ryan felt guilty. He didn't like the idea of having to rely on the Cohens for everything. He wanted to contribute, and the only way he knew how was by getting a job. That's the way it had always worked in his family.

Kindness and doing your chores didn't get you very far in the Atwood household. You had to earn your keep. Pay for yourself. And if you didn't, then you were either on your own or standing over a chair, waiting to get slapped.

Of course, Seth couldn't argue with Ryan's logic, and the images evoked by Ryan's stories made him uncomfortable. So Seth reluctantly agreed that Ryan should take the job, and watched him leave that morning.

But now Seth was alone in the middle of summer with nothing to do. He'd tried to mask his anxiety and anger earlier by telling Ryan he was ready for some "me" time, but none of that looked appealing right now. He didn't want to write his novel, or catch up on his comic books, or take Chester sailing.

He hadn't realized how accustomed he'd grown over the last few weeks to having someone around.

He looked at his watch and plugged in his iPod. Only two more minutes had passed. This was going to be hard.

Marissa and Summer lay on the beach soaking up the sun. This was the first time Marissa had been out in public since Cotillion — since her dad was knocked unconscious and Luke had broken up with her. She had been spending most of her time indoors reading magazines or listening to music, sneaking alcohol when her parents weren't around. Gossip traveled fast in this town and she hadn't been ready to face its wrath up until now. She was just glad that school hadn't started and she didn't have to face her peers every day.

A cloud floated above and blocked the sun for a second. A sign, she thought. She shifted on her towel, adjusting the sand beneath her.

Marissa felt insecure in this new world. As much as she had been begging for change, and hoping for someone to ride in and turn her world upside down, she hadn't been expecting any of this. All she'd ever wanted was a new dress. A new look and a new Marissa. But now her life was completely twisted, unrecognizable.

Summer flipped over onto her back and turned her head toward Marissa. "I'm totally crispy. Let's go do something. Shopping. Get exfoliated. Anything."

Yeah, of course. Marissa sat up on her towel. After Cotillion, she had discovered why Holly's dad had hit hers. Jimmy had essentially been stealing money from all of his clients, which pretty much meant all of Newport. Which meant that Marissa now had all of Newport hating her too. And she felt guilty asking her parents for any money.

"And I'll pay for it how?" Marissa asked as she tried to smile at Summer. "My dad's credit cards got shut off yesterday."

Summer looked at her, horrified. Marissa nodded, full of embarrassment. "We're now officially broke."

Both girls sat silent for a beat, letting the sun hit their faces. Each knew that things were going to change in Newport.

"What about Luke?" Summer asked. "I mean — he can pay for you. He is your boyfriend." Summer, fishing for an answer. After Cotillion she wasn't sure what their relationship was. "Right?"

Marissa remembered the last time she had seen Luke, right before she had run out onto the golf course and collapsed in the sand trap. And she thought of Ryan. "I don't know . . . We left things kind of up in the air."

"Have you guys even talked since Cotillion?"

But Marissa hadn't talked to anyone. Only Summer. She shook her head no.

Summer faced her, a serious look on her face.

"Okay, Coop? That is so not the way to handle this. You're gonna become depressed. And then you're gonna need medication. And then you're gonna stop, like, feeling anything." She paused. "According to my stepmom."

But Marissa was scared. There was a bit of truth to what Summer said. She didn't want to become depressed or take pills and have to go to therapy. She was stronger than that. She looked at Summer. Wasn't she?

"Let me buy you lunch. My dad gave me his credit card for emergencies — and, well, this is an emergency."

                    *   *   *

At the Crab Shack, Ryan was learning how to bus
tables, when Marissa and Summer entered. Marissa
stopped upon seeing Ryan, surprised.

"Hey," he said as she approached.

"Hey."

They both paused awkwardly. Both wanting to
say so much. Answer so many questions. But they
couldn't. She couldn't. She smiled at him. He put
down the tray of glasses he was carrying. The last
time she had seen him she had run away and left
him alone with Luke. And she was sure he had
heard the news about her dad, about how her family was broke and she was embarrassed.

Ryan wanted to tell her that everything would
turn out fine. That he knew what it was like to have
your family fall apart, to have secrets revealed. And
he wanted to tell her that he was on her side. That
no matter what happened, he would be her friend,
like she had asked him to be.

They both smiled at each other, but said nothing.

Summer waved Marissa over to their table. Ryan
noticed.

"I should get back to work," Ryan said as he
picked up a towel off the counter, not wanting her
to go.

"Right," Marissa replied, turning to walk away.

A pause shot through the air between them.
Ryan didn't want her to go.

"You wanna hang out sometime?" Ryan asked.

He couldn't hold back any longer. Marissa turned back, surprised. "Go out?"

"Like, on a date?" she asked with hesitation. Unsure if she was ready for this.

"Not a date. Just . . ." he answered quickly.

Marissa shifted her weight from the left to the right, gently swaying as she pondered Ryan's question. Not sure she could answer. Every bit of her wanted to say yes, but she couldn't do it. She couldn't accept the change. Admit that she and Luke were over for good.

"I can't right now. With, you know . . ." The image of her father unconscious on the ballroom floor flashed through her head. Her hand trembled slightly.

Ryan understood. He knew her secrets, her troubles, and he didn't want to pressure her. "Right. Of course." He took a step back and reached for the tray of glasses he had set down earlier.

"But, thanks?" Marissa smiled weakly, trying to hold on to any bit of friendship they might have had.

Marissa settled in to the table next to Summer and started to look through the menu.

She was starving and the Crab Shack was known for its sand dabs and clam chowder. Marissa set her menu on the table and looked at Summer smiling. She was glad to have a friend who cared.

But then Marissa soon realized what Summer was smiling about. It was Luke. Standing behind her. Summer had orchestrated the whole thing. She quickly got up and let Luke have her seat.

Marissa was alone with Luke, unsure what to say. Unsure whether he would know what to say.

"Sorry I haven't called you back," Marissa started, about to explain everything that had been happening in her life. Tell him how she had hid in her room for the last few days, not talking to her father. How upset she was.

"No worries. We don't have to talk about it."

But Marissa *wanted* to talk about it. She needed someone to share her pain — someone who would understand her. She looked over Luke's shoulder to see if Ryan saw them together. But he was nowhere to be found. "We should talk about it," she told Luke.

"Why? Talking about stuff is just gonna make us all bummed out. So let's just do something." Luke grabbed her hand, gently holding it in his. Marissa succumbed to his touch and softened for a moment. "Holly's beach house? Party?" Her hand clenched.

"I don't really want to. . . ." she started, remembering how Holly's dad had knocked Jimmy unconscious. "It's kind of weird. Her dad just beat up my dad at my debutante ball," she whispered, holding Luke's hand tight, hoping he would feel her pain.

"You can't blame Holly for that. I mean — your dad stole their money —" But he let her hand slip out of his and took a sip of his Coke. Marissa's hands fell to the side as she boiled with anger and hurt. Luke would never understand her. Never feel her pain. She got up from the table and ran out of the restaurant, holding back tears as she jetted past Ryan.

*　　*　　*

Back home, Seth was going insane. He'd won every game of Jenga he'd played against Captain Oats, downloaded every one of his favorite songs, and organized all of his comic books, putting them in plastic sleeves with cardboard backing to preserve them. He looked at his watch, 5:45, relieved that more than ten minutes had passed since this morning. He grabbed his skateboard and said goodbye to the horse. If he left the house now, he'd be at the restaurant right when Ryan got off work.

Ryan and the other busboy, Donnie, had discovered they had more in common than just their jobs.

"You're from Corona?" Ryan asked Donnie. "Chino," he said, pointing to himself.

Donnie slapped him a high five and started clearing off the table in front of them. "Long way from home. Chino, man. That place is no joke." Ryan nodded yes, remembering his house and Theresa and their neighborhood and the ghetto birds they used to hide from as kids. "Newport must make you sick. These kids? With their trust funds, their big-ass McMansions, their tricked-out SUVs . . ."

"Sounds like you're a fan," Ryan said as he wiped down the table with his towel.

"I like the surf. I like the tips." A beautifully

tanned girl walked by in a bikini top and a skirt. "I like the girls." Both guys smiled. "And it's not all like this," he said, indicating the restaurant. "There's some real people here."

"Yeah?" Ryan asked, curious. *Maybe we'd have something in common.*

"I know of a party later. Want to come?" Donnie held out his fist and the guys bumped knuckles.

Six o'clock on the dot Seth arrived at the Crab Shack just as Ryan stepped out the front door. Seth skated up to him.

"So, the craziest thing. I was in the area, looked at my watch — six o'clock. I thought — celebrate your first day on the job perhaps?" Seth asked, trying to play it cool, but desperately wanting Ryan to join him.

Ryan hesitated. He could feel Seth's unease and felt bad for making other plans.

Donnie came outside just as two girls walked up beside him. He put his arms around them and shouted for Ryan. "Let's go, son."

Ryan looked at Seth. *I'm sorry.*

Seth fought back his disappointment. "Okay, so — I guess I'll — see you at home. Tomorrow? Tonight?" Seth stopped himself from continuing on. He wasn't Ryan's keeper. "Have fun."

Ryan felt Seth's pain and knew how hard this was for him. But Seth had already said he didn't want to join them.

"You sure you don't wanna —?"

Seth shook his head no. *I'll be fine. I'm Seth Cohen. I was born alone.* Ryan smiled weakly at him, trying to apologize. But Seth just smiled and waved and rode off into the sunset.

Seth skated along the boardwalk and across the Balboa peninsula until he found himself at the harbor where he taught sailing lessons. The docks were empty, just the clinking of the boats as the waves rushed into them. Seth walked along the docks until he found a small little catamaran and sat down on the webbing that spread across the boat.

The waves continued. His mind was still but his body swayed with the movement of the ocean. Seth had had enough "me" time. Enough contemplation and self-reflection. His entire life had been "me" time and he wanted more.

He thought about the night Ryan had arrived at his house. About Operation Criminal Friend and its success, and he wondered what had gone wrong.

Even though he had a friend, a brother, he was sitting alone. Just like he always had, just like he might always do. Seth fought the tears as he lay on his back watching the starry sky shimmer above him, and wondered what Summer was doing.

Ryan grabbed a cup and was filling up his beer when a big bald guy with tattoos came over and asked him for five dollars. "No one drinks for free," the guy said to him. Ryan smiled and immediately paid up. He knew the drill. The bald guy thanked him and ran off to make the next guy pay. Ryan stood in the middle of the party looking for someone he knew. A familiar face, but he saw nothing. No one.

Even at a party that felt just like home, he still felt alone. That he didn't fit in, that he might never fit in.

Marissa lay on her bed at home, contemplating her life, her future. Her parents and sister had gone out to dinner, but she hadn't wanted to join them. She still hadn't spoken to her father and she wondered when he would ever say sorry, tell her that things were going to be okay, that their lives were going to go back to normal.

Even though she had change, a break in the monotony, she still felt pain and she wanted to be numb. She went downstairs to her dad's liquor cabinet in the dining room and took a couple shots — a little from each bottle so no one would notice. Then she went back up to her room and lay there alone with a buzz, trying to forget the things she had gone through so far this summer. Trying to numb the pain.

After all they'd been through, they were still alone. Seth on the boat. Ryan at the party. Marissa in her bed. Three outsiders.

17

Overnight Ryan had found new courage. He had realized that he was no longer part of Chino, no matter how much he missed Theresa or wanted to see his brother, he couldn't go back. Being at the party with Donnie had made him realize these things and he knew that it was time. Time to take his first real steps to becoming part of Newport. He wouldn't hide anything or hold anything back anymore — it was time for him to show the golden city who he really was and take charge of his own life.

His first step in this direction was Marissa, so when he saw her by the beach just down from the Crab Shack he stopped to talk.

"So, I was thinking," he started as he hopped off his bike. His newfound courage pushing him forward. "When I asked you if you wanted to hang out? I was asking you out." Ryan smiled. The truth felt good.

"I know. . . ." Marissa answered.

"Just wanted to clear that up. 'Cause I'm gonna ask you out again."

Marissa looked at Summer, completely thrown. She hadn't expected Ryan to ask her out again. Not after all she'd done. Not after all Luke had done.

"You are?" she asked with a smile. He nodded, waiting for her reply.

She thought for a moment. Why not explore the option? She and Luke were over anyway, right? And what did she have to lose? What else could go wrong this summer? She pressed the temples of her head, trying to erase the residual pain of the shots she had taken the night before.

"Do you wanna do something tonight?"

"Okay," she said, smiling at Ryan. Instantly agreeing. "I have to babysit for Kaitlin. But I will be cooking. Macaroni and cheese. My specialty."

Ryan hesitated. "So that's a yes?"

Marissa nodded. It was a yes. She'd accepted the change. Admitted that things were different.

"Time for a new plan," Seth said to Captain Oats as he scrambled around his room, rummaging through his drawers.

He was tired of sitting at home alone. And it was time he took matters into his own hands. Either he was going to hang out with Ryan tonight or he would have to find a new friend.

In the corner of his room, Seth finally found what he was looking for: a copy of *The OC Weekly*.

He sat at his desk and thumbed through the newspaper pages, black ink smearing on his sweaty palms. Half the magazine was filled with advertisements for plastic surgery and spiritual advisories, but he soon came upon the section he was searching for: the entertainment section.

Page after page of shows, local bands, comedy, dancing, and movies. Seth flipped through them all but knew that they'd have to see some type of movie. Ryan had told Marissa that he didn't really listen to music and, after Cotillion, he knew how much he loved dancing, so a movie it was.

And then Seth saw it. A full-page ad for the shark movie at the IMAX theater. It was the best he could do on such short notice.

The sun had begun to cool on the beach and Summer and Marissa decided it was time to head in for the night.

They loaded up Marissa's Jeep with their towels and sunscreen and watched as all the surfers began to hit the sand to catch the 5:15 tide that was coming in, their hard tan bodies glistening under the rays of the summer sun.

"So hot," Summer said as she shut the back gate of Marissa's car. "Let's watch."

Marissa turned and saw the groups of surfers headed to the beach and giggled at her friend. "A few minutes. I have to get home and —"

"Get ready for your date with the Chino kid. I know. I was there when he asked you," Summer said, finishing Marissa's sentence.

"No. I have to babysit Kaitlin. And Ryan just happens to be stopping by," Marissa returned.

"Right. If that makes you feel good. Then sure, Ryan is just stopping by."

"He is," Marissa finished, fidgeting with the fringe on her denim skirt.

Summer nodded okay to Marissa and winked at a passing surfer who flashed her the hang-ten signal.

Marissa was nervous. What if this didn't go well? What if her date or her "stopping by" with Ryan turned out to be a disaster? Would that be one more thing to add to her list of things gone wrong this summer?

Summer saw Marissa pull the frayed pieces off her skirt and knew her friend was nervous. "Coop — there's no pressure. Your life will stabilize. Your parents will work it out. Luke will come around, and if he doesn't? Maybe Chino just stopping by will be a good thing. Stop worrying and enjoy the summer."

Marissa nodded okay. Summer was right. Maybe if she stopped worrying things would just work themselves out. And if they didn't, at least tonight would be fun.

Six P.M. on the dot and Seth was at the Crab Shack with the IMAX tickets in hand. He found Ryan just as he was pulling off his apron and getting ready to leave.

He approached the counter.

"Hey. How do you feel about a little something I like to call —" and he held up the two tickets —

232

"the IMAX experience." Ryan just looked at him, not excited. "This town sucks. Best I could do."

Ryan hesitated, feeling guilty yet again. "Uh. I can't. I'm hanging out with Marissa tonight."

"Okay. We can get a third ticket. I really don't think it's sold out." Seth wasn't giving up on his plan. Ryan was coming out with him tonight.

But Ryan explained that he was going over to help Marissa babysit Kaitlin and that they probably couldn't leave.

"Ohhh. I see . . . 'The babysit.' Good move. Taking it to the next level," Seth said, trying to seem cool. He'd want Ryan to do the same for him if he was going to Summer's house. But unfortunately that threw off his plan, and he now had an extra ticket to the IMAX.

Donnie entered and started to pay out Ryan's tips. Seth got an idea and gathered the courage to execute it. If he couldn't hang out with Ryan, he'd find a new friend.

"Hey, Donnie. I have an extra ticket to the IMAX. It's a shark movie. Very violent. Hammerheads."

"A shark movie? What are you, like, eight?" Donnie laughed at him.

"You got any better ideas?" Seth asked, oblivious to the dig at him.

And Donnie did — a party in Long Beach.

"You wanna come with?" Donnie asked him.

"Is that cool . . . I mean . . . yeah," Seth answered.

233

Ryan turned to Seth as Donnie walked away to clean up. "You're not going." He knew what kind of party Donnie would take him to and he didn't want Seth to get hurt.

"Oh. Okay, Mom. Except — I am." Seth started to walk away. Determined.

"Seth — guys like Donnie? You don't really know them. And they don't really know kids . . . like you."

"Oh. I get it. 'Cause I walk around with an ascot, talking about Grey Poupon," Seth retorted.

"How you gonna get there?" Ryan asked, trying to find a way to stop Seth from going.

"I got my mom's Range Rover," Seth answered. Ryan looked at Seth — *exactly what I was talking about.* "I'll park it down the street," Seth quickly covered. "Donnie's cool, right? Maybe . . . this way . . . we can all be friends. Hang." Seth smiled. He liked the sound of that, of all three of them being friends.

Donnie returned from the back and Ryan could see that Seth was not staying. He was determined to go. Ryan took a deep breath and thought about Marissa, how he had gotten the courage to ask her out, how he was taking control of his life. But now as he stood staring at Seth with Donnie, he knew he had to go with them. That someone needed him more than he needed himself.

"We'll go for an hour," Ryan said and shuffled the guys out the door.

*   *   *

234

Marissa was boiling water for the macaroni and cheese when Kaitlin entered.

"Is Luke coming over?" Kaitlin asked, grabbing an uncooked noodle and cracking it between her teeth.

"No," Marissa answered quickly.

"How come? He always does when Mom and Daddy are out."

"Yes. And tonight isn't always," Marissa snapped. She didn't want to have to explain everything to her sister.

Kaitlin felt the snap. "You don't have to be so grumpy like they are. I was just asking." She walked out of the kitchen.

Marissa turned to say she was sorry, but Kaitlin was already gone. She felt bad. This whole time she had been so concerned about herself, about the way her dad's problems were affecting her, that she hadn't even thought about her little sister's feelings.

She turned up the heat on the stove and looked at her watch. Where was he?

*   *   *

Ryan and Seth followed Donnie to the party and arrived just in time to enter the stream of people flowing into the house.

The party was crazier than Seth had imagined. There were all the drugs and the drinking that the parties in Newport had, but this one had edge. Something special that set it apart from all the rest. Something that made Seth feel comfortable here.

Seth looked up to find a girl dancing in her bra and panties against a pole on the platform above him. She winked at his smiling eyes. Yes. This party had edge. And it wanted him. The stripper bent down and pulled on Seth's collar. *Come here.*

Seth succumbed to her smile, leaving Ryan to wander the party alone.

The water was boiling and overflowing.

"Kaitlin," Marissa called as she pulled the pot off the stove. "Dinner. Come down here."

Kaitlin came trudging through the kitchen. "It's not done," she said as she sat down at the kitchen counter.

"Give me a minute," Marissa said as she poured the noodles into a bowl and started to add the ingredients.

"Ew. Not butter. Mom would never use butter. How fattening?!"

Marissa put the butter back in the refrigerator and grabbed the soy butter, which supposedly had less fat. She held it up and Kaitlin nodded her approval.

"Can you get out the bowls?" Marissa asked as she started to mix the macaroni with the cheese and the rest of the ingredients. "Three of them."

"I thought Luke wasn't coming," Kaitlin said as she walked over to the cabinet.

"He's not. Ryan is."

"Who's Ryan?" Kaitlin asked.

"He lives with the Cohens now." Marissa smiled.

The macaroni was done. She set the bowl on the counter and helped her sister get out the silverware and the smaller bowls.

"With the geek?" Kaitlin laughed.

"Seth's not a geek," Marissa said, realizing she had just defended Seth Cohen. "He just hasn't found his place yet."

Kaitlin nodded sure, but Marissa wasn't paying attention. She looked at the phone. Silent. And there was no one at the door. Where was Ryan?

The stripper had gotten off her pole and was talking to Seth. He had found heaven. A girl talking to him. His place in the world.

But Ryan was starting to get antsy. He finally had a date with Marissa and he was already late. He went inside the house and found a phone.

The phone rang in the kitchen. Marissa picked it up. Kaitlin listened as she ate her macaroni.

"Marissa?"

"Hey. Where are you?" Marissa asked, the noises of a party distinct in her ear.

Ryan looked around him. Tried to place his hand around the phone and block out the noise. "I got dragged to a party. But I'm leaving. I'm on my way." He looked out the window at Seth, the stripper playing with his hair. "I just have to get Seth away from the stripper."

"Stripper?" Marissa asked, unbelieving. Kaitlin laughed. Marissa shot her a look.

"It's a long story," Ryan said guiltily. "I'll be there soon. Save me some macaroni and cheese?"

"Sure. See ya." Marissa hung up the phone, clearly disappointed. Kaitlin noticed and started scraping the macaroni from the extra bowl back into the big bowl.

Marissa stopped her. "He'll be here." Kaitlin put the bowl down and went back to eating her own.

The two sisters continued to eat in silence. *He'll be here.* Marissa repeated to herself. *Won't he?* She took a bite of macaroni. *He has to be.*

Ryan and Seth emerged from the party to find their Range Rover demolished. Seth ran to the car, inspecting the damage. The graffiti of white spray paint, the broken glass, the smashed-in headlights. He was doomed. His parents were going to kill him.

Seth knelt down next to the car. "I'm screwed, Ryan."

"Maybe not," Ryan started even though he wanted to scream, *I told you so*, and be at Marissa's.

Seth looked at him and looked at the damage. *What are you talking about?*

"How often do you lie to your parents?" Ryan asked, remembering when he used to be the golden child. When Trey was the only one who got in trouble.

"Like, never," Seth said, opening the door.

"So if you made up a story they would . . ."

"Have to believe me." Seth hopped into the driver's seat, understanding Ryan's thoughts. "They

238

trust me. And of course by deductive reasoning, and logic, they would have to figure that I was telling them the truth. They would recognize my behavioral pattern and suspect — well, nothing. To be exact." He looked at Ryan. "Ryan, you're a genius."

Ryan smiled. "Now can we go home?"

"Yes," Seth said, starting the car. "To Marissa's."

Marissa slowly wrapped up the leftover macaroni and put it in the fridge. Kaitlin had gone to bed long ago. *He wasn't coming.* She knew.

She went into her father's office and sat at his desk. Wanting to feel comfort. Safety. When would the pain stop? She picked up a photo of herself that sat next to the lamp on the desk and stared at it. How had she grown from daddy's little girl to being all alone? She turned out the light and held the picture to her heart. Her eyes closed, imagining her life to come. And she fell asleep in his chair, the smell of his cologne her blanket.

When they got home it was too late. All the lights at the Coopers' were off. Ryan had missed his chance. There would be no date. No giant leap into Newport. No taking control of his life and making his own decisions.

Just Ryan alone in the pool house.

Seth awoke with a horrible pang of guilt. "It was all my fault," he said to Captain Oats as he got out of bed.

"I have to make it up to him," Seth thought aloud. They were friends and that's what friends did.

Marissa heard a knock on her bedroom door. She had awoken late last night and climbed into her own bed. The smell of her father's cologne still lingered in her hair as she pulled on her robe. It was already two P.M. She opened the door with caution. *Ryan? Dad?*

But was surprised to see Seth.

"Your dad let me in," Seth said quickly, noticing Marissa's surprise.

What are you doing here? "So how'd it go with the stripper?" Marissa asked, remembering the night before, wondering what Seth wanted.

"That's what I came to talk to you about. Last evening? Totally my bad. And Ryan was quite bummed that he missed his Blockbuster night." Marissa shook her head, *so?* "Look — I know you're going through a lot." Marissa stood still. *Yes, I am.* She took a step back. She didn't want to discuss her problems with Seth. She wanted Ryan or her dad. "And the last thing you needed was to get stood up." Marissa dipped her head yes. "So . . . sorry," he ended with a sweet apology.

Marissa paused. "That's really . . . thoughtful." Seth Cohen really wasn't a geek.

"Yeah. Well. He's pretty mad at me. So help a brother out." Marissa smiled at him. "How about another date? Ryan is an excellent cook."

Seth waited a beat for an answer, hoping he

could make this right. Get his friend back. Marissa nodded yes and Seth smiled. Things were finally working out just as he had planned.

Seth found Ryan at the Crab Shack, clearing off a table.

"Seth Cohen — your friendly neighborhood pimp. At your service." Ryan just stared at him, still wiping his towel across the table. *What?* "I had a little conversation with Marissa. It's totally handled."

"What are you talking about?" Ryan asked as he finished wiping the table.

"Ryan, I am quite skilled at getting a date — provided it's not for me. You'll have the house all to yourself. She'll be coming over shortly. And you'll be cooking."

Ryan smiled. Who knew Seth had such skill? He was impressed and thanked Seth by friendly-whipping him with his dirty dish towel.

"Ow," Seth said, laughing.

Donnie approached them. "Whaddap, guys? What's on the agenda for tonight? Any plans?"

Ryan shook his head yes, but Seth said no, hoping Donnie would know of a party where he could meet some more strippers or dancers. But Donnie didn't have any plans and no prospects.

"You know of nothing going on?" Donnie asked Seth as Ryan walked off to clear another table.

"Just this, like, lame beach party. Typical Newport scene," Seth responded, trying to play it cool, as if he had been invited and had chosen not to go.

"You know what — we should go," Donnie said.

"Mmm. Nah. Not for me," Seth started, trying to get Donnie to change his mind. "Just, like, a bunch of water polo players and their girlfriends."

"I don't get the whole water polo thing down here."

"Nor do I. Just a bunch of dudes who enjoy wearing Speedos." Seth laughed, thinking he had convinced Donnie to not go to the party.

"But the girls are hot. So with the right attitude? Some cocktails? It could be fun. And if not, we'll make it fun."

Oh no. Seth got nervous, but tried to smile. Donnie did have a point. Life was what you made of it.

"We'll go. Drink their beers. Dance with their honeys. I'll call some of my boys. We'll make it fun."

Seth put up his fist and bumped knuckles with Donnie. How bad could it be?

Seth turned around to find Ryan glowering at him.

"Enough with the whole moody-scowl thing. It's not a big deal," Seth said, trying to get Ryan to agree with him.

"You're taking him to a Newport party?" Ryan asked, remembering the disaster with the Range Rover the night before.

"Yes. And besides. Summer will be there," Seth answered.

"I don't know, Seth. . . ."

"I do. I'll be fine. Now, go. You, my friend, have

a date." Seth ushered him out the door. "Make me proud."

Ryan hesitated at the door, uneasy about letting Seth go alone with Donnie. But Seth smiled at him and mouthed that it would be fine. The worst that could happen was a fight and they'd already been in plenty of those.

"Where you going?" Kaitlin asked as she entered Marissa's bedroom to find her playing with her hair, trying to get it perfect.

"Out," Marissa said as she pulled her hair back.

"With Ryan?" Kaitlin asked, drawing out Ryan's name, implying that it was a date.

"Yes," Marissa said, allowing her hair to fall around her face.

"You look pretty."

"Really?" Marissa asked as Kaitlin sprayed some of Marissa's perfume in the air. Kaitlin smelled it, but it was too strong. Her nose squinched.

"You always do," Kaitlin said as she walked toward the door, escaping the perfume.

"Thanks." Marissa smiled as her sister left.

The cool summer air ran through the Cohen backyard as Ryan lit the grill. Tonight was his night. His night to take control of his life, embrace Newport and his new life.

His family had said goodbye and Theresa's image was slowly fading, a distant memory. It was time to move on.

Marissa walked through the sliding glass doors of the house and approached Ryan. His face lit up. She looked amazing and perfect and beautiful. Ready to change his life.

"Hey. I brought some leftovers," she said, holding up a small Tupperware bowl. Ryan took the bowl out of her hands and placed it on the shelf next to the grill.

"That should go well with grilled cheese." He laughed. Her eyes lit up at the sound of his voice. "My specialty."

She smiled and laughed at him. Glad that Seth had convinced her to give Ryan another shot.

For the first time in a long time, she felt happy and free. The image of her unconscious father a void in her memory, Luke a distant past.

Seth and Donnie arrived at Holly's to find a party raging in full force. The margaritas were flowing and the girls were dancing.

"Kinda lame, right?" Seth said, looking around at all the water-polo-playing Abercrombie and Fitch guys.

"I'm seeing nothing but potential. We just need to change up the vibe," Donnie said as he grabbed a beer and turned up the music.

Seth followed him as he made his way through the crowds of the young Newport elite until he spotted Summer. Seth smiled at her.

Donnie was right. Life was what you made of it.

* * *

"Dinner is served," Ryan said as he flipped the last grilled cheese onto a plate and handed it to her.

"Looks good. Very fancy."

"You're welcome," he said as he gestured to the edge of the pool and sat down, his feet dangling in the water.

Marissa sat down next to him and took a bite of her sandwich.

"So," Marissa said, trying to ease out of the silence.

"So." Ryan looked at her. Her tiny mouth filled with grilled cheese.

"This is nice," she said, looking at all her surroundings. The pool house, the patio, the infinity pool.

"Yeah," Ryan said, still in disbelief that this was his home. "It is."

She took another bite of her sandwich. Ryan sipped his drink.

An awkward silence overcame them as their feet splashed in the pool. Both thinking about their lives, their futures, how they'd ended up here together tonight.

Marissa watched Ryan's toes move through the water. So strong and soft, she thought as they glided against the ripples. She moved her feet alongside his, a synchronized movement. A connection. And she remembered Luke's feet, torn and dry from years in the chlorine and the salt of the sea. Her left foot brushed Ryan's. A tingle ran through her leg.

Ryan's leg trembled. His heart pounded.

She took the last bite of her sandwich and turned to him, breaking the silence. "Wow. That was the greatest grilled cheese ever."

He smiled. "Thanks. Your mac and cheese was pretty good too."

"Tasted better last night," she joked, playfully tapping him on the arm.

"Ouch," Ryan said, laughing as he splashed a little water on her legs. "But hey. We're here now."

She smiled, *yeah*. "I'm glad we are."

"Where's Marissa?" Holly asked Luke as they stood on the back patio of her beach house, the moon shining bright overhead.

"She's at home." Luke sipped his beer. "We're kind of taking a break." He gently kicked the sand with his feet, a little mound formed.

"You are?" Holly asked, moving in to him, touching his arm. "Are you okay?" She batted her eyelashes and lit the night with her smile. He looked at her, suddenly feeling a little better.

Ryan's feet continued to move through the water. Marissa's moved beside his.

"So . . . how are you?" he asked. "With everything?" He put his head down, watched her tiny feet glide in the liquid and he wanted to hold her, take away the numbness and the pain.

"Okay. I guess." Her feet stopped moving. "I still don't really know what's gonna happen. My parents are fighting all the time." He circled his foot, pushing water at her. Hoping it would give her the strength to start moving again. "My family's not perfect." She thought about Kaitlin at home alone with her mom, her dad asleep in his office. "Not even close. But." Her foot jerked through the water. "I don't want us to fall apart."

Ryan's feet stopped moving. Floated next to hers. He understood and he didn't have the strength to move, to forget that he had a family, to help her heal hers.

He grabbed her plate, the stillness weighing heavy on his chest, and he stood up.

"Let's go do something fun," he said, offering his hand to help her up. "You can still have fun, right?" She took his hand and he pulled her up off the ground. She shrugged, unsure. "What if you don't have a choice?"

"What does that mean?" she asked, curious.

He put his arms on her back and faked pushing her in the pool. She screamed. Playfully.

"Do. Not."

He took a step back. She smiled at him and before he knew it, she was pushing him in. He struggled against her, but his balance was off and he started to fall.

"I'm taking you with me —" he yelled, grabbing her by the arm, as they both fell into the water.

Their feet hit the bottom and when they came up for air, they both started laughing. Giggling. Smiling. Two kids on the best vacation ever.

They splashed and played in the water, letting their troubles wash off them, as they both dunked each other under.

And when they came up for air, the water dripping from their faces, they caught each other's eyes and felt that feeling — the same feeling they had on the driveway the first night they met, the same feeling they'd had in the model home, the same feeling they'd felt at Cotillion, the same feeling they'd had all night. The same feeling that made them want to kiss . . .

Holly pulled off her shirt as Luke continued to kiss her. His hands moving all over her body, exploring.

Downstairs, Donnie tried to get Summer to talk to him, but she pushed him away. "Ew."

Seth saw Donnie with Summer and immediately tried to pull him away. But Donnie was pissed and he pulled back his shirt, revealing a gun.

Seth took a step back.

But Donnie stopped him. "Relax. It's just for fun. I'm not going to shoot it. Just put a little scare in them if I need to. Like this." And Donnie reached for the blender and pushed it onto the floor.

Margarita mix and glass went flying.

Through the chaos downstairs, Luke continued to kiss Holly. She wasn't Marissa, but she would have to do.

*   *   *

248

Ryan pulled Marissa out of the water and they stood on the patio freezing, shivering. The moon was darkening, but they hadn't kissed.

Marissa's dress clung to her, the dampness exposing her insecurities.

Her teeth chattered. "Hurry up. I'm freezing."

Ryan went into the bathroom and returned with some towels. He wrapped one around her and rubbed her arms, her sides, trying to warm her. Her body shivered in his hands. He held her tighter, closer. Their eyes locked. They moved toward each other. Their lips were inches apart. About to kiss . . .

Luke came downstairs to stop the commotion and found Donnie, ready to fight anyone. Luke stepped up and accepted the challenge.

"What are you looking at?" Donnie asked, his fists tightening.

"Come on," Luke said, hitting his chest. Nordlund and Saunders stood behind him.

Donnie's boys joined him and there was a standoff.

Seth tried to stop them but couldn't. He couldn't talk his way out of this one. He needed help.

He called Ryan.

They moved closer. Their lips almost touching . . . closer.

But the phone's ring pulled them apart. Seth needed Ryan.

Ryan backed away from Marissa. "I gotta . . . go get Seth. He's at Holly's, if you wanna —"

"I can't go there," Marissa answered, remembering her father, his unconscious image returning to her head.

"Right. Okay. Well. I'll be back in, like, no time. I'm sorry," Ryan said as he left. Holding her gaze, not wanting to leave.

Donnie and Luke moved closer. Fists drawn and ready to punch.

"All right. Let's go. You're done," Luke said as he shoved Donnie.

Ryan arrived, but it was too late. Donnie whipped out his gun.

Luke backed away.

"Who's the bitch now?" Donnie screamed, pointing the gun at Luke.

"Put it down," Ryan said soothingly, trying to stop anything bad from happening.

Marissa sat at home, alone, ditched again. No Luke. No Ryan. No father.

Ryan had no choice but to reach for the gun and tackle Donnie. But a shot rang out and Luke was down. Bleeding. Ryan ran to help him as Donnie bolted out the door.

He held Luke's arm tight. And when he was carried away in the ambulance, Ryan called Marissa and told her the news.

Marissa entered the hospital to find Ryan and Seth in the waiting room. She locked eyes with Ryan. *This wasn't how the date was supposed to end.* And she walked off to see Luke, leaving Ryan alone with Seth.

As he watched her walk away, Ryan knew it was over. His chance at Newport was gone. He had lost her to Luke. Again.

18

"So, your grandpa. He's your mom's dad, right? The one who basically owns Newport Beach?" Ryan asked Seth as they unloaded groceries from the Range Rover.

"And much like yourself — he comes from humble beginnings. I believe you guys are gonna hit it off."

"I burned down one of his homes," Ryan said, thinking back to his beginnings in Newport, to the night he told Marissa to leave and encountered Luke. He sighed.

He had forgotten that having a family meant more than just a brother and parents. And it scared him. He tried to remember his own grandparents but couldn't place a face with a name. He was four the last time he saw any of them, before his immediate family had started to fall apart. He reached for the band around his neck, but it was gone. He looked over at the Cooper house, but the door was closed.

Just when Ryan thought no one else could enter his life to complicate things, Caleb Nichol arrived.

"Seth," he said, embracing his grandson.

"Grandpa. This is Ryan," Seth said as he backed out of his grandfather's grip and motioned to his friend.

Ryan smiled and extended his hand. He didn't look so bad.

"So, you're the kid who burned down my house," Caleb said, shaking his head as he dragged Seth into the house.

This was not going to be easy, Ryan thought as he shut the back gate on the car and followed them inside.

Marissa sat on her bed and picked up the newest issue of *Cosmopolitan* from the nightstand. She flipped through the pages and found much of the same — "How to Make Sex Hotter," "The Best Swimsuit for Your Body Type" — and nothing really interested her. She had spent a lot of time lately reading magazines at Luke's bedside while he recovered in the hospital, and she was getting bored. She was about to put the magazine down and call Summer to get her out of her indoor rut when she saw an article that caught her eye, "Six Signs You're Really Meant for Each Other." And she started to read, her curiosity piqued.

She hadn't seen Ryan since their date had ended with the news of Luke's injury. Her last words to him had been about Luke. She had left him alone to go see Luke an hour after they had almost kissed and now she wondered if they would ever have that chance again. If they would ever kiss, become more than just friends. She looked at the article again and wondered if she even wanted that chance.

She put the article down, afraid to find out the truth, and was startled by a knock at the door.

"Hey, babe," Luke said as he entered her bedroom and gave her a quick kiss.

"Hey. What are you doing here?" she asked, quickly turning over the magazine so Luke wouldn't see the article headline.

He sat down on the bed next to her. "I just came from the doctor, got my stitches out. I thought maybe we could celebrate by hitting the beach."

She looked at him, but couldn't get the thought of Ryan out of her head. "Don't you think it's too soon? You should go home and get some rest."

But Luke didn't want to rest, he wanted a second chance. He handed her a tiny teddy bear with a red heart that said *I love you*.

"I've been an idiot." He placed his hand on top of hers. "I never should've broken up with you. And now — with all the stuff that's going on with your parents . . . ?" Her heart dropped — was Luke understanding her? "The thing is. You were there for me. The whole time I was in the hospital. And now I want to be here for you." He leaned in and kissed her cheek. Gently. Tenderly. "Everything's been so crazy. . . . But summer's almost over and — I wish we could be together. Like it was."

Marissa looked at the overturned magazine. Unsure. The picture of Ryan still in her head. Their lips close. "I . . . don't know. . . ."

Luke squeezed her hand, reassuring. "You don't have to. We can go slow." She looked at him. Thinking. Contemplating. "Tell you what. Let's just hang here. Sit by the pool. Watch a movie. Whatever you want." He grabbed her hand and helped her off the bed.

She turned away from the magazine, the article. She could find out later. She didn't need to choose. "Okay," she agreed and followed Luke downstairs and out to her pool.

Seth and Ryan floated in their pool, admiring Caleb's new girlfriend, Gabrielle, who sat in the hot tub. She was twenty-four and gorgeous.

Seth was in shock. "Dude, that could be my grandma. Is it wrong to find my potential grandmother hot?"

Ryan splashed him. *Stop.* Then he whispered, "Not when she looks like that."

Gabrielle waved the boys over to join her in the hot tub.

"So, what's up?" she asked, once they were all seated. "This birthday party for Caleb? Is it gonna be, like, a who's who of Newport? That should be wild, huh?" The guys said nothing.

Caleb's birthday was the following night and

Kirsten had been planning the party for the last two weeks. It really *was* going to be the who's who of Newport.

"So, who are you guys bringing to the party?" Gabrielle asked, running her fingers through her hair.

Seth thought about Summer, but after Holly's last party, he knew he was slowly slipping off her radar. "Pretty much no one," he said.

Ryan remembered the last time he had seen Marissa. And she had gone to look after Luke. "Yeah, same," he added.

"You're kidding, right?" The guys shook their heads no. "There are no girls you want to invite? Two hot young guys like yourselves?"

The guys looked at each other. Should they tell her their troubles?

"Her name is Summer," Seth blurted.

"And? Did you invite her yet?"

"Well. I mean," Seth stammered. "I had, like, a plan —" Gabrielle looked at him. *And?* "No."

"She can't say yes if you don't ask her." Gabrielle laughed.

Right, Seth thought. "That's very wise, Gabby." And his mind started racing. She was right. If Summer was ever going to be his date to anything, he needed to ask her. And he needed a plan.

"What about you?" Gabrielle asked, leveling her eyes at Ryan, maybe just a bit too seductively.

"Did you ask Marissa?" Seth asked.

Ryan shrugged. The last time he had seen her,

she was with Luke. "I haven't talked to her in a few days. I don't think she'll want to go."

"And why not?"

"Her family's kinda falling apart. And she's got this boyfriend — I think they're back together. They've been going out since fifth grade."

"Fifth grade? She needs to change it up. She's known that guy since he was eating paste."

Seth laughed. "I think he still does."

But Ryan sat for a moment, considering. Maybe Gabrielle was right. Marissa did need change. And maybe he could be that difference. Maybe they could finish what they'd started.

Marissa and Luke were toweling off from the pool and making a snack inside when the doorbell rang.

Marissa came to the door and opened it to reveal Ryan. "Hey. What are you doing here?" she asked, surprised to see him.

"I was on my way to work, and . . ." Ryan's hand fidgeted. ". . . we haven't talked in a while. . . ."

"I was gonna call you —" she started.

"It's cool. . . ." Gabrielle's advice came to his mind. She needed a change. "So, Kirsten's dad is in town, and they're having, like, a —"

But before he could invite her, Luke appeared in the doorway.

"How ya doing, man?" Luke asked, his new cheery self.

"Um. Fine," Ryan answered. Thrown by Luke's niceties.

257

"I never got to thank you. For taking me to the hospital. Calling Marissa."

"Yeah. No problem." Ryan nodded. Uncomfortable.

"Do you guys have any Motrin? Arm's a little sore from the stitches," Luke said as he smiled at Marissa, gently brushing the hair off her face.

Ryan cringed. Maybe Gabrielle was wrong.

"Check in my parents' bathroom."

Luke nodded and headed off. Marissa smiled at Ryan, trying to cover. She didn't want to choose.

"So — what's up?"

"I just was wondering if you —" But he couldn't ask her. Not after seeing Luke. "I wanted to see how you were doing." He smiled at her. "But you seem good. So. Good." He backed out of the doorway. He couldn't do it. "I gotta get to work. Later," he said as he turned and left.

Marissa sent Luke home soon after. She wasn't ready to choose.

From her bedroom, she could hear her parents arguing down the hall. She picked up her magazine and started reading.

She needed to know the signs. Were they really meant for each other? Luke or Ryan?

How would she know?

Seth sat at the bow of his grandfather's sailboat, the ocean breeze blowing in his face. The two had set out for an afternoon of sailing, but all Seth could think about was Summer.

How would he ask her?

He needed courage. A plan. He looked to his grandfather for direction, but found he was on his cell phone making business deals.

And Seth wondered when he would have the confidence to make deals himself. Ask Summer out.

"So — you're living in this pool house. And then what? What's next?" Gabrielle asked. She had found Ryan at the Crab Shack, while Seth and Caleb were out sailing.

He shrugged. "What's next for you? Traveling the world in a private plane?" he asked, trying to change the subject. Not ready to talk about Marissa or the uncertainties of his life.

She laughed as Ryan smiled at her. Their eyes met and they held the glance for just a beat too long. Ryan pulled away and turned his head. Her eyes were trouble.

He looked over at the door, trying to find a way to escape. Gabrielle continued to gaze at him. And then he saw his escape: Marissa.

"I'll be right back," he said to Gabrielle and turned to walk over to her.

She forced a smile as he approached.

"Do you have a minute?" she asked, motioning to the patio outside the restaurant.

"What's up?" he asked as he followed her out-doors.

"I wanted to talk, but —"

"Luke was there," Ryan said quickly.

"Right," Marissa began, uneasy. "He wants to get back together."

"What'd you tell him?" Ryan asked. *What about us? Our connection.*

I know. She smiled. *I can't choose.* "I told him I needed to think about it." *How do you feel?*

Marissa played with her purse, swinging it back and forth, waiting for Ryan to say something.

But Ryan just nodded and kept quiet.

"I don't know what I should do," she said, her purse falling to her side.

"I don't know either," Ryan answered, not want-ing to pressure her or make her feel things she didn't.

"No. I know that," she said. Her feet shifted. *Do you feel the same?*

"Look. If you're here 'cause you want me to help you choose —"

"Of course not," Marissa said quickly, trying to cover her thoughts. *I just need a sign.*

"Good."

Both stood silent. Gazing at each other. Each wanting the other to make the choice. To make them together. But they couldn't do it.

And finally Ryan couldn't stand the uncertainty anymore. The idea of seeing her with Luke. She had to choose.

"Why don't you let me know when you've made up your mind. Okay?"

And she nodded okay, trying to stay strong. The pain building. *I choose you.* But she couldn't say it. And it pained him to watch her walk away. Would they ever get their chance?

"Dude. You played some hardball with her." Seth skated beside Ryan as they made their way down the boardwalk toward the pier.

"What was I supposed to do?" Ryan questioned, thinking back to hours before, wondering if he'd made the right decision.

"I hear you, man. That guy ate paste, shaves his chest, and wears a Speedo. It should be no contest."

Seth was right, but still Ryan felt insecure. He hadn't felt this way about anyone since the last time he and Theresa had broken up, and he and Marissa were never even together. But he didn't want to talk about it.

"What's up with you and Summer?"

"I picked up the phone to call her and got through six of the seven digits."

"You're almost there." Ryan smiled.

"I don't know why I become paralyzed with fear around women."

"Because they're hot," Ryan answered, Marissa on his mind.

"Right . . ." Seth said as they continued to move along the boardwalk.

"If he just said *something*. I just wanted him to say anything. . . ," Marissa said as she and Summer walked along the beach to the taco stand by the pier.

"You can't expect him to choose, Coop." Marissa nodded. She knew Summer was right, but all she wanted was a sign. "He comes from a place where they have, like, knife fights, and drag racing, and, like, sex on the hood of a car."

Marissa laughed. "That's from *Fast and the Furious*."

"Well, that movie was based on a true story," Summer said as she turned to order her food.

"No. It wasn't."

"Whatevs. All I'm saying is — it's up to you to choose. Not him or Luke. But you better choose soon. School's almost starting. . . ."

Marissa grabbed her food and followed Summer to a table in the sun. Summer was right. She would have to choose. But when? And how?

"It's fate. It's destiny. We both like burritos," Seth said as he and Ryan approached the pier and saw Summer and Marissa eating their lunch.

"You wanna eat somewhere else?" Ryan asked. The sight of Marissa made him cower.

But Seth wasn't backing away. He had a plan. A mission. And he was determined.

"Who's winning — me or my hair?" he asked as he headed off to the girls' table.

Ryan reluctantly followed.

Summer saw them approach and immediately stood up. She knew that Marissa and Ryan needed to be alone.

She stumbled into Seth.

"Hey. There. Summer." He held out his hand. "Seth Cohen."

But she ignored him and grabbed his arm. Dragging him over to the salsa bar. Leaving Ryan and Marissa alone together.

Ryan sat down across from her.

"What's up?" she asked. The air cool between them.

"Nothing," he responded. Not sure where to go from here.

The awkwardness was palpable and she smiled, trying to warm the air.

"Okay," he started. He couldn't resist her smile. Maybe he would have to make the choice. "You need to figure everything out. I get that. But in the meantime — Seth's grandfather is having this big party —"

"I know," she said. *You should've asked me earlier.* "I'm going." Ryan looked at her. *How?* "He asked me this morning."

Ryan nodded. Okay. Awkward for showing her how he felt. Exposed.

He had to get out of there. "Cool. Well. I'll see you . . . and Luke . . . tomorrow."

"Yeah. See you." Marissa watched as he walked away. Wanting to run after him. Wanting to choose. Make a final decision. But she couldn't. Not yet.

Seth had just about finished scooping out the salsa, when Summer looked down and saw a to- mato chunk on her finger.

"Ewww. Are there any napkins?" she asked, turning to Seth.

He looked all around but there weren't any. She looked at her finger again. Disgusted.

"Lick it," she said, holding up her finger to Seth.

"What?" he asked, getting nervous.

"I just had my nails done. It'll ruin the polish."

"You lick it," he said.

"I don't like picante. It's for Marissa," she an- swered, shoving her finger closer to Seth's face. Seth looked at it and looked at her smiling at him. He had to do it. If he ever wanted to be on her radar and take her to Tahiti he had to do it. He bent down and quickly and very froglike he licked her finger.

She smiled at him. "Thanks. Now. Are you gonna invite me to your grandpa's party?"

"I'm sorry, Summer. Could you repeat that?"

"Your grandpa's having, like, this awesome party. It's at your house. And I thought we were friends."

Seth liked the sound of that, but he was skep- tical. "Do you want me to ask you because you wanna go, or 'cause you wanna go with me?"

Summer just looked at him. She wasn't saying.

"Fair enough. See you at eight."

And the licking of the picante was definitely worth it. He had a date to the party.

*　　*　　*

Dinner that night at the Cohen house ended in a fight between the adults, which left the kids and Gabrielle out in the pool house.

"This game sucks," Gabrielle said, holding up the Game Boy in her hands.

"Lemme see." Seth took the game and looked at it. "Ryan — you've been playing the pirate game? That's a bit minty."

"What else do you have?" Gabrielle asked as she gave Ryan a wink.

"I'll get *Pro Skater 3*. Awesome," Seth said as he headed out the door, leaving Ryan and Gabrielle alone.

"Does he always yell like that?" Ryan asked, still uncomfortable with the power Caleb seemed to have over the family.

"Pretty much," Gabrielle said, moving closer to Ryan. "He's the boss. And every relationship is a business relationship to him."

"Even yours?" Ryan asked, oblivious to her advances.

She shrugged. "He'll only ever love one woman. And she passed away years ago. Now he's just looking to stay entertained. Keep from being bored. But aren't we all?"

She placed her hand on his thigh. Traveling up his leg.

"I am. *So* bored."

Ryan's body tensed. "Uh. Do you think —"

"Don't think," Gabrielle said, her hands moving

265

up his body. She grabbed him and pulled him close. And before Ryan could react, she was kissing him. Hard.

Caleb's voice yelling for Gabrielle interrupted the kiss, and Ryan hastily retreated. This was all wrong.

19

The Cohen house sparkled with white lights, bottles of Dom Perignon, and Newport's elite. As more people swarmed the house, Ryan found himself caught up in the glamour. He looked down at his suit, the one Kirsten had bought for him, and thought about the life he was leading and smiled. How had an Atwood come upon such luck? He remembered the cigarette Marissa had smoked the first time they had met. She was lucky.

Ryan looked up from his thoughts just in time to see Marissa enter with Summer and Luke close behind. She was beautiful, but then she always was. He smiled. Her eyes gazed at him and she smiled back.

Seth walked over to greet them in the entrance. Marissa and Summer handed their coats and wraps to a valet.

Ryan stood back, waiting for the right moment to approach.

"Hey, Cohen. Good to see you," Luke said as he extended his hand to Seth.

"It is?" Seth asked. A little thrown by the new Luke. The nice Luke.

Luke nodded yes and Seth shook his hand. *Why not?*

"So this is your house? It's beautiful, man."

"Uh. Thanks . . ." Seth stammered, still wondering what had gotten into Luke.

But then Seth realized why Luke was so happy when he took Marissa's arm and escorted her over to the bar. Once they had gone, Seth got nervous for Ryan. He looked over at his friend. Had Marissa chosen Luke? Ryan shrugged back at Seth. *I don't know.*

But Seth had bigger things to worry about. Summer was still standing in front of him waiting to be escorted into the party.

"C'mon," she said, grabbing his arm. "Don't you want to show me off?"

Seth smiled. He couldn't argue with that. And so, he too entered the party.

Ryan stood back and watched as Marissa stood by Luke's side. His hand never leaving the side of her back or the inside of her palm. Her gaze rested on Luke. Their lips met every few minutes. Ryan took a deep breath. He wanted to move to her, but as Luke pulled her in for another embrace, Ryan realized, there would never be a right moment. For the two of them. For her to choose. Not tonight.

And he walked off to the pool house to be alone.

Summer led Seth around the party, forcing him to introduce her to some of the wealthiest young bachelors in Orange County.

"Seth," she said, turning to him and slyly pointing to her left. "Is that David Manpearl?"

Seth looked over at a well-groomed twenty-something in a buttoned-up suit. "Yeah." He nodded. It was David Manpearl, one of the wealthiest Harbor School graduates. He was somewhat of a legend around the Cohen household. He'd been a few years younger than Seth's aunt Hailey, but his grandfather had always liked him, much the way he had always felt about Jimmy when he and Kirsten were in high school. But Seth thought he was boring and overrated.

"Well," Summer started. "Aren't you going to introduce me?"

Seth shook his head. *Why?* Summer had been asking him to introduce her to guys like Manpearl all night and he was starting to get frustrated. She was supposed to be here with *him*, and now all she wanted to do was meet every other guy at the party.

"Please, for me, Seth," she begged, batting her eyelashes and smiling at him.

But Seth couldn't say no to her. "Okay," he said, reluctantly leading her over to Manpearl, falling away from his plan.

Ryan sat alone in the pool house playing Game Boy, hiding from the outside world. He didn't feel much like Newport tonight, trying to blend in, become one of them. Marissa was with Luke and he felt like he didn't have a reason to try anymore. But even so, he still felt pain. He looked to the door, hoping Marissa would come running in to tell him that she had chosen him — that he was the one.

"This party rocks," Summer said as she stood in front of the mirror in the bathroom with Marissa. "I can't believe David Manpearl's here!"

"Who?" Marissa asked as she applied a fresh coat of lip gloss.

"He's Senior Vice President of the Wealth Management Division at McKenna. You know — the venture capitalist firm?" Marissa looked at her, but Summer continued, overwhelmed by the wealth and power that she had met tonight. "He manages wealth! As a job!" Right, Marissa thought, nodding at her friend, not the least bit surprised by her feigned interest in Seth just to get to the wealthy. "I've been reading *Forbes*," Summer finished, reaching for Marissa's lip gloss and applying a fresh coat to her own lips.

"So, I guess you chose Luke, huh?" Summer asked, completely changing the subject. "Chino didn't stand a chance. I told you Luke was the one."

"No, you didn't," Marissa answered. *And I haven't chosen.*

"Well . . . I meant to," Summer replied. "You're all over each other. Did you . . . did it . . . happen?"

"No," Marissa said quickly. Summer hadn't even chosen who was right for her. How could she have given up her virginity?

"His willpower is amazing. The fact that you two haven't —"

"Summer," Marissa begged.

"Coop. What more do you want? He's beautiful. Sweet. Totally crazy about you. What are you waiting for?"

"I don't know," Marissa said. But she did know. She couldn't give herself to someone until she knew he was right for her. That they were meant to be. She had waited this long and held Luke at bay forever. She still dreamed that her first time would be special. That it would be love, but now that Ryan was in the picture, she had to choose.

"Well, you better figure it out," Summer stated as she combed her hair with her fingers. "Because he's not gonna be able to wait forever."

Summer was right. He wouldn't wait forever and neither would Ryan. But maybe Luke was the one. They had been together forever and all signs pointed to him. But why couldn't she get Ryan out of her mind? Why did she feel like it was one or the other? She needed to be certain. Tonight she would have to choose. Tonight she would decide whether she stayed in the monotony, Marissa and Luke, or stepped into the colorful unknown, the Pucci dress.

She had to find Ryan. If she saw him, she would know. If he invoked doubt in her relationship with Luke, she would know Luke wasn't the one.

Ryan heard a knock at the door. *Marissa?*

But it was Gabrielle. His face fell.

"Somebody's hiding," she said, approaching him.

"No. I was just —" He put down his Game Boy.

"Bored?" she asked. "I'm bored too. . . ."

"I've heard," Ryan answered as she took a step closer. He could smell her perfume.

"She's just a girl."

"I know," Ryan said, not wanting to believe it.

"So why are you hiding from her?"

"I'm not," Ryan answered. *I'm waiting for her.*

"I don't believe you," Gabrielle said as she grabbed his hand and pushed him onto the bed. Their lips about to kiss.

Ryan held back for a second, looking to the door, but it stayed closed. Marissa wasn't coming. And he gave in to Gabrielle's kiss.

Marissa ran through the party. Searching.

Ryan looked to the door again. Marissa wasn't coming. She must have chosen.

Marissa continued searching.

He looked to the door. One last time, but she wasn't there. He closed his eyes, accepting his fate. But when he opened them again he saw what he had done.

Marissa was standing in the doorway. Her eyes

wide-open. Stricken. Humiliated. She had come to find him, to see if he was the one, and he had ruined it.

"Sorry. I thought —" *I came to see you. Choose you.* "Never mind." He sat up, wanting to take back all he had just done, but it was too late. Marissa was already out the door.

There was no doubt now. She knew what she had to do, and she headed straight for Luke. He was the one.

Seth was sitting alone at one of the tables by the pool when Summer found him.

"Hey. What are you doing?" she asked. "I want you to introduce me to —"

But Seth stopped her midsentence. He couldn't do this anymore. He didn't want to be a pawn in her game. He wanted to be with her. "You know what, Summer? No."

"What?" Summer asked, a little thrown that a guy had stood up to her. Especially Seth Cohen.

But Seth had confidence. "This whole night — all you've done is use me to meet rich, older guys." He wasn't going to let her control him.

"That's not true," Summer said, trying to cover. Seth glared at her — he wasn't buying her excuses. "Okay. Maybe a little," she said, trying to apologize.

But Seth didn't want her apologies. He wanted her to know that he couldn't sit back and watch as she flirted with other guys. "Do you have any idea

how pathetic it is to watch you babble about merg-
ers and acquisitions, while some guy just stares at
your boobs?"

"Which guy was staring at my boobs?" Summer
snapped quickly.

"Who cares?" Seth answered. "The point is, he
doesn't know you. He doesn't care about who you
really are. He has no idea that every day of third
grade you shared your lunch with that skinny squirrel that kept having its nuts stolen by that fat
squirrel."

Summer's face softened. "I hated that mean
squirrel."

And Seth continued with confidence, remembering the little pony Summer used to hide in her
desk. "And none of those guys were there when
you had to read your poem in front of the class, and
your hand was shaking because you were nervous
and cared what the other kids thought."

"Poem? What poem?" Summer asked, now curious.

"'I Wish I Was a Mermaid,'" Seth answered
softly.

"You remember that?" Her smile brightened.
"That was, like, sixth grade?" Her heart opened.

Seth paused for a moment. He knew every line.
He had written it on the first chart he had ever made
for their sail to Tahiti. He needed to tell her. "'I wish
I was a mermaid and was friends with all the fish. A
shiny tail and seashells that would be —" But be-

fore he could finish, Summer's lips were on his, kissing him. His heart swelled, pumped.

"'— my wish,'" he finished.

His hand quivered and she bit her lower lip. The best kiss either had ever had. They smiled at each other and held their breath. There was something magic about that kiss.

But Summer took a step back, not ready to accept fate. She had to return to the party, to her scheme. Seth nodded and smiled.

Even as she walked away he knew he was on her radar. One day they would sail to Tahiti.

Luke and Marissa lay on his bed — their bodies entangled. He kissed her gently and then with passion. She let his hands wander. She had made her choice.

"I love you so much," he whispered as he kissed her ear.

But she didn't respond, she just kept kissing him, touching him. Their bodies pressed closer.

She knew there was no turning back. This was her choice. Ryan had left her none.

"Do you . . . are you . . ."

"Okay," she answered. He wouldn't wait forever.

"So — should I get a . . . ?"

"Yeah. Okay," she answered as he got up and reached for the condom.

She lay still, quiet. She had made her choice.

He returned and kissed her. Together they made love for the first time.

But it wasn't love, it was just sex.

Marissa couldn't say the three words and she felt empty. A piece of her missing.

She looked to Luke for comfort, for assurance, but he was still. Asleep. And she felt shut out.

She was all alone. She turned her back on him and held the sheets tight against herself.

Ryan sat on the balcony of the Cohen house overlooking Marissa's driveway. He had to apologize, tell her he had made a mistake. That he wanted her to choose him. That he was confused and hurt and only wanted to be with her.

Luke's truck pulled up front and Ryan took a step back, hiding, and then he walked around the side of the house and down to her yard, where he waited.

"You want me to walk you in?" Luke asked as he pulled Marissa to him.

"No. Thanks," Marissa answered, wanting to be alone.

"Okay. I love you," he said as he kissed her good night.

But she just nodded. She couldn't say it back. The night had been a night of passion, but passion for the wrong reasons.

Luke drove away and Marissa held her purse

close to her as she walked to the door. Nothing would ever be the same again.

Ryan approached from behind the bushes. Ready to tell her everything, but when she looked at him, he knew. . . .

"You're too late," she said softly as she turned around and walked into her house. Shutting Ryan out.

And he stood there still. His world shattered.

She watched him from the tiny window beside the door as he walked back up his driveway and away from her.

A tear ran down her cheek and she went straight to her room.

Her body trembled as she fell onto her bed. *What have I done?* But there was no turning back.

She turned on the radio and Jeff Buckley's "Hallelujah" played.

Hallelujah. And another tear fell.

She pulled the blankets up. *Hallelujah.*

And as she lay awake in her bed, the music playing, she wondered if she should make Ryan a new CD to replace the one that had burned in the fire. *Hallelujah.*

20

Summer in Newport Beach was coming to an end. Fashion Island was full of back-to-school specials and the summer renters had begun their long journeys home. Ryan stepped out onto the grassy area surrounding the pool house and looked out at the ocean far below, the top of Marissa's house to the left, Seth's sailboat on the shore to the right, and he thought of the first night he had ever spent at the Cohens'. His fear, his doubt, and his longing for a family seemed far away now. He smiled at the thought that maybe things were going to be all right. He touched his neck and felt the bare skin soft against his hand. He hesitated, then took a deep breath. His lungs filled with salt-tinged air and for the first time since his arrival he accepted that Newport was now his home, a part of himself, his life.

From up here he could hear the echo of a car door slamming shut in the Cooper driveway. His thoughts stilled and he held his breath. He hadn't seen Marissa since the night of Caleb's party. *You're too late* echoed in his head, and an image of

Marissa with Luke flashed through his mind. But she had made her decision and there was nothing he could do. He took a deep breath. This was his new life now, with all its flaws, drama, and pain. He was home.

Seth came bounding outside and ushered Ryan into the pool house.

"Shh," he said as he sat Ryan down on the bed. Then he pulled out a sombrero from behind his back. "Are you ready, Ryan?" he asked as he stuck the hat on Ryan's head.

Ryan shook his new hat, and gave Seth a questioning look.

"Tijuana, Ryan. On the last weekend before school, one goes to Tijuana. It's a tradition. A rite of passage. We leave boys, and we return men. What happens in Mexico stays in Mexico."

"And what do you think is going to happen in Mexico?" Ryan asked, remembering all the things that had gone wrong so far.

"I don't know. Because it stays there! That's why we must go."

But Ryan was still hesitant. He took the hat off of his head. "I don't really know about lying to your parents."

"Okay. I respect that. I'll lie to them," Seth said. He had a plan and it was foolproof. An alibi. There was a Comicon convention in San Diego that he went to every year and it was this weekend too. His parents would never suspect that he would be going to Tijuana instead of the convention.

He looked at Ryan. *Please?* But Ryan said nothing. He had already lost Marissa and he wasn't ready to lose his new family, his new home. He couldn't get into any more trouble.

Seth sensed Ryan's hesitation. "Dude. Tijuana's a big town. You won't even see Marissa."

"I don't care about seeing Marissa." Ryan paused, trying to cover his feelings. "Or not seeing her." But he did care. He knew she had made her decision, but still, there was a part of him that thought he still had a chance — that they had a connection. But he didn't want to make her life more complicated than it already was, and he knew that if he saw her things would only get worse.

But Seth was persuasive; besides, he couldn't let him go alone. So, finally, he agreed.

An ecstatic Seth handed him a bound document.

"What's this?" Ryan asked.

"An itinerary for our trip," Seth replied matter-of-factly.

Ryan flipped through the pages. "Seth — it's twelve pages long. We're going for twenty-four hours."

"If you're gonna get over Marissa, you need activities."

Ryan handed back the itinerary. *So that's what this is about?* He didn't want pity and he didn't want to feel the way he did about her. He just wanted to forget about it. "I don't need to *get* over Marissa. I *am* over Marissa."

Seth sat on the edge of the bed. "Ryan. This is me, amigo. Look. I know you're hurting. You need to unburden your soul. I'm here to help —" Seth said, trying to offer comfort.

Ryan paused, then responded, "My soul is . . . fine. Marissa and me . . ." Her image flashed in his head. *You're too late.* He couldn't turn back. "It's better this way." And he paused, not wanting to hear the words come out of his mouth. "It never would've worked." But he knew it was true.

Seth nodded at him. *Okay. I'm here if you need me.* And he left the pool house to start packing.

Marissa and Summer sat in Marissa's room painting their toenails over magazines so as not to drip on the carpet.

Summer read the cover of hers. "Six signs to tell if you're meant for each other." It was the *Cosmopolitan.* "Did you read this?"

Marissa nodded yes.

"So? And . . . you and Luke are meant for each other. That's why you . . ."

Marissa barely nodded yes. She had chosen him. Ryan had chosen someone else and she had chosen Luke. All signs had told her he was the one.

Summer sensed her friend's apprehension. "What about Chino?"

"Ryan?" She paused, not wanting to admit this. "It just . . . never would've worked."

"No kidding," Summer started, trying to assure Marissa she'd made the right decision. "It's so

281

much better this way. He was all, like, brooding. Wounded. 'Somebody save me.'"

"I thought you liked that," Marissa said, re-membering Cotillion when Summer had wanted Ryan as her White Knight.

"It's too hot to save anyone," Summer said, quickly changing the subject. "Speaking of hot . . . I can't believe you and Luke — that you guys did it. You have to tell me everything. I've been waiting for this forever."

"Summer. It's a sacred act between two people," Marissa said, not really wanting to discuss the details. Not wanting to explain that it was just sex and nothing special.

"It was a letdown, right? Kinda hurt. Totally awkward."

"It's not like I have anything to compare it to," Marissa responded. It did hurt and it was awkward, but it was her heart that hurt. The choice. The decision.

"So? Do it again. I mean — you're gonna, right? It's way better the second time."

Marissa hesitated. "I'm supposed to go over to his place this afternoon. . . ." She didn't know if it would ever get better.

"Trust me, Coop. Get back on the horse." Summer laughed. "Giddyap!"

Luke and Marissa lay on his bed.

"I can't wait to go to Tijuana. It'll be so roman-tic," he said as he kissed her neck.

282

Marissa stopped him. "It's kinda gross there."

"So we won't leave the hotel room," Luke said.

"I don't know." Marissa pulled away from him.

"It'll be better the second time," he assured her.

But Marissa wasn't so sure; pangs of doubt troubled her.

The Crab Shack was full of Harbor High students, most of whom were planning their trip to Tijuana. Seth sat at the counter eating sand dabs while Ryan worked in front of him. Behind them sat Summer and Holly and some of Luke's buddies eating their own meals.

Seth looked back at Summer, waiting for her to notice him, but she was caught up in her friends. He turned back to Ryan. "You know what she's doing? It's textbook. Playing me hot and cold. Trying to pretend like our little kiss didn't happen."

Ryan just shook his head and smiled. Seth's hopeless romanticisms always made him laugh. "There were no witnesses. I mean, I didn't see anything."

"I guess I'll just have to make magic happen again," Seth responded.

Ryan smiled, impressed by Seth's confidence.

But his smile faded as he looked up at the door and saw Marissa enter with Luke. He looked at her, but she was cold.

"Hey. How've you been? Haven't seen you in a while," he said, trying to warm her.

But she continued her icy stare. "Yeah. Last time I saw you, you kinda had your hands full."

Ryan absorbed this as she walked away. He really was too late. He threw his dish towel down and walked into the back kitchen, his towel almost landing in Seth's meal. But Seth knew better than to say anything. He could sense the tension. He knew that Ryan wasn't over Marissa.

Seth looked over at Summer. At least they were still okay.

Marissa sat down next to Holly in the middle of a gossip session. All her friends were talking about their plans for Tijuana, but she was silent. She thought about her dad at home. How he had been so distracted and stressed and she wondered if maybe she should just stay home. Avoid Tijuana and spend quality time with him.

Marissa turned to Summer and whispered, "I don't think I'm going to go to Mexico."

"What do you mean you're not going?" Summer asked aloud. Overhearing the conversation, Ryan and Seth exchanged a look.

"I just . . . can't . . ." she responded, knowing that she couldn't explain.

"But how am I gonna get there? The guys are all going tonight for that stupid freshman hazing and Holly's car is full," Summer demanded.

"I'm sorry," Marissa answered. She just couldn't do it.

"I'm totally stranded," Summer sulked. But behind her, Seth had heard the whole thing.

He walked over to her table. "Hello, Summer. Seth Cohen. I believe you remember." But she said nothing. "I heard you need a ride tomorrow?" he asked. Her face lit up. Seth was in.

Summer went over to Marissa's house to say good-bye before she left. But she was trying to convince her to go to Tijuana.

"I told you. I can't go," Marissa said as she walked into the living room, Summer following close behind.

"C'mon, Coop. I got us a ride. Just grab some stuff and let's go —" Summer tried again.

But she wasn't budging. She was distracted as her dad walked into the room.

"Hey," she said, happy to see him.

"Honey, what are you still doing here?" he asked.

"I thought I'd stay home this weekend," Marissa said, waiting for his excitement.

"What? Why? I thought you were looking forward to this trip." The excitement didn't come. Marissa was taken aback.

"I was. I just thought maybe — we could hang out. . . ." *Catch up. Talk like we used to.*

"We can't. I'm sorry. You said you were going, so I made other plans."

"Are you sure? Because . . ." *I want to share with you. I want things to be like they were.* She looked at him. Waited for his response. But he snapped at her.

285

"Marissa, please. I can't take care of both of us."

Marissa took a step away. Hurt. But she couldn't let it show.

"Okay . . ." she started as she turned to Summer. "Let me grab my stuff." She had no choice.

Marissa opened the car door to find Ryan sitting in the other seat.

"Oh," she said as she slid in next to him. This is going to be fun, she thought as she shut the door behind her and turned to look out the window and away from Ryan. He folded his arms across his chest. They sat in silence as Seth started the car.

"We're going to T.J.," Summer shouted from the front passenger seat as she motioned to Seth to put the car in reverse. Seth smiled at her and looked to the backseat for a smile of enthusiasm, but he got nothing.

Seth pulled out of the driveway — the ride to Tijuana had begun.

As the gold of Newport disappeared behind them, Marissa and Ryan continued to sit in silence. Both their minds wandering. Wanting to say so much, but saying nothing at all.

In the front seat, Seth and Summer bickered over the speed Seth was driving.

"I'm going seventy in a sixty-five zone," Seth said as he looked down at the speedometer.

"Eighty is the new seventy," Summer retorted.

"What? Who talks like that?" Seth asked, laughing but a little annoyed. He looked at her and thought, Tahiti might be a little rougher than planned. He'd have to readjust some things when he got home. Put a limit on the amount of complaining Summer was allowed to do.

Ryan and Marissa looked at each other. Seth and Summer were driving them nuts with their fighting. Ryan reached down and grabbed a bottle of water out of the cooler, then grabbed another and held it out for Marissa.

"No. Thanks," she said, then quickly turned back to staring out the window, ignoring him.

Your choice. Ryan looked at her, hoping she would turn back around, that he would get the courage to tell her all that he felt. That he was sorry. That he had only let Gabrielle kiss him because he thought she was with Luke. Had he known she was coming for him, it would never have happened. *Please. Look at me.* His eyes lay heavy upon her. But she didn't turn around.

Her own mind was racing. She had chosen Luke, but now she was sitting next to Ryan. Some sort of cruel joke fate and destiny had played on her. If she had made the decision, why was she stuck here now wondering, staring — forced to face the result of her decision. A slight pang of doubt entered her mind. She could see Ryan's hand out of the corner of her eye, and a part of her wanted him to reach out and hold her. Tell her she had made the wrong decision — or push her away and tell her she had made the right decision. She clasped her arms closely around her chest, trying to force the doubt away. Why hadn't she felt this before? Before she'd given herself to Luke.

Up front Summer and Seth continued to bicker.

"Still no service?!" Summer said as she looked at her cell phone. "This is a nightmare. I'm sweating to death, driving ten miles an hour on, like, a rickshaw, listening to this *music*."

Seth turned up the volume. "Do not insult Death Cab."

"It's just like one guitar and a whole lotta complaining," she said, turning the volume back down.

"Hey. That reminds me of someone else who's doing a lotta complaining . . . YOU," he started. As much as he liked her, he couldn't take her whining anymore. "I'm the one who's driving. At the speed I feel comfortable. It's my music. My snacks —"

Summer looked in the bag of groceries and reviewed the options. "Kudos and Goldfish. What are you, eight?"

That was it. Seth had had enough. If he didn't put an end to this now, it would continue forever. Tahiti would be ruined. He switched lanes. "Ryan. Marissa. Say good-bye to Summer."

"What are you doing?" Summer whined.

"Leaving you on the side of the road." Seth switched lanes again.

"No. You're not," Summer said, grabbing the steering wheel.

"What are you —?" Seth fought back, pulling the wheel the opposite way. Summer pulled back, but Seth fought harder as they began a tug-of-war over the steering wheel.

Ryan looked at Marissa, who had turned forward. *Help.*

"Uh. Guys . . ." Ryan gasped, trying to stop the war, getting a little freaked himself.

But Seth and Summer weren't listening. Summer pulled one way and Seth pulled back. She tugged again, but this time Seth jerked the wheel hard and they went barreling off the side of the road into a ditch. Ryan threw out his hand to protect Marissa from flying forward and Summer started screaming. "Seth!" The car plowed through the ditch with an awful sound, a crack and a thump, then came to a sudden stop.

Marissa looked down and saw Ryan's hand in front of her. Strong. Almost touching her. The doubt returned. She quickly moved back. Ryan pulled his hand away.

"Seth, you . . ." Summer started flinging open her door.

Seth threw open his door and went after her. "Not my fault," he said. "If you hadn't been complaining we would still be on the road. And we would be in Tijuana in approximately three hours." He looked at his watch. "But now? Who knows." Seth walked back to the car and grabbed a package of Goldfish out of the backseat and started eating them as he sat on the grass next to the car.

"Cohen," Summer screamed as she ran up next to him. "What are you doing?"

"I am having a snack, Summer. Do you want one?" he asked, offering her a handful of Goldfish.

"Ugh," she said as she turned to Ryan and Marissa, who were just getting out of the backseat. She looked to Ryan. "What do we do?"

Ryan looked at the tires. The front two were flat and one appeared to be completely off track. "Two flat tires. And that looks like a broken axel."

Summer looked at him. "So?"

"Even if we had two spare tires, which we don't, it's still undrivable."

"Way to go, Cohen," Summer snapped as she grabbed a Goldfish from his hand. "Now what?"

Ryan looked at Seth, but Seth seemed to have no plan whatsoever. He held up his cell phone. No service. The girls held theirs up too. The same. So Ryan thought of the only thing he knew how to do. The only thing he'd ever done growing up when his mom's car had broken down. "We hitch a ride."

Summer and Marissa exchanged glances. This didn't sound like a good idea.

"You got a better idea?" Seth asked Summer as he looked to Ryan for assurance that this would be okay. Ryan nodded.

The two guys headed up the road to start looking for a ride. The second car that passed them was a pickup truck loaded with chickens.

Ryan and Seth turned back to the girls. "You coming?" they screamed. Marissa and Summer glanced at each other, then back at the broken-down car. They had no choice.

By the time they had hitched a ride to a service station and had their car towed, night had begun to fall. The four sat in the waiting room, where they got the diagnosis that the car wouldn't be ready until the following morning. Everyone sighed, but they had no other option.

Seth and Ryan couldn't call home, because they were supposed to be at Comicon and not on the way to Tijuana. Marissa didn't want to bother her dad, and there was no way Summer was turning back now; she still wanted to go to T.J.

They had to stay here. "Excuse me," Summer said as she approached the mechanic behind the counter. "Is there a resort around here where we could stay for the night until our car is done?"

The mechanic looked out the window and pointed to a dilapidated building with the word *motel* flashing on and off in neon lights out front.

"That's it?" Summer asked.

"Yes, that's it. Our finest resort." The mechanic smiled maniacally. Summer stepped back, frightened.

"Okay, thanks," Ryan said as he escorted everyone out of the station. "Maybe it's not so bad on the inside."

Seth perked up. "I like your optimism, Ryan."

"Sweet. Do we have to pay extra for the lice?" Summer asked as they opened the door to their room. The bed was lopsided and the couch looked like it had been sitting outdoors for the entire summer. The carpet smelled of mildew and dust and the air was thick and warm. "This is so gross. You guys, we can't stay here."

Ryan looked around. The place was pretty bad, but he'd seen worse. And they had no other options. "Well. Unless you feel like hitchhiking again . . ."

Summer removed a feather from her hair. "No, thank you. I've spent enough time in a truck full of chickens."

"We're lucky that guy stopped for us," Marissa said, trying to get her friend to stop complaining.

"You know what would've been even luckier? If Cole Trickle hadn't driven us off the road."

"Who the hell is Cole Trickle?" Seth asked.

"Tom Cruise. *Days of Thunder*?" Summer answered as if Seth should have known.

"Why don't we try to be positive here?" Marissa said, trying to stop another argument.

Seth looked at Summer. "Okay. I'm positive this is Summer's fault."

"I'm positive that I'm leaving this place with a rash," Summer said as she took another glance around the room.

Then Summer glared at Seth. "Ugh," she finally sighed as she walked off into the bathroom and slammed the door shut behind her.

Ryan looked at Seth and Marissa. He'd had enough. "I'm gonna go get some food," he said, reaching for the door handle.

"Omigod. Coop! You gotta see what's crawling in the shower," Summer screamed from inside the bathroom.

Marissa looked to Ryan. "Maybe I'll come with you?" she asked.

Ryan looked at her and nodded okay. She smiled a tiny smile and followed him out the door.

In Tijuana, Luke and his friends were already pretty drunk by the time they got to Señor Frog's to meet up with Holly and the other girls.

Holly and her friends were dancing on the bar when Luke and his crew entered. Luke smiled at the girls and ordered a beer. Holly made her way down the bar and stopped in front of Luke, her legs at eye level.

"Hi, Luke," she said flirtatiously as she bent over and kissed him on the cheek.

"Hey," he said, taking a step back. Not sure he wanted to start something with her . . . to cheat on Marissa.

But the bartenders started harassing him. "Ay, muchacho. Si no quieres besar la chica, podemos besarla?"

Holly sat down on the bar, her legs dangling. "They said —" she motioned for Luke to come closer — "if you don't want to kiss me, they'll do it for you."

Luke looked at the bartenders. All staring at him, waiting for him to make a move.

Holly wrapped her legs around his waist,

pulling him in close to her. "Please. Save me?" She reached for his face and drew him near.

Her sweet smell intoxicated him and he couldn't resist. He kissed her and the bartenders applauded.

Holly grabbed on to his neck and hopped off the bar. "Thanks," she whispered in his ear with a slight flick of her tongue. "See you later?"

Luke watched her walk away, his eyes trained on her backside. He took a swig of his beer.

Summer finally emerged from the bathroom dressed in a little nightgown, but Seth was too annoyed with the situation to even care. He flipped through the static on the TV, trying to find something to watch.

"Get off the bed," Summer started. "The sooner I go to sleep? The sooner it'll be morning and this nightmare will be over."

But Seth didn't move. He just stared her down and motioned to the grimy couch.

"I'm not sleeping on that couch. It's stained and smells foul. You sleep there."

Seth looked at her. "After you've made it sound so appealing?" He turned and closed his eyes. "Good night."

"C'mon. Get off the bed," Summer said as she tiptoed across the dusty carpet.

"Nope," Seth refused.

"Be, like, a gentleman?"

"Chivalry's dead, sugar."

Summer was infuriated. She picked up her feet and marched over to the other side of the bed. Carefully climbing under the sheets so as not to let too much of them touch her body.

"If you make a move, I'll rip out your jugular," she said to Seth.

"Oh, hey. Pillow talk . . ."

She glared at him. Daggers pierced his skin. But nothing fazed him. It was all part of his master plan. Eventually she'd warm up to him.

Holly dragged Luke to the back of the club and pressed her warm body up against his.

"Thanks for saving me earlier," she said, her hand moving up his chest.

"No worries," he replied.

She kissed him and he hesitated for a moment, a slight tinge of guilt. But then he looked around and couldn't find anyone he knew. Marissa would never find out.

He kissed her back, their tongues touching, bodies moving.

"Wh-e-ee-e-e-t. Tw-we-ee-e-t." A whistle blew near their ears.

"Grape or cherry?" a scantily clad woman with a tray full of shots asked them as they pulled away from each other.

Luke looked at Holly. *Your choice.* "Grape," she said and tilted her head back as the woman poured the shot and blew her whistle.

*   *   *

"Ding-Dongs or Cheese Stix?" Ryan asked Marissa as they stood in front of a vending machine outside the motel. *Your choice.*

"I don't care. Pick whatever," Marissa answered. She didn't want to have to choose.

"I don't really care either, so . . ." Ryan couldn't choose. It was her decision. *I can't decide for you. I never could.*

"So I guess we'll just starve?" Marissa remarked. *Couldn't you have just given me something? A sign.*

"Uh-huh. Are you ever gonna stop being mad at me?" *You made the decision. I had no choice.*

"I'm not mad at you," Marissa answered quickly.

"Right." Ryan pushed his toes against his shoes, holding back his anger, his hurt and regret.

"Why would I be mad at you?" she asked, feigning naïveté.

Are you really going to make me spell it out for you? "Uh. Because. You walked in on me. With another girl?"

"I think she was a woman," Marissa retorted. The image of Ryan and Gabrielle surfaced painfully. "But why would I care about that?"

"I dunno," Ryan said, not giving in. "There shouldn't be a problem."

"There isn't a problem."

"Except." Ryan gestured to the vending machine. "Ding-Dongs or Cheese Stix?"

He smiled at her, but she didn't smile back.

"I don't care, Ryan." *I'm not choosing. I made my choice. Don't make it worse.* "I don't care about Ding-Dongs and I don't care about Cheese Stix and I *really* don't care that you were with some girl." *You made a choice too.* "Or woman. Whatever."

"The only reason I was with that chick was because you were very clearly back with Luke," he stated, finally letting her know how he felt.

I had to choose. Why didn't you tell me? Give me a sign? "I wasn't back with Luke."

Ryan took a step back. *Did I choose wrong?* "Well. You are now. Right?" *I change my mind.*

You're too late. "Right," she answered.

"Good." *I missed my chance.*

"Great. So we'll just get to Mexico. Split up. And we never have to talk to each other again."

"Sounds like a plan." But Ryan hated that plan. *This isn't that simple. You were the lucky one.* "But by the way? You could've knocked first." He turned it on her.

But she turned it right back. "Did you ever wonder why I came to the pool house to find you?"

"Every day." He paused and looked into her eyes. "So here's your chance. Clear the air. Tell me."

And she hesitated, wanting to tell him everything. Tell him that she had come to see if he was the one. She wanted him to be alone and she wanted to find him waiting. That would have been her sign — the decisive factor — but it didn't happen.

"Cheese Stix. I hate Ding-Dongs." She'd already made her decision.

Luke led Holly back to his hotel room, his mind made up. Marissa would never know.

He shut the door and dimmed the lights. They fell onto the bed, laughing.

"Do you have any . . . ?"

Luke nodded and reached into his bag for the condoms.

Holly smiled at him and began to undress, her clothes slowly falling around her. Luke's lips touched hers.

"We can't tell —" Luke started.

But Holly put her finger to his lips. "I know."

And Luke breathed a sigh of relief.

Marissa and Ryan walked slowly back to their hotel room.

"You have a key?" Marissa asked.

Ryan reached into his pockets, fishing, but when he put the key in the lock Marissa's phone started to ring.

It was her dad.

"You have a minute, kiddo?" he asked.

Marissa looked to Ryan. "Yeah. Is everything okay?"

Ryan looked at Marissa. Knew this wasn't good.

"No. Not exactly . . ." Jimmy answered.

Marissa paced. Nervous. She knew this wasn't

good. Ryan looked at her, then went inside, sensing her need for privacy.

"What is it?" Marissa asked as she sat down on the sidewalk outside the motel room door.

Ryan pulled out the sofa bed. Seth and Summer were asleep, their backs toward each other.

"There's no easy way for me to say this." Marissa felt her eyes fill with tears. "When you get home tomorrow? I'm not gonna be there. Your mom and I are —"

But Marissa already knew what he was going to say. She had been around the house and felt the tension, but she had denied it. "You're getting a divorce."

Ryan paused as he tossed a sheet onto the bed. He could hear through the paper-thin walls and he wanted to reach through them and hold her. No matter what had happened between them, he still cared.

Marissa stood in shock outside the room as her father choked up over the phone and tried to explain, but she could barely hear. Her life was melting away before her. The monotony had turned into a catastrophe and she wanted to escape.

The tears poured onto her cheeks. And when she went inside she tried to hide them from Ryan.

"I can sleep on the floor if . . ."

"It's okay," Marissa whispered as she kicked off her flip-flops and got into the sofa bed.

Silence fell over the room as they both lay on the pullout. Together. Alone. Miles between them, lying so close.

Ryan looked at her but her back was turned. He wanted to hold her. Grab her hand. But he couldn't do it.

"I'm sorry," he said as he turned away from her.

"Thanks," she said softly, wanting him to hold her. Grab her hand and tell her that everything would be all right.

But he didn't and she fell asleep. The tears drying in her eyes.

Luke held Holly as they fell asleep in his bed, their bodies sweaty and exhausted. He looked at her and smiled. Neither would tell.

She felt safe. That when she woke her lover would be by her side. All her problems would be erased, and she would know he was the one. Marissa woke from her dream to find his arm around her. But it wasn't Luke, it was Ryan. She breathed in his smell and took in the image of his hand so strong and soft around her, holding her. Telling her things would be all right. She let his hand stay as she closed her eyes again. *He was the one.*

Ryan woke and slowly removed his arm from Marissa, unsure of what she'd think if she awoke.

                    *   *   *

Holly awoke to find Luke gone. And she slipped
out of the bed and into her clothes and made her
way back to her own room. She would see him
tonight.

"You think we should've woken Ryan and Marissa?"
Seth asked Summer as they sat at the motel diner
eating breakfast.

    "Nah. They looked so cute together." She took
a bite of her toast. "Vomit."

    "Gee, Summer. That's a real sentimental streak
you got there." He sipped his coffee.

    "Trouser it, Cohen. It's too early for your so-
called comedy."

    "You enjoy my comedy. And you know what
else I think you enjoy? Me."

    "That's because you're mentally unstable."
Summer took a bite of her eggs.

    "Be that as it may. The facts speak for them-
selves. Might I remind you of a little something I
like to call 'the time you kissed me by the pool at
my grandpa's birthday party'?"

    "What are you talking about?" she asked, put-
ting down her mug.

    "I know denial is a powerful coping mecha-
nism." Seth put down his fork. "But it's about time
we paid lip service to our lip service."

    "Two words, Cohen: no tongue."

    "You did agree to take this little trip with me
down Mexico way."

                        301

"I needed a ride."

"We shared the same bed."

"I wasn't going to sleep on that couch. It smelled like . . ." She looked at her plate. ". . . these eggs."

"You ate my toast, Summer."

"I like crusts," she answered quickly.

"Face it." Seth looked into her eyes. "Our chemistry is undeniable."

"You know what else is undeniable?" Summer picked up her fork, not wanting to admit that maybe Seth was right. "The pain this fork will cause when I jam it into your eye." Seth stared at her, a bit scared. "I suffer from rage blackouts." She smiled.

Seth backed away. "I'll get the check."

Marissa let the warm water of the shower pour over her body. The pain of her father's news still stuck to her. An indelible ink.

"Where's Coop?" Summer asked as she and Seth returned to the hotel room.

"In the shower," Ryan answered.

"I hope she's wearing shower shoes."

Seth handed Ryan a Styrofoam container. "Brought you some breakfast. The chariot is repaired and out front. Let us away."

Ryan looked at the bathroom door. It was still closed. "I'm not sure we're going."

"What?" Summer asked, shocked.

"Marissa's dad called last night with some bad news."

302

Marissa walked out of the bathroom with her hair still wet.

"What's going on?" Summer asked. But the look on Marissa's face said it all. "They're getting divorced. . . ." Marissa nodded and Summer went to her. Held her. Hugged her. She understood the pain. "Whatever you wanna do, Coop. But if I may? Speaking as a child of divorce? You do not want to be home right now. And this is our last chance for freedom. We get back to Newport it's, like, school and reality." She hugged Marissa again and stepped away. "Let's go to T.J. Have fun. Life will suck soon enough."

Marissa looked to Ryan for support. A decision. She needed his help.

"She might actually be right," Ryan said, smiling at Marissa. She looked at his hands so soft and strong.

"Let's go to T.J.," Marissa said with a tiny smile.

Tijuana was dusty and crowded — the streets covered with partying teens, vendors selling souvenirs and cheap drinks, and cars everywhere. Seth and Ryan had checked into their room and were waiting outside the hotel for Marissa and Summer, who were upstairs still getting ready.

"This is T.J., Ryan," Seth said as they sat on the steps waiting for the girls, observing their surroundings. "What do you think so far?"

A girl in a soaking-wet white T-shirt passed in front of them. Both guys stared. "I think . . . I could get in less . . . You know what? I think I could enjoy it here."

Seth smiled. "Me too."

Summer and Marissa arrived ready for a night out on the town. The sun was starting to cool above them and they needed to go meet up with all their friends.

"So everyone's probably at Boom Boom," Marissa said as she led the way through the crowded streets, passing by taquerias and ristorantes.

"Let me just run into the pharmacy," Summer said as she paused in front of one of the storefronts. "You can buy whatever you want without a prescription. I need to make a pit stop for my step-mom. I guess she's already taken all the Vicodin available in Orange County."

"I should do a pop-in. Pick up an antihistamine. Allergies," Seth said as he joined Summer in the store.

Marissa and Ryan stood outside waiting for their friends. Their eyes met, but she quickly turned away.

"You don't have to come with us if you don't want. I mean. . . ." She paused. Uneasy with the truth. "I'm going to find Luke."

But Ryan didn't care. This wasn't about her decision. It was about two friends being there for each other and he didn't want to leave her alone. "You're not walking there alone." He paused as she looked at him. "It's cool. Really."

Inside Club Boom Boom, the music was pumping and the drinks were freely poured. Holly found Luke lined up at the bar with his friends, taking shots. She put her arms around him and tried to dance with him, kiss him.

"C'mon, Luke."

But Luke wriggled free. He had woken up this morning feeling guilty. "That's cool," he said, taking a step back.

But Holly wasn't taking no for an answer. "Marissa's not even coming," she started as she kissed his ear. "Besides, what happens in Mexico stays in Mexico." Holly pressed her body against his, her hand moving down his back. She winked at him and he couldn't resist.

The guilt masked by the knowledge that maybe Marissa would never know. That dancing was harmless.

He followed Holly up the stairs and to a dance floor above that looked over the entire club.

Down below and out of sight, the foursome arrived to find themselves caught in a massive crowd of drunken teens.

Ryan motioned toward the bar area where there seemed to be fewer people. They could search for their friends from there.

Upstairs, Holly and Luke began to dance. Her body close against his, moving to the music.

At the bar, the four took some shots out of a water pistol as a bartender squirted it into their mouths. They laughed as they swallowed the pungent liquid. Marissa looked to Ryan, who smiled at her. A trip to T.J. was just what she needed.

Holly and Luke danced closer and closer. His restraint falling to the wind yet again. Her body irresistible.

Ryan grabbed Marissa's hand and led her through the bar as Seth and Summer followed close behind. "Up there," Ryan shouted over the music as he motioned to the dance floor high above them.

They made their way up the stairs, past throngs of people. Weaving in and out of the crowds.

Luke pressed his lips against Holly's. He had succumbed to her pressure once again. She kissed him back. Their bodies still moving to the music.

Marissa and Ryan moved along the dance floor, still searching, laughing as they were pushed and pulled by the massive crowds. Marissa dragging Ryan behind her — across the room — until suddenly she stopped short.

She could see him. Luke. With Holly. Her hand let go of Ryan's. Her heart shattered. Luke and Holly, kissing, their hands all over each other. The music pounding the beat of the pain.

But Marissa couldn't hold herself back any longer. And she rushed Luke, tearing him away from Holly.

"What are you doing?!" she screamed above the music.

"I'm sorry! I had no idea —" Luke said as he tried to step forward and comfort Marissa.

She shoved him away. "How could you? After everything!" *I chose you.* She pounded at him, but he grabbed her arms, holding her back.

"I'm so sorry!" Luke tried.

"What? That you got caught?!" she screamed, breaking free from his grip just as Seth and Summer and Ryan ran up to help her.

Rage engulfed her and the pain made her tremble with anger. She turned to Holly. "Don't ever talk to me again!"

"You are such a bitch!" Summer yelled over the chaos, backing up her friend.

"Please!" Holly started, turning toward Summer. "He hooks up with everyone!"

"What?! What did you say?!" Marissa asked, now even more enraged.

"I said he hooks up with everyone! Freshman girls! Girls from Modern Day! From UCI!"

Marissa stepped back, her whole world shattered before her eyes. The monotony was never monotony. "Is that true?" she asked, turning to Luke. But Luke couldn't answer and Marissa knew. He had lied to her.

She ran down the stairs and straight out of the

307

club, onto the streets of Tijuana and into the crowds of people. Seth and Ryan ran after her.

Summer found Marissa back at the hotel, her eyes red and swollen from the tears. Her body convulsing with pain.

"Thank god. Coop!" Summer exclaimed as she ran to her friend and hugged her. Marissa's body shaking in her arms.

"Did you know, Sum?" Marissa asked softly.

"I promise. No way." Summer held her tighter.

"I slept with him," Marissa cried. *He wasn't the one.*

"I know, sweetie." Summer smoothed her hair.

"Half our school was there." Marissa sobbed even harder as Summer continued to hold her. The tears moistening her arms.

"I gotta call Ryan and Seth," Summer said as she pulled back and reached for her purse.

"No. I don't want to see them." She didn't want to admit she'd made the wrong choice. "I'm so embarrassed."

"It's okay," Summer started, calming her friend. "It's just . . . we'll go home."

But Marissa's eyes filled with more tears. "I can't go home. My dad is gone. My mom will be back. I have . . . no one."

"You have me," Summer said as she rifled through her purse and found her phone. "C'mon, Coop. Let's get outta here. I'll grab our stuff."

Summer went into the bathroom and began to

pack up their stuff. She called Seth and told him to meet them at the hotel. They had to get out of there quick.

But when she came out of the bathroom she discovered that Marissa was gone. She had disappeared again. Summer grabbed her purse, but when she went to zip it she noticed that the Vicodin she had bought for her stepmother was missing.

Marissa had gone with the pills.

She ran through the streets and away from the crowds. She didn't want to see anyone. She found a bar off the beaten path where she could drink and not be bothered. There were no high school kids in here. There was no one from Newport. Just Marissa, the bartender, and a few locals.

She ordered a shot of tequila and swallowed it in one gulp. Her pain too strong to handle.

And she reached into her pocket and pulled out the bottle of pills. The painkillers. She wanted to be numb.

She poured the pills onto the counter and lined them up. One for each pain she felt. The monotony. Her mother. Her father. Luke. Holly. Ryan. Each for a different reason, but each a pain none the less.

And one by one she picked up the pills and swallowed them with shots of tequila. The pain racing down her throat, coating her stomach, and burning inside her.

Her hands shook and her world became blurry. Slowly numbing. Slowly disappearing.

309

She drank more and more. Each pain slowly erased, and she drank until she could feel no more.

Her vision blurred by tears and pills, she felt the pain escaping. The numbness overtook her and everyone was out to get her — not just her family and Luke, but everyone, including the three locals staring at her.

She ran out the door and down the street. Her body shaking, the pain seeping, numbing. She ran into an alley. To hide. To vomit. To cry.

She was numb. She could never turn back. She was not Newport.

Then she lay down in the dust and the whole world went black.

When they found her, she was blue and cold and barely alive. Ryan went to her. Shook her. But she didn't move. He placed his hands underneath her, the coldness radiated against him, and he lifted her. Seth held Summer and they watched as Ryan walked toward them, her lifeless body in his arms.

He looked at her eyes. Shut out from the world. And he whispered *goodbye*. Perhaps forever.

The O.C. — where everything and everyone appears to be perfect. But everything *isn't* perfect and everyone has a secret. Now the story continues . . .

THE MISFIT

Coming in
October 2004

Catch up on all the action of
TV's hottest show!